About the Author

Katherine Livesey is a Young Adult Fantasy author living in the historic Northumberland countryside. She was born and raised in the wilds of Lancashire and spent much of her childhood running ragged across the moors or lost in a sea of books.

Katherine takes inspiration from folklore, fairy tales and the classics of the Fantasy genre, as well as the ever-changing but ever-present natural world that surrounds her home. When not writing, Katherine can usually be found knee-deep in mud walking her two Alaskan Huskies with her partner, baking up a storm in her little kitchen or watching an old favourite period drama.

katherinelivesey.co.uk

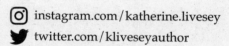

instagram.com/katherine.livesey
twitter.com/kliveseyauthor

Books by Katherine Livesey

Sisters of Shadow
Sisters of Moonlight
Sisters of Midnight

SISTERS OF SHADOW

KATHERINE LIVESEY

One More Chapter
a division of HarperCollins*Publishers*
1 London Bridge Street
London SE1 9GF
www.harpercollins.co.uk
HarperCollins*Publishers*
1st Floor, Watermarque Building, Ringsend Road
Dublin 4, Ireland

This paperback edition 2021
3
First published in Great Britain in ebook format
by HarperCollins*Publishers* 2021

A catalogue record of this book is available from the British Library

ISBN: 978-0-00-846770-8

Printed and bound in the UK using 100% Renewable Electricity
by CPI Group (UK) Ltd

Where sunless rivers weep
Their waves into the deep,
She sleeps a charmed sleep:
Awake her not.
Led by a single star,
She came from very far
To seek where shadows are
Her pleasant lot.

— Christina Rossetti, 'Dream Land'

Prologue

Nobody really noticed when Alice Blackwell disappeared. The 'witch-girl', as the village folk came to know her, lived alone in a hut nestled amidst tall ferns and ancient oaks in the mountains that surrounded Alder Vale. No one knew where the hut was exactly, or whether Alice lived in a hut at all, but they felt sure that she was the kind of girl who *would* live in one, and so the presumption had become a widely circulated fact. She was strange, you see. Only a strange person would choose to live a quiet existence away from the chatter and bustle of the town. At least, that's what they whispered to one another.

The only soul in the entire town who did know where Alice resided was a girl of a similar age who made the trip through moss-covered forests and up into the cold mountain air to visit Alice several times a week. She usually brought little bundles of fresh herbs, baked goods, and an apple or two, and they would spend hours talking and laughing before the girl disappeared back down into the valley, leaving Alice alone again.

Contrary to what the townsfolk whispered, Alice lived a solitary life not by choice, but because she had no family to speak of. Her father and mother had raised her in this cabin. They'd loved her, cared for her, and cherished her for the first six years of her life. Then one day they'd kissed her goodbye and ventured out on a short but routine hunting trip.

And never returned.

Loneliness had stopped tugging at her heart years ago, very soon after she started receiving visits from the girl from Alder Vale. Something else tugged at her heart though, and it tugged with relentless abandon. The irony of the townsfolk calling Alice the 'witch-girl' was that Alice was sure that she possessed no real magic. She knew very little about her lineage, except for what was in her beloved grimoire that sat proudly on her crooked bookshelf. It was an ancient leather-bound tome, filled with spells and incantations, that she'd inherited from her mother, who had inherited it from *her* mother, and so on. For Alice, this book proved that she came from a line of women who were all gifted with real, visible magic, but she'd never seen any proof that it actually existed. The only skill Alice had was in reading cards and tea leaves – hardly useful in the world of real witches. A world she wasn't even sure existed.

In truth, Alice was quiet and introverted; she enjoyed the solitude. Never once had she shown an inclination to leave her hidden mountain home. Oh, she dreamed of the world beyond the Shadow Lands: castles shrouded in mist, and schools where magic was taught to those who possessed the gift. She spent much of her time in her head dreaming of such things, but home was home. It was comfortable, peaceful; a reminder of her past, a physical memorial to her parents. She could never really, truly commit to the idea of leaving.

One evening in late autumn, all that changed.

A deafening storm rolled over the mountainside, pelting the wooden roof of Alice's cabin with rain. She stoked the fire and tried to ignore it; she'd never liked storms. She was acutely aware that living out in the wilds with no real means of income meant that if a tree came down and crushed her cabin, she'd be homeless. Over the years, she'd learned about essential maintenance from some of her father's old books. She'd treated the wood, cleaned every inch of the cabin inside and out, and even replaced three beams in the roof where it had started to leak last winter. She had done everything she could to weather-proof it, time-proof it, but tree-proofing it? Alice was sure there was nothing that could be done to protect her or her cabin if a tree decided to hurl itself down upon them. She'd managed to avoid destitution for eleven years, but when the wind howled, she couldn't help but worry that her little wooden sanctuary wouldn't protect her for much longer.

Night fell with alarming haste. Alice placed a kettle on the stove to boil as she prepared the root vegetables she'd collected earlier for her dinner. The rain sounded like it was weakening a little, but not enough to calm her nerves. Something didn't feel right about this storm, about this night. Something Alice couldn't quite put her finger on.

She'd already consulted her tarot deck twice in the last hour but the answers were confusing and inconclusive.

A gust of wind rattled the windowpanes and the heavy curtains that were pinned to the frames fluttered. At the same moment, the candle she was working by was extinguished by the draught. Only the faint flickering fire embers illuminated the room and the shadows were heavy and thick like melting tar. Through the storm, Alice heard an unmistakable noise: knocking. Three slow, deliberate knocks on her heavy oak door. Her head snapped towards the noise. Someone was out there on her porch, at her cabin that sat in the middle of a forest, miles away from the nearest town. There were no hiking routes nearby, no reason for anyone to be just passing through.

A chill crept up Alice's spine. Standing up from the small table, she kept hold of the knife she'd been using to prepare her food, the ivory handle sitting uncomfortably in her sweat-drenched palm. She inched towards the door, the blade of the knife glinting in a sliver of moonlight. Gathering her frayed courage, she reached for the handle and pulled just as a thunder crack echoed through the night sky.

Alice squinted through the pouring rain into the oppressive darkness but saw nothing. She frowned, the wind whipping through her raven hair, raising goosebumps on her arms. Another roll of thunder rattled above and Alice stepped back, suspicious and frightened, intending to close the door and shut out the creeping night. Just before she could, she noticed a patch of white on her doorstep.

A letter.

It was crisp and bright in the gloaming, entirely dry even though it sat on the saturated floor, completely exposed to the weather. As she bent to retrieve it, she failed to notice the pair of eyes that watched her from a shadow-shrouded spot in the trees.

Inside the cabin, with the door firmly closed and locked, Alice tore open the letter. As her eyes flicked over the words written in an exquisite scrawl, she felt fear strike her heart. Yet, alongside the fear, a tiny glimmer of hope. Could it be possible that such a small thing, a simple combination of ink and paper, could give her the opportunity to be who she'd always yearned to be? Alice knew in her heart of hearts that, truth or fiction, she needed to discover the source of this letter; she needed to know where it had come from and what they knew about her, what they knew about *everything*.

Her heart pounded in her ears even more loudly than the rumbling thunder outside, but she mustered her courage, swallowed her fear, and clutched that sliver of hope like a lost child clings to a doll.

Alice stumbled back and forth, stuffing her belongings into a black carpet bag. In mere moments, she was ready to do what had always felt impossible. She wrapped a heavy emerald-green travelling cloak around her shoulders before lacing up her strongest leather boots. Strength, she wagered, would be exactly what she needed on this journey.

With a shaky breath, she stepped out into the storm, lifting the hood of her cloak over her ebony hair.

She didn't get very far.

5

Chapter One

L ying in the shadow of a great oak tree, Lily Knight held out a hand and let the dappled light of the early morning sun dance between her fingers. She had her other arm behind her head and revelled in the feeling of the dewy grass beneath her stocking-free legs and bare feet. She definitely should not have removed her stockings. According to the matronly busybodies of the town, it was *most improper for a young lady to wander about in such a manner*. But, rolling her eyes when recalling their scolding, she had removed them anyway and taken great joy in imagining the shocked expression on old Orla McHail's wrinkly face if she could see her now.

Nature was Lily's tonic. In those precious moments when the sun was awakening, as the world was bathed in pale, warm light, she felt the most alive. She was sure that this was the only real magic that existed in the world: the magic of birdsong, starshine, burnt-orange leaves, crisp early morning air, and glittering river water.

She sat up, resting her weight on her elbows, enjoying the coolness of the autumn breeze on her bare arms and legs for a few minutes more. Before long, she would have to return home to her little valley town, Alder Vale. Although for now she was content to watch a small nuthatch hopping between branches on the tree above her. Lily wished for a fleeting moment that she too could grow wings and fly up into the sky.

This was a conversation topic that often cropped up when Lily was with her closest friend, Alice Blackwell. They would lie by the river near Alice's woodland cabin and take turns vocalising their hopes and dreams, speaking them into existence. Lily's dreams didn't often stretch much further than the boundaries of Alder Vale, but they always included flying up to the top of a tree or a tall mountain to gaze at the world below, just like the wild birds could. Her hopes were modest and revolved around preserving the little slice of normality that she had come to know and love. She had always pictured herself taking over her uncle Alf's apothecary, which would make her the first female business owner in the village, perhaps even in the whole of the Shadow Lands. *A fine goal to have,* she thought.

Lily's dreams had always been the complete opposite of Alice's. In fact, almost everything about the two girls was different. They should never have got along. Alice contrasted Lily's light and easy manners with darkness and awkwardness. They even contrasted in appearance, with Alice's poker-straight, inky black hair that fell in a thick curtain to her waist. Black hair that shimmered in the moonlight, unlike Lily's warm, strawberry-blonde hair that was meant to shine under bright, clear sunlight. If Lily was the sun, Alice was the moon, glowing in the rays of Lily's kindness, and infinitely warmer because of it.

Where Lily's dreams were practical, responsible, and quietly ambitious, Alice's dreams were fantastical. She would speak of unearthing lost cities and tracking a coven of witches to teach her magic. She would spend hours every day checking her future in her hand-illustrated tarot cards or flicking through her grimoire, whispering spells under her breath, hoping to wish her magic into existence. Her biggest dream was to harness the magic she had never been able to conjure. Yet, in their jumble of future plans, the two girls remained sure of one thing: their friendship would outlast everything else.

Once, years ago, Alice had suggested that they call themselves the Sisters of Shadow, for although they were not related by blood, they were attached at the heart, two souls who loved each other fiercely. One filled with light, the other darkness, casting their shadows on the world around them.

Under the old oak tree, Lily's thoughts strayed to Alice, her uncle Alf, and the apothecary. She found herself feeling incredibly fortunate for all she had been given in life. How could she ever wish for anything else, when everything she needed was right there within her grasp?

With that contented thought giving her the strength to leave behind the bliss of the magical dawn light, Lily stood, fastened her boots, and ran as fast as she could back to the village. The faster she ran, the faster the day would go and the sooner she could go up the mountain to see Alice and spend the evening by her log fire.

Lily ascended the creaking wooden staircase that led to her room after her habitual morning outing. She had so far, in her many years of sneaking out in the early hours, managed to hide it from Uncle Alf. She knew he would disapprove of her bare-footed escapades. That morning however, she had dallied in the fields for a few seconds too long. Her uncle appeared at the top of the stairs, looking through narrowed eyes at her dishevelled appearance. He was a round-bellied, rosy-cheeked man in his early fifties who loved Lily like a daughter and reprimanded her like one too.

'Lily Saoirse Knight, where on earth have you been at this time of the day?' he asked, frowning through his bushy greying eyebrows. Uncle Alf had never been very good at disciplining her, as she was a naturally wild creature with a strong will and a habit of forgetting rules the moment she stepped foot outside. She was sensible when it mattered and feral the rest of the time.

Lily looked up to him and exaggerated her apologetic face, mimicking the facial expressions of the six-year-old child she had been when she arrived twelve years ago, orphaned, turbulent, and already possessing the knack of making others bend to her will with kindness in her heart and mischief in her eyes. Uncle Alf grinned. 'You know, if you're going to sneak out and roll about in mud or whatever it is you young 'uns do, you really ought to try not to get all that moss and twigs in your hair. It does rather give the game away, lass.'

Amused, Lily climbed the last few stairs. 'I would say I won't do it again'—she lifted her hand to her hair, picking out the bits of foliage that had found their way into her curls—'but you insist that no one tells lies in this house so...'

She smirked, went up on her tiptoes to kiss her uncle's cheek, and then skipped past him, disappearing into her room. Just before she closed the door, she called out to him, 'I'll be down to open the shop before we even catch a sniff of the first customer of the day, I promise!' and then she vanished in a flurry of skirts.

———

Uncle Alf's apothecary was a breathtaking space and it was practically impossible to walk past his window without stopping to gaze at the myriad wares on offer. In the centre of the room sat the workbench where he concocted natural remedies, salves, herbal teas, and tinctures. This bench, much like the entire shop, was organised chaos. It was covered in old, dusty books that smelled of must, afternoon sunshine, and petrichor. The books were stuffed with separate pages of notes and sprigs of lavender to mark particularly important chapters. To the untrained eye, it was a mess that needed a good tidy. But to the Knights, it was their creative space; it was organised exactly as it should be without a page or speck of dust out of place.

The rest of the room was similarly wild in its

organisation. On the right wall, hiding the staircase up to the residential rooms beyond, stood a hulking walnut cabinet which housed every single remedy Uncle Alf and Lily had ever made (and not yet sold). The cabinet was bursting with dark glass jars and bottles filled with dried herbs, unlabelled liquids, and other less distinguishable products that gave the entire room a sweet, rich smell. In the window, to brighten the room and catch the eye of passers-by, Lily had wrapped crystals and sea glass in old string and hung them just above the window frame where they refracted the sunlight that streamed through the huge open windows. Drifting in the breeze they hung there, glass tears falling silently, frozen in time.

Lily's parents had died when she was a small child, long before Lily could remember the sound of their voices singing lullabies or telling ghost stories. Uncle Alf had taken her into his care and started to teach her the wonders of nature and its healing properties. He had thought that a useful vocation could help to distract this bright-eyed, wild-natured child from her grief. Uncle Alf had taught Lily how to brew every single potion he knew, so that now the two of them could quietly create new remedies from the base knowledge they both possessed. Bunches of lavender, nettle, marigolds, sage, and thyme hung from the ceiling, drying in preparation to be ground up and used in a variety of concoctions. These hanging herbs were the main reason why Lily frequently had petals and leaves caught in her curls. She had long since given up ducking and fighting her way around them. Instead, she'd made a habit of charging through them, much to the chagrin of her uncle.

As if by magic, Lily appeared downstairs as punctually as she had promised. She had even attempted to tame her wild mane, which hung loosely around her shoulders. Reluctantly, she agreed to adhere to society's idea of 'appropriate attire' while she worked in the shop, which included battling with a corset and lacing herself into constricting gowns. But the one thing Lily absolutely refused to do was tie up her hair. 'There's no point even trying,' she'd say whenever her uncle commented on the impropriety of it. 'You know it would fight its way out of the pins and end up looking like an unfortunate bird's nest anyway.' And, with a begrudging sigh, her uncle would agree. The compromise they had settled upon was that Lily would try to make her hair at least look neat – or, as neat as she could manage. Today, she had created a makeshift hairband from an old leather scrap, which she had used to push the curls away from her face, keeping the corkscrews out of her eyes so she could work without her vision obscured.

As punctual as ever, Lily unlocked the front door of the shop and fastened it open so the cool autumn breeze could dance around the room. Perching herself at the workbench, she tucked a pencil behind her ear and began to organise and bottle up the orders that were due to be collected.

As she was preparing a bitter-smelling remedy she had recently concocted to ease the pain of a gout sufferer who lived in a nearby hamlet on the edge of the town, her uncle appeared from the storeroom behind her.

'Ah, you're already down!' Uncle Alf exclaimed, as if Lily didn't surprise him with her punctuality every morning. 'Good, well, stop what you're doing because you're out on deliveries today.' Lily let out a melodramatic sigh and buried her head in her hands. 'Pull yourself together, child, Frank has a sick mother to look after as well as three younger siblings, which is why he will be late in today. Count yourself lucky.'

'Do I really have to?' Lily asked, slowly lifting her head from her arms. 'You know old Orla has been dying to clip me around the ear ever since she caught me picking figs from her tree last week.'

'Well, if she does,' Uncle Alf smirked, 'I might just have to let slip to Jemima Darroch exactly which remedies Orla has on order, and you know Jemima can't be trusted with gossip like that!' He let out a belly laugh at his own mischief and his cheeks glowed red under his speckled grey beard. Lily often felt her penchant for mischief came directly from her uncle. He was her father's brother, and he had taken her in without a second thought when she was six years old, after her parents' untimely deaths. They had been encouraging each other's mischievousness ever since.

'Ha!' Lily exclaimed, 'and you berate me for insensitivity!' Lily continued with just the slightest flicker of devilry in her eyes. 'Just because Orla has an issue with incontin—'

'Woah there, lass, I don't need to hear you say it!' Uncle Alf spluttered through his stifled chuckles. 'Anyway, it's not her I'm sending you to see today. Your Alice requested a fresh delivery of mandrake root, valerian, coltsfoot, and a few other bits and pieces last week to be delivered today or tomorrow. Well, I thought Frank could do the local deliveries when he arrives later, and you could manage the longer journey.' He dropped an overflowing wicker basket on the table in front of her. 'I told her I'd send you up and I thought maybe you would be grateful to see her and those beloved forests of yours. You've been working far too hard lately. It's not good for a young lass like you to be cooped up in here, much as I appreciate your help.' He ruffled her already messy hair. 'I thought you may as well take some food with you and stay for the rest of the day. There's not much to do here for once, so make the most of the free time.'

Lily leaped from her seat and embraced her uncle, gratitude glowing from her bright eyes. 'Thank you, Uncle!' She grinned and kissed his cheek, before throwing her arms around his neck and pulling him into another melodramatic embrace.

'Be careful, mind.' Alf held her shoulders in his firm grip and looked her straight in the eyes. 'You've heard the tales they're telling, the rumours, haven't you?'

Lily shrugged. 'Nonsense. I'd bet my life on it.'

'Well, I'd rather you didn't. If there's talk of strange folk wandering around these parts, of people going missing, of *murders*... I know you're sensible, and I know how much good it does you to head up into those mountains so just—'

Lily held her hands up in surrender. 'I'll be careful.' She drew his hands from her shoulders and gave them a gentle, reassuring squeeze. 'I promise.'

Chapter Two

With the basket of wares hung on her arm, Lily hitched up her dress and started out on the old familiar track she'd roamed along hundreds of times. Before she left, she had quickly changed into a less restrictive dress that matched the colours of the dazzling autumn leaves, and she had removed her corset so she could breathe freely in the mountain air.

As Lily left the confines of the town, the cobbles gave way to a grassy driftway, which in turn became a lightly trodden unmarked path up the side of the mountain. It was a rugged landscape, but it was entirely hers. She knew every pinecone, every animal track, the grey corries and mountain ridges that obscured the horizon; it all felt like home. Far more than the whispering thatches of Alder Vale.

Once she was sure she was out of sight, she bent to unfasten and remove her supple leather boots and tucked the hem of her dress through her belt, so her legs and feet were free from the heavy folds of material. She needed the feel of the grass and moss between her toes like a flower needs water and sunshine; it was a necessity she simply could not live without. Lily tied the laces of her boots in a knot around her belt so they could hang there, out of the way until she needed them. Continuing up into the forest-covered mountain, the morning breeze whistled sweet melodies through the canopy.

Even though they saw each other for a few hours most days, Lily felt overcome with joy at the thought of having a full uninterrupted day to spend with her friend. Alice had lived in the cabin her whole life, but since her parents' disappearance she had been received coldly by the rest of the Alder Vale residents. Alice was quiet but headstrong and unusual, and something about her presence made most people descend into gossiping whispers whenever she walked by.

One of those people, who called herself Alice's 'governess', was a middle-aged woman filled with pity and self-righteousness. When Alice's parents first disappeared, she took to making sure Alice ate occasionally and taught her how to keep a fire burning in the grate. Alice had been a pale and sickly-looking child back then, but her dark eyes were fierce and her temper was fiercer, and the woman had packed up and left less than a month after Alice's parents.

'She tried to curse that poor woman,' Jemima Darroch commented to the shop girl in the bakery a few days after the woman had left. 'That's why she left so fast. Take it from me, love, that child, she's a witch, and I'm as sure as I am that the sky's blue. A witch through and through, and the sooner she leaves the better.'

As unkind and unpleasant as Jemima was with her gossiping, the 'witch' notion spread through the village like a plague. Within a week, it wasn't simply a rumour muttered in bad taste, but an accepted fact. By the age of eight, Alice was only going down to the village every other week for food and supplies, and even then she made sure she was seen by as few people as possible. She hid her hair in a cap and skulked in alleyways, sneaking from place to place, before disappearing into the shadows again. She became a part of the local lore, 'the witch in the woods', 'the strange Blackwell girl', and every accident, every case of bad luck, every injury, was blamed on her.

There were only two people in the village who opposed the persecution of Alice Blackwell, and they were Lily and her uncle. So as soon as Alf heard that Alice's parents, loyal customers of his, had gone missing, his immediate concern had been for their daughter. He thought, if nothing else, perhaps Alice needed a companion and sustenance. Barely a few hours after he heard the news, he packed a wicker basket full of cakes, herbal remedies, candles, and apples, and sent Lily up the mountain to visit her.

They had been just young children, awkward and shy, but their connection was instantaneous. From the moment they met, Lily knew they were kindred spirits and she felt sure that Alice had been sent specifically so they could be companions. She told Alice so that very first day, when they had sat together by the open log fire in Alice's home. They shared a hunk of bread with some cheese, and enjoyed a mug of hot cocoa each, which Alice had just learned to make. Their friendship was forged that day, and Lily had visited Alice several times a week ever since.

Sometimes Alice would read Lily's future in tea leaves or with her tarot cards, sometimes they would plan her eventual takeover of the apothecary, and sometimes they would just sit in comfortable silence, enjoying the presence of each other's company. What they never discussed, however, was Alice's life, her past, her future. Lily had learned to stop asking, because Alice would shut down and change the subject, but her eyes would always flicker towards the ancient grimoire that sat on a dusty makeshift bookshelf next to the fireplace.

Alice was less open with her emotions, but even without words, the two of them could communicate their love for each other with a squeeze of the hand or a head rested on a shoulder. Friendships like theirs were rare, and they treasured each other.

As she continued to trudge rhythmically up the mountain trail, Lily realised that she was particularly anxious to see her friend. The last time they had been together, two days previously, they had argued, which was something they never, ever did. Alice had been distracted and melancholic for weeks and Lily had wanted to help her friend in any way she could.

Lily had convinced Alice to come down from the woods and join her underneath her favourite oak tree, where they could gaze out across the endless farmers' fields and pastures. Alice had reluctantly agreed. The look in her eyes foretold a relief to be in the company of a friend, but also a tentativeness, a fear that if she let the emotion overcome her, she'd reveal too much.

Alice was frequently troubled by one thing or another, but on this particular occasion something was different. Her forest-green eyes had been ringed with the tell-tale blackness of insomnia, her pallor was death-like, her skin an even lighter shade of ivory than usual. Even her straight black hair looked unkempt and she'd let it hang loose over her shoulders instead of pinning it up off her face like she usually did. Her hands shook, though whether through cold or fear it was hard to tell. The Alice that Lily loved was usually full of wisdom and imagination; she was mysterious and she played upon it. But when she had seen her those few days before, Lily recalled a distance in Alice's eyes. She had looked lost.

She had looked haunted.

'Alice,' Lily had begun tentatively, careful not to push her too hard, 'you know you can tell me anything. What's going on?'

Lily had reached for Alice's hand, meaning to hold it, warm it, anything to stop it from shaking.

But Alice had flinched and pulled away.

'You wouldn't understand. This...' she paused, contemplating her choice of words, 'thing, I can't move past it. I've tried to wish it out of me, I've tried every potion to get rid of it, but I can't. You couldn't even begin to understand.' She whispered, but Lily heard the unmistakable edge of venom in her voice.

'I'm not asking to understand, Alice'—Lily tucked a piece of hair behind her ear—'I'm simply asking to help you carry your burdens. They're weighing down so heavily on you. A friend doesn't need to understand all of your troubles to help lighten them a little.' Lily half smiled, suddenly terrified that if she pushed too hard, Alice would close herself off altogether.

It had been said, ever since her parents' disappearance, that Alice had been abandoned by them. Even Alice had started to believe the stories: she was too strange, too fractured and unpredictable, and it had scared them away. It had scared them enough to leave her alone in the cabin and never return.

What if running away was in the Blackwell blood? Suppose, if Alice became any more scared, she ran away too. Just like her parents. Scanning her memories, Lily remembered the look in Alice's eyes that fateful day.

'Oh, Lily,' she had sighed, 'how I wish I could view this world like you do. To you, everything is simple. Everything can be fixed with a hug and a cup of tea.' She had frowned, her eyes darkening. 'But that will not fix me and neither will your words. I am unfixable. From the moment I was made—' She had stopped, seeming to change her mind about what she was about to reveal. 'From the moment I was made as I am, my life was destined to be hollow, sorrowful—'

'Wait,' Lily had interrupted, 'this is about your lack of magic?' Lily had been so surprised. Considering the recent onset of her troubles, she had presumed the issue that had been bothering Alice was new. The absence of magic in Alice's life was something they spoke of sometimes, even joked about if Alice was in a good mood. 'But Alice, you know that magic is really, really rare.' Lily's brow had furrowed with concern and trepidation. 'We don't even know if it exists at all...' Her voice had trailed off and she had swallowed hard, barely daring to look her friend in the eye.

'I told you that you wouldn't understand,' Alice had growled, standing up suddenly and flattening down her skirts. 'This world, *your* world, just isn't designed for me, Lily. I wish you could see that.'

With that, she had spun on her heels and run full speed back towards the mountain. She had disappeared beyond the horizon before Lily had even had a chance to comprehend what had happened. Pulling herself up slowly, lost in thought, she wandered in the direction Alice had disappeared. Trying to catch her in that kind of mood was pointless. Alice could outrun even the fastest adults in the town when she put her mind to it, and had done so on several occasions. No, Lily had decided that she would walk through the tall grass, stop off at her uncle's apothecary and discuss things with him first, before attempting another exchange with Alice.

She had intended to visit Alice first thing the next morning, hoping that overnight her temper might have softened and she would be willing to forgive Lily for pushing. However, the apothecary had been overflowing with orders and Lily hadn't been able to take a single hour off from dawn until dusk to go and visit her friend. She knew Alice wouldn't be angry anymore, but that didn't make her any less anxious to go and see her and smooth things over. They never fought and she didn't intend to start now.

Aside from her selfish concerns, Lily also wanted to make sure that Alice was okay. Whatever had been tormenting her, whether it was the magic or something else, it was seriously impacting her health and Lily decided that she would do anything to make sure her friend felt safe and cared for.

She walked the familiar path, her bare feet skipping lightly over the rocks and the plants, lost in her thoughts. As she idled along through the forest, Lily spotted several patches of wildflowers which she knew would brighten Alice's often dark cabin, so she placed the basket down and knelt by the flowers, careful to hitch up her dress so as not to get it too muddy.

She picked chicory, harebells, and field pansies (Alice's favourite), and several other pieces of foliage like rusty-coloured bracken, rowan, and unripe blackthorn berries, arranging them into a little bunch and tying them with some string she found lurking at the bottom of the wicker basket. Alice could never resist a fresh, wild bouquet, and Lily figured that if all else failed, at least the flowers might cheer her up a little.

Amongst the hedgerows, the blackberries still clung to their stems, and they were abundant. Crafting a makeshift bag from a napkin, Lily plucked the berries from their hiding places, ensuring that she left enough for the wildlife that would still need them for sustenance. With her bunch of flowers and her wicker basket in tow, Lily wandered the last miles of the journey in an optimistic frame of mind.

She finally broke through the treeline and caught sight of the familiar cabin nestled in the centre of a small, open meadow, far away from the prying eyes of passers-by. The meadow was completely surrounded by a dense wall of forest on all sides, and the only sounds that could be heard from where Lily stood on the edge of the glade were the trickling of a nearby brook, the birdsong, and the wind whistling through the trees. As she looked at the small, homely cabin, encompassed by nature, she felt like she understood why Alice was so content to spend so little time down in the village. With all of this natural beauty, and only the sky to judge her, it was leagues away from the muttered rumours and hurtful superstitions of the townsfolk.

Wouldn't it be nice if I could convince Alice to come for a swim today? Lily thought. *The air is warm, the water will be cool, we could spend the rest of the day pretending to be the free, uninhibited children we used to be.*

Those idyllic thoughts were banished from her mind when she noticed that the cabin looked different. She was unable to immediately place her finger on what exactly it was, and for a moment she just stood, staring blankly, until it dawned on her like a cloud passing over the moon.

There was no smoke.

Alice was always cold, even in the height of summer, and therefore very rarely did she forget to light her log fire.

Lily shook her head. *Silly superstitions making me paranoid*, she thought. It'll be nothing.

She walked the final few steps around the side of the cabin and stepped up onto the porch that led directly to the entrance. Her frown deepened when she saw that the door was hanging open, carelessly left to swing in the forest breeze.

This, she knew, was wrong.

In all their years of friendship, Alice had always been intensely private. Her door was closed and locked, even if she was only leaving for a stroll.

Lily felt her heartbeat quicken as she placed the basket and the flowers down on the warped wood. She didn't know what she was going to find inside, but she felt sure she would need both of her hands free if she was going to face it.

She was suddenly reminded of the tales that had spread through the village a few weeks earlier, and the warning Alf had given her earlier that day. There had been whispers and mutterings of children being taken from their homes in the dead of night. Of violent unsolved murders and disappearances. Of blood-soaked beds and gurgling cries in the darkness. Of the Lightkeepers of local lore blackening their light and venturing out with their cleavers to seek out waifs and strays. But the tales had come from the unreliable mouth of Jemima Darroch and her hoard of cronies and conniving gossips, who had said that the stories originated from the coast, many miles away. To most, though, they felt close enough to encourage caution in even the bravest of souls.

Lily, who had always been dubious about anything that didn't have a logical explanation, had ignored the cautionary whispers and decided that these rumours were nothing but scary stories designed to frighten children, just like the ones she herself had been told.

And yet, something about the scene before her eyes – the darkness of the cabin, the open door, the eerie silence – made her stop and wonder whether she should have done more to protect Alice, whether she should have left her alone, so far away from other people. But at seventeen, Alice was hardly a child. She was sensible and capable, if a little unstable at times. Surely there would be a reasonable, logical explanation and things would become clear the moment she stepped over the threshold. Still, Lily felt sure that something was amiss and, gathering her courage, she entered the cabin.

The interior was small and cramped. Alice had insisted once when Lily had commented on its size – or lack thereof – that it was 'cosy', but Lily still found it to be oppressive, as though the ceiling was pressing down on her from above. It was single-storey and set out as one room. The windows let in a small amount of daylight that cast gloomy shadows across the stone floor. Alice didn't own many possessions, and a swift glance around the room confirmed to Lily that she had left in a hurry, maybe even just hours after their argument. The fire in the grate had died out, drawers were hanging open and empty, and Alice's beloved tarot deck and the huge grimoire were also missing. It was unnerving.

The one thing that remained was a discarded piece of parchment, left lying on a desk one the far side of the room, illuminated by the light that shone from the window above it. Lily walked across the room, her still-bare feet growing cold from the stone floor. It wasn't a piece of blank parchment, she realised, but a letter. She reached out and picked it up, her hands shaking.

27

For the Attention of Alice Blackwell,

I have a proposal for you. I knew your mother and I know that, like her, you possess the gift, amongst other supernatural abilities. It has come to my attention that you are in possession of a particular gift that requires nurturing. Should you be interested in learning how to wield your special talents, then I advise you to meet with me. I will show you how to navigate a world that is filled with more magic than you could ever imagine.

I will be passing through Kelseth village when the next full moon rises. If you should wish to join me, and I should clarify that it is in your best interests to do so, meet me by the harbour, beneath the lamp, at midnight. Do not waste your time writing and sending a reply. Be there, and do not tell a soul where you have gone. This is of the utmost importance. You are entering a world of incredible power, and our organisation requires total discretion and absolute secrecy.

Until then,
Your friend,

Hecate Winter
High Priestess of the Shadow Sect

Lily looked up from the letter and gazed, unseeing, out of the window. She let the parchment fall to the floor, questions racing through her mind. *What did this mean?*

How could this woman, this Hecate Winter, know of Alice's existence, let alone of her 'gift', whatever that was? And why did she seem completely set upon meeting with Alice so secretly, and so urgently?

Lily knew that this letter must have arrived moments after Alice had returned from their argument. She had been in a vulnerable state, and Lily had no doubt in her mind that Alice would have gone if she had any hope of gaining the magical ability for which she yearned so desperately. But leaving so suddenly, without even leaving a note... Alice's behaviour was reckless and out of character.

Lily was missing something. She knew she must be.

What was this 'Shadow Sect' and why, out of everyone in the world, did they want Alice?

Lily gathered up the basket, retrieved the letter, and set off back down through the forest. Her uncle had lived here longer than he cared to admit, and if anyone would know anything about this mysterious letter and its contents, it would be him. She thought that maybe he could help her convince the local warden to look into it; perhaps he could even contact the warden in Kelseth and see if anything suspicious had happened there. She hoped that someone would be able to read the letter and decipher its meaning without the distraction of emotion and concern that clouded her own logical thinking.

At least if Alice had gone willingly, she would have been guarded and sensible. And last night was the full moon, so the warden in Kelseth might have some information to share. Lily tried to regulate her breathing. Alice would be fine ... wouldn't she? She was more than capable of looking after herself. Hadn't she survived all this time against all the odds? And this woman, Lily thought, this Hecate Winter, she wanted to nurture Alice, to help her, not hurt her.

But for some reason she couldn't relax. She couldn't help but feel that hidden somewhere in between the lines of the letter, there was a threat. A threat to hurt Alice. The thought made Lily's hair stand on end. She knew that if someone, anyone, hurt Alice, then they would be tracked down and punished. She just wasn't sure who would track them down, and who would punish them. Because it couldn't very well be her ... could it?

Chapter Three

Lily hurtled into the apothecary, letting the door slam shut behind her, the bottles on the shelves rattling precariously.

'Uncle!' she shouted.

She didn't know what she should do, only that she felt like she needed answers and in order to get answers, she was going to have to find Alice. The thought had occurred to her several times as she was running back to the town, but she had pushed it from her mind each time.

Mysteries, lost friends, magic ... these were all things that happened far away, beyond the peace of Alder Vale or in dusty old novels. The rest of the world had left behind the people of the Shadow Lands because they were gentle, simple folk; they had no use for the new technologies, weapons, and societal structures that the world beyond relished and valued. This was the world in which Lily belonged and she knew it in her heart of hearts: she was a quiet, settled girl in a quiet, settled country. Adventure had never once crossed her mind. She couldn't just run away from her life to chase a bad feeling.

Even if she could manage it physically, could she ever be strong enough emotionally?

Her fears were momentarily abated when her uncle materialised at the bottom of the oak stairs that, only a few hours ago, she herself had skipped down, fresh and bright from her morning excursion. His presence was an eternal comfort to her, even in her darkest moods.

'What is it, child?' His brows furrowed, lines of concern stretching across his forehead.

She held out the letter, her hand shaking. He frowned, curious, and beckoned her towards the work desk. He sat behind the desk, placing his half-moon spectacles on his nose.

'Alice is missing,' Lily began. 'I found this in her cabin... I don't understand why she would leave without saying goodbye. She didn't even leave a note.' She placed the crumpled letter down in front of her uncle, flattening it and then watching his face for any sign of recognition.

Uncle Alf's eyes traced the lines on the paper slowly, deliberately, until he reached the final line. The creases on his forehead grew deeper and his face drained of colour. He dropped the letter and rested his face in his hands.

'Wait,' Lily asked, 'what is it? What does this mean?'

'The Shadow Sect. I knew them. Or-or-or at least,' he stuttered, 'I knew *of* them. They haven't shown themselves around these parts in a very long time. Last time they were in the area, there were a series of disappearances, grisly unexplained murders, missing children, that sort of thing.

They disappeared after a while, no doubt to stalk through a different area. I never dreamed that they would come back. I heard the rumours from the other village councillors when I last went to pay our rents to the baron, and I suppose I hoped they'd got the wrong end of the stick, y'know?'

'You heard about this the last time you went to the borderlands? But ... that was so long ago. Why didn't you tell me?'

He shrugged. 'I didn't think anything of it. There's always strange stuff said out on the border ... I think the baron likes to start rumours; he fought on the other side during the wars, you know. I don't think he likes that we were left to our own devices; he thinks we should all be joined as one fiefdom, with the Brotherhood ruling us all.'

'What? What brotherhood? Alf, how much have you been keeping from me? You always said your trips to the border were quiet, uneventful. None of this sounds quiet or uneventful.'

He looked up from his hands and met Lily's eyes. He went to respond, and then caught himself, his mouth opening and closing like a codfish. He shook his head. 'It doesn't matter now. You're right – maybe I shouldn't have shielded you for so long but ... there's no time now. If they really do have Alice, then you have two options. You give up and accept that your friend is gone – and by the sounds of things, she's gone willingly, so they might spare her life. Or...' He paused, hoping, perhaps, that Lily would be content to let her friend go. Instead, she knew there was a terrified defiance in her face, a fierce refusal to accept Alice's disappearance. 'Or you go after her. You go after her and hope with all of your might that you catch her before they get under her skin. But you have to be willing to accept that the Alice you find may not be the Alice you remember.'

'Does it have to be me that goes? Could you not contact someone in Kelseth? The warden would help, I'm sure he would. We could write to him and send it on the afternoon mail coach... It would reach him by this evening, and we could have an answer by tomorrow, or perhaps the day after. Or come with me and we can ask around, see if anyone has seen her?' But Lily knew she was asking too much.

Deep down, she knew that Alice was her responsibility, but she still dreaded the idea of leaving her home, her forests, her life. She hadn't even stopped to consider what she would do when, or if, she did find her friend. What if she didn't want to come back?

What if it wasn't safe? What if all the rumours were true...?

'You know the answer to that yourself, love,' her uncle said sympathetically. 'I can't go with you, we'd lose too much business, and if she has gone willingly then it isn't wise to inform people that she has joined them. If she can be saved, we need to make sure you've got as many people as possible on your side when you both return.' Lily nodded, understanding. 'What I can do to help though is arm you with knowledge. I can share with you what I know about the Shadow Sect, and maybe you might be able to outsmart them. They will be counting on your generation being ignorant of their crimes.'

Lily grabbed her worn notebook and a pencil, poised to

record anything and everything her uncle could share that might help her with this seemingly impossible task. If she was going to do this, she would do it logically, with notes and plans and schemes.

'The Shadow Sect are a group that leave death and destruction in their wake. They target poor areas and vulnerable girls and young women, hoping that they can mould and shape any early signs of their potential.'

Lily interrupted, 'But why? There must be a purpose, a ... goal or end point that we aren't aware of, surely?'

Alf shrugged. 'Perhaps. Whatever it is, they've not brought it to our attention; we've only ever known of the murders and the kidnappings. If your friend Alice has gone to them willingly then you'd better hope that she shows signs of potential, because it will buy you more time to save her.'

'But ... why would they go to all of this effort just for Alice? No one else has disappeared around Alder Vale ... have they?' Lily felt panic-stricken: she was convinced that the Sect had recruited Alice by mistake.

'Who knows, but either way I hope she's thought this through, because it's going to take you a while to track them,' Alf explained, his heavy brows shielding his eyes.

'How do you know all of this?' Lily asked, for the first time realising that Alf had an awful lot of knowledge for a man who knew of the Sect 'in passing'.

'Hearsay, you know. People talk; they love nothing more than a good gossip over their morning tea. All you need is a good pair of ears and a trustworthy position in the community and you'd be surprised how much you can learn. The apothecary is the hub of all gossip, you should know that. There's not a single thing that happens in this town that you and I don't hear about.

'Anyway, how I gain my knowledge doesn't matter now. What matters is that you go upstairs, pack as lightly as you can, and go after her. She'll only have a day's head start on you. You may be able to catch her before too much damage is done.'

Lily begrudgingly accepted Uncle Alf's evasion of her question, but promised herself that she'd ask him how he had acquired such extensive knowledge when she returned. Preoccupied with unease and the million questions spinning around her head, she rushed upstairs, grabbed her tattered travelling bag and threw it on her bed. She snatched a few warm dresses, a heavy woollen cloak, a few leather hair ties, and thick cotton scraps in case her courses came early; she didn't know whether she'd be gone a couple of days or a couple of weeks and it never hurt to be prepared.

With her bag packed and slung over her broad shoulders, Lily sprinted downstairs and raided the kitchen and the apothecary stores for food and a few of her favourite tinctures and salves for minor injuries. She tucked a tiny bottle of anxiety-reducing smelling salts into the deep pocket of her dress, keeping it close at hand in case anything got too overwhelming.

The sun was yawning in the burnt autumn sky and dusk was chasing it away with his shroud of darkness. As Lily wrapped her cloak around her shoulders, her uncle reappeared, carrying an old leather-bound book. 'This may come in handy, if it's the same group as last time. When you're alone and you're sure that you're not being watched, open it to page one hundred and thirty-seven. It may be more helpful than it initially appears, so be patient with it. Don't allow your logical brain to stifle its true meaning.' He passed the book carefully to her, and Lily examined the cover.

'*Fifty Folk Tales of the Shadow Lands and Beyond*?' She frowned, but didn't question it any further when she saw the severity of her uncle's face.

'Just read it.'

Lily dropped it into her bag and fastened the bronze clasp, before passing the strap over her shoulder and securing it in place with a shaking hand. The bag felt double the weight with the addition of the book nestled amongst her vast collection of 'essential' belongings. The side of her mouth twitched in an attempt at a smile of gratitude, but her confidence and her courage were waning dangerously fast.

'And here,' Alf continued, 'I've written some basic instructions that should get you to Kelseth – where to stop for the night, which stagecoaches to avoid, all those sorts of things. It's the least I can do.' Handing her a crumpled piece of paper, Alf also slipped a few coins into Lily's hand. He closed his hands around hers and squeezed with the tender affection of a father.

'I don't know if I can—'

'Alice needs you, Lily. Do it for her.' Alf embraced her, a tear slipping from his eye and rolling silently down his bearded cheek. 'Now go. Remember: page one hundred and thirty-seven.'

With a deep breath, Lily turned away from her uncle and left the apothecary, holding her head high, trying desperately to retain any semblance of courage she could muster.

She'd barely covered two strides when a voice as shrill and unwelcome as the early morning cockerel broke her resolve in an instant. 'Apothecary!'

Chapter Four

A lice Blackwell opened her eyes.

The world was black, suffocating. There were no stars that night, no moon to illuminate the sky. She had no idea where she was. All she knew was the pain of the splitting headache that resonated from her right temple, the side to side, bone-shaking movement of a horse-drawn cart, and the sound of the hooves that echoed on the cobbles below. Her brain felt foggy and her eyes were crusty with dried tears, and she found herself growing increasingly disturbed and confused.

She scrunched her eyes closed and then opened them again, trying to focus in the darkness. *Where am I?* Panic started to creep in. *How did I get here?*

She breathed in deeply and felt a strange material brush against her lips.

The brain fog disappeared in an instant when she realised the world wasn't black.

There was a heavy bag over her head blocking out the

sky, rendering her blind and helpless. Frightened, she tried to reach up to tear the bag away from her face. Pain shot through her as coarse rope dug into the delicate skin around her bony wrists.

Her hands were bound.

An attempt to separate her ankles confirmed her legs were also tied together. She felt the terror rise in her throat, her breathing became laboured, and she grew unbearably hot with the thick wool pressing against her face.

She couldn't think. She couldn't breathe.

'Help me!' Alice attempted to scream. A gag prevented the words from forming and instead all that escaped from her mouth was a pitiful shriek, muffled and only audible to those nearby. The panic only increased, bile filled her mouth, and sweat dripped mercilessly down her forehead, running down the back of her saturated neck. Alice's heart was hammering so hard she feared her ribcage might actually shatter in her chest. In the distance, she heard the driver of the carriage command the horses to halt and the rumbling of the carriage wheels beneath her stopped.

Disorientated, Alice screamed again, feeling sure that this time she would be heard, now that the carriage was still. She imagined everyone within earshot running to her aid, rescuing her, telling her everything would be all right. She imagined her best friend appearing out of nowhere to hold her hand and guide her home.

Instead, she heard heavy boots walking towards her. The owner of the boots kneeled by her side and Alice could feel the pressure of a hand at her throat as her captor leaned over her and growled. Another pair of boots joined the first, but this second person stayed standing. Alice could feel the power emanating from them both.

'What should I do to her?' the person leaning over Alice, a young-sounding woman with a high-pitched, eerily excitable voice asked.

'Just shut her up and get back to work, all right? There'll be plenty of time for *fun* when we arrive.' The way the second voice, a richer, deeper female voice, paused on the word *fun* made Alice's skin crawl. Her repulsion and her terror at that sentence was the last thing she felt for a while. The first person, evidently frustrated, grumbled and cursed, before Alice felt a heavy blow to her temple.

The world fell silent and black once more.

Chapter Five

Oh, no ... not her, not now. Lily expelled a heavy breath and turned slowly, painfully towards the direction of the unwelcome speaker. *Why doesn't she just call me by my name?*

A short middle-aged woman was charging towards Lily, her cheeks flushed with exertion. The woman had greying hair scraped back into a bun that forced her face into a permanently surprised expression. Somehow, through the stretched skin, she still managed to arrange her features to display complete and utter disdain with a sprinkle of meddling curiosity.

'Apothecary,' the woman said again, now practically nose to nose with Lily, panting from rushing across the square to catch her. Her breath smelled of rancid fish.

'I'm actually just in the middle of something, Jemima, so I can't stop to chat today. Terribly sorry.' Lily attempted to go around her, but Jemima stepped sideways to block her path, an asinine smile plastered across her face.

'Off to pander to the beck and call of the witch-girl, are we?'

'Excuse me?' Lily growled through gritted teeth. She could feel her face growing hot and her eyes were prickly with tears. She wasn't ready for a showdown with Jemima Darroch; she just wanted to get on a stagecoach and disappear before she could lose any more of her fading courage.

'I said—'

'I heard what you said.'

'Now then, child. Your uncle is an upstanding member of our community. Any more of that attitude and we'll be forced to assume he hasn't brought you up as well as he should.'

Lily blinked, dumbfounded.

'We've all stood by whilst you've spent your time dawdling up to wherever her little hovel is, but no more. You've heard the tales, haven't you? She's cursed our town, but that wasn't enough, so now she's cursing the whole of the Shadow Lands. Demons are haunting us, demons of her creation, I'm sure of it. She's conjured an army of shadows to do her bidding. And now look! Children missing, livestock slaughtered and stolen from their barns, strange goings-on across the moors and down to the sea.

'Isn't it time she moved on and left us all in peace? We won't stand for it anymore, and we certainly won't stand for one of our own sympathising. If *you* don't tell her to get gone,' Jemima poked Lily with a wizened finger in the centre of her chest, 'believe me, child, we will.'

Lily swatted the hand away. 'Don't touch me. And don't

you dare threaten me.' She swallowed the lump in her throat and tried to make herself look bigger, more imposing. 'The last person in Alder Vale that you should be threatening is the person with the power not only to unleash the secrets of your...' Lily snarled, *'problems*, but who also has the power to make them a whole lot worse.'

Jemima stumbled backwards. 'How dare you!'

'No, how dare you. Now, if you'll excuse me, I have somewhere to be.' Lily shouldered past Jemima and marched towards the waiting stagecoach. Fury was burning in her veins.

Through the anger, Lily felt a strange gratefulness for the cantankerous woman and her unpleasant, judgemental ways. Jemima Darroch had just made leaving Alder Vale so much easier.

She wiped her face of tears and handed her heavy bag up to the driver, before taking a seat inside the shady, wooden coach that would take her onwards.

Towards Alice.

Chapter Six

The stagecoach rolled into the sleepy village of Ardnaroch just as the sun was awakening. It stopped with an unexpected, forceful jolt and the driver climbed down from his seat at the front. The next thing Lily saw was her large travelling bag flying past the window, thrown carelessly by the driver with a complete disregard for its contents. It landed in a crumpled heap on the dusty cobbled village square. He yanked open the door and demanded that the lone traveller remove herself from the coach and be on her way. 'This is as far as I'll go, lass. There's no point complainin'. Out you get, c'mon.' He silenced her objections before climbing back up to his perch.

Lily clambered out, confused, dejected, but too tired to hold onto any anger. Her courage had left her for the hundredth time since she left home, somewhere on a nauseatingly winding road in the middle of the night. She had woken from an awkward sleeping position to find herself trapped between a plump man and a withered old woman clutching a grumpy-looking hen. It had been an uncomfortable journey to say the least. The last thing she needed was the driver to refuse to take her where she had paid to go: Kelseth.

She looked up at him with tired eyes, attempting to appeal to his sympathetic side and began, 'Why won't you take me? And why didn't you tell me yesterday morning, when I paid you?'

He turned to her slowly from his position high above her, impatience clearly marked on his lined face. 'I just don't go there anymore lass. A lot of us don't. The entire place is accursed, if you ask me. I'm sorry, but I'd really best be on my way. Best o' luck with the rest o' your journey.' With that, he whipped his horses and turned the stagecoach around, disappearing like a ghost into the fog, back down the road in the direction from which they had come.

Lily stood staring until the coach was completely out of sight. She closed her eyes, took a deep breath, and then stooped to pick up her bag. She had no idea how far away Ardnaroch was from Kelseth, or how she was going to get there. She consulted the notes Alf had given her before she left, but found no reference to Ardnaroch, or any suggestions for a place to stay nearby.

I just need to find someone to talk to, that's all. She tried to comfort herself, refusing to let her worrying mind take over this early on in her journey. *I'm sure there's someone around here who wouldn't mind helping. Maybe they'll have a map or something. It'll be fine.* She breathed in and out a few times, trying to slow her raging heartbeat, and looked around.

Ardnaroch was an old-looking place, with clusters of strangely misshapen houses and shops built from crumbling bricks. Most of the roofs were thatched, but not in the careful, pretty style she was used to seeing back home. Instead, these were far more ramshackle, as if someone had just thrown bunches of branches and twigs in the general direction of the roofs, hoping they'd stick there long enough that no one would notice the job was only half-done.

Lily couldn't quite believe she was less than a day's travel from Alder Vale. Even the glowing, sanguine light of the approaching dawn couldn't brighten the mottled atmosphere of this village.

Where were the people? Where was the birdsong?

Lily knew the Shadow Lands had been left behind after the Wars of Change, when those from beyond their shores tried to force their new ideas of progress upon them, but she hadn't realised that a place could feel so … soulless. Lily wondered whether the wars had been harder on these people, whether they were still recovering all this time later.

Ardnaroch was built around the one road that snaked into, and then out of, the village through an uneven cobbled square. There were squat houses behind the few shops, but everything looked desolate and uninviting. There were no comfortable hearths in Ardnaroch.

The only sound that broke the silence was a rhythmic hammering coming from a smithy in the corner of the square. A hulking man – the blacksmith, Lily presumed – didn't look up from his anvil. The *tap, tap, tap* echoed out across the moor. A death knell, a warning.

This kind of place should be bustling, Lily thought. There must be people toing and froing all the time on their way across the country. But then … where were they?

In the centre, a large wooden sign pointed backwards to a village called Barley – which she remembered passing through a little while before the coach dropped her off – and onwards to Kelseth. The sign gave no indication of distances and she was reluctant to set off walking if Kelseth was still days and days away.

Lily knew all too well the dangers of underestimating this rural, pastoral landscape. The countryside all across the Shadow Lands was pock-marked with little villages sprouting awkwardly from the moorland. Sometimes the villages were only a small distance apart, often visible one from the other on a clear day. However, some villages were separated by deep, damp bogs or thick forests. In those conditions, even a place just half a day's travel away as the crow flies could take a week with the effort and navigational skill needed to venture across the difficult terrain. Kelseth could be close by, but Lily knew she would need local expertise if she was to venture there safely.

From her position in the centre of Ardnaroch's village square, Lily examined the crooked buildings, looking for any sign that she wouldn't be thrown out the minute she stepped inside one of them. She sighed. The entire place had a general air of desolation, as if every single villager knew that she was from elsewhere and that was all they needed to know about her in order to want to keep their distance. It was such a contrast from her home, where the windows glowed with warm light and the townsfolk welcomed almost everyone who passed through.

It felt like a different world.

On her third round of squinting through the dawn sunshine at the surrounding structures, disappointed to find that none of them appeared friendly whatsoever, she decided that the apothecary was probably the best place to start. If nothing else, their shared trade would hopefully allow Lily to gain the apothecary's trust.

She walked towards a building with a hand-painted sign hanging outside depicting a bubbling cauldron encircled by bunches of herbs. She stood tall, trying to make herself appear confident, carefree, and distinctly non-threatening in the hope that someone might decide she was worth helping.

A bell chimed as she walked through the door and went up to the counter. There were a few other people waiting to be served, standing in the early morning light that was shining through the grubby windows. A young girl was unsuccessfully trying to clean the glass panes, clearly impatient that her work was being disturbed by the presence of customers.

Several of the people waiting to be served turned to look at Lily, suspicion clear in their judgemental eyes. Strangers were clearly not common here. Lily tried her best to ignore them and instead let her eyes wander around the interior of the room. It was very well organised, she had to admit, although there was something unsettling about how clean and tidy it was. There was no life in the walls of the place, no soul, no story. This apothecary couldn't have been more different from the one Lily called home.

Lily's was always full of bright, glowing sunlight. There were wild herbs everywhere, flowers in cracked, hand-painted vases and a sense of hope hiding on every shelf. This space was something else entirely, filled with shadowy corners, dark, dusty bookshelves, and smoke from candles and burning incense that caught in the back of Lily's throat and made her feel like she needed to cough. The bottles stacked high on shelves behind the counter were filled with dark, ominous-looking liquids with brown handwritten labels in a scrawl that Lily couldn't make out. The whole room had a surreal, haunted atmosphere, much like the village outside the door. It was oppressive, disquieting.

Lily's eye was caught by several advertisements stuck to the front of the counter. Most of them were to be expected, such as 'Missing Cat' signs and vacancy notices. One poster, however, caught Lily's eye. It was frayed slightly at the edges, as if it had been stuck up for weeks. Lily was unable to get close enough to read all the text without drawing more attention to herself, but she could clearly see the heading: 'MISSING CHILDREN', and underneath that was a series of sketches of little faces, all young and scared, drawn to reflect the horror of their disappearances. Her heart skipped a beat.

This tattered forgotten sign was proof that she was heading in the right direction, but instead of affirming her belief in herself and in her task, she found herself growing even more unnerved. Each hour brought her closer to being reunited with Alice, which could only be a good thing. But each hour also brought her closer to facing an unknown foe that made her skin crawl and her hands tremble. Somehow, she, an apothecary far better suited to treating wounds than causing them, had to figure out a way to rescue Alice.

Someone loudly cleared their throat, which brought Lily out of her thoughts with a start, and she looked around, realising that everyone else in the room had left. A woman who Lily assumed was the apothecary had been the one to clear her throat, no doubt impatient to serve Lily and send her on her way – preferably back to from whence she came.

'Can I help you, madam?' she asked, with stiff politeness. She was ageless, tall and slender, with dark circles beneath her eyes as if she hadn't slept properly in weeks. They looked as haunted as each other.

Lily suddenly realised she didn't actually have a plan if anyone asked her what, exactly, she was doing. How would she know who to trust? *Or*, she thought, *perhaps I can't trust anyone at all*. She cleared her throat and tried to look self-assured. 'I-if you don't mind,' Lily stuttered, 'I'd like to know how long it would take me to walk to Kelseth from here please, and how I might go about getting there...' Lily trailed off when she saw the expression that flickered over the apothecary's face.

'K-Kelseth?' she stuttered. 'Why on earth do you want to go there, child?'

'I just really need to get there as quickly as possible.' Lily stood tall and firm, hoping the apothecary wouldn't question her any further.

'That *place*,' she snarled, as if unable to utter *Kelseth* again, 'is still another three, maybe four days' travel on foot.

It's hard going and there's only one coaching inn between here and there and even then, a lot of coachmen refuse to go further than here. Tell me this: is your reason for going there honourable? That is, you're not going to...' she paused to whisper, '*join anyone,* are you?' This final question sounded more like an accusation, as she exaggerated every syllable in an attempt to convey some secret meaning of which Lily felt completely ignorant.

'I promise you that my intentions are good and honest. I wouldn't be going if it wasn't entirely necessary.' Lily's heart was battering her ribcage, but the apothecary's face softened. Could she actually be getting somewhere?

The woman sighed. 'We've all been worried, see. You've probably seen the poster?' She pointed at the tattered sign Lily had seen earlier. 'We've been worried that whatever has taken those kids down Kelseth way will come up here, and then you turn up looking suspicious and, obviously, we had to assume the worst. But, I don't know ... you don't look the type. Just, give me a second.' Lily nodded and the woman disappeared. Lily could hear tense muttering between two people and then a door slammed.

A few moments later, the apothecary reappeared, holding a folded brown parchment in her hands. She handed it to Lily with an apologetic smile. 'I'm afraid this is about as much as I'm able to help you. It's seen a few decades, and passed through many a hand, but not much changes around these parts. I'm pretty confident it'll set you on the right course.'

Lily unfolded the parchment to reveal a beautiful, if a little faded, map of the whole of the Shadow Lands; she'd never seen anything quite like it. The edges were worn but beautifully hand-illustrated and she could clearly see the path she needed to take to find her way safely to Kelseth. It far surpassed anything she could have hoped for. But, looking at the distance between Ardnaroch, the coaching inn, and Kelseth, when there was no scale to judge how far it would actually be on foot, Lily felt nauseous. This really could take days. It could even take weeks…

'Thank you. You've been a great help.' Lily nodded, swallowing a lump of hopelessness that caught in her throat and turned to leave.

'I'm sorry I couldn't be of more assistance but … help can be found if you look hard enough for it. When you see a sign'—something about the look in the apothecary's eyes made Lily feel strange—'take it.' There was an intensity in the woman's face, like she was silently trying to convey some hidden message in her words. A shiver passed down Lily's spine as the woman disappeared once more into the back of her shop. She didn't re-emerge.

Just as Lily reached out for the door handle, it swung violently open and a hulking man in long golden robes stood silhouetted in the doorframe. He stomped past Lily, ignoring her, and rapped his fist on the counter. 'Hello?' he cried out, and then glanced over his shoulder at Lily. 'Do you work here?'

'N-no.' Lily stuttered, and turned to leave. The man, in his impossibly pristine robes, made her uneasy.

'Who are you then? I haven't seen you around here. Where are you going?'

Lily didn't know what to say. Why was he so interested?

'I said...' He took a threatening step towards her. Hanging around his neck, and sitting large and glinting on his chest, was a pendant – a strange symbol that looked like a knotted tree encircled in more shimmering gold. 'Where are you going?' His upper lip twitched into a snarl.

'Brother?' The apothecary had reappeared and the man whirled around.

Lily took the opportunity of his distraction and bolted out of the door, her forehead dripping with sweat. *What was all that about?* She didn't want to hang around to find out.

She shouldered her bag and walked away from the apothecary as quickly as she dared, hoping not to draw any further attention to herself.

Ardnaroch was still eerily quiet. A roll of thunder rattled in the distance and the early morning sun had been shrouded by thick, heavy grey clouds. A storm was brewing. No wonder all the townsfolk were hiding away; the threat of bad weather *and* the presence of a strange unknown woman wandering about the place were enough to put anyone off the idea of heading out of doors.

Well, she thought, *perhaps if I'm lucky a coach will pass me on this road, but I'm not going to stick around this creepy old place.* With a deep breath, she left Ardnaroch behind, hurrying away from its furtive glances and whispered suspicions.

She couldn't shake the unease the man had sparked in her. She had never seen anyone so finely dressed in all of her life. Could he have been from beyond the Shadow Lands? And what was it the apothecary had called him? Brother? Where had she heard that before?

She didn't stop until Ardnaroch was barely a speck in the distance behind her. She felt vulnerable enough without the prospect of being followed.

Even so, it was a relief to get moving – if she ignored the sense of foreboding that she was never, ever going to reach Kelseth, let alone conserve enough energy to actually be able to help Alice when she got there. After so long cooped up in one attitude, squeezed between grumpy people in a rattling stagecoach, the simple act of walking along a driftway was a comfort.

She stretched her arms above her head and rolled her shoulders, encouraging the stiffness away from her muscles. Her heart slowed to a more comfortable rhythm and her speed dropped off to a sustainable fast walk. If the man had intended to follow her, she'd have spotted him by now.

No, he was just a bizarre, nosey man wanting to know what a young girl was doing wandering about alone. He was no different to anyone else.

She rearranged the bag on her shoulder; it was growing heavier as she walked. She wished the book Alf had given her had been less of a physical burden. But even with the weight of it, she couldn't bring herself to rip out the relevant pages and abandon the rest of the book by the side of the road. Books were too precious for that.

A furtive glance behind her confirmed that Ardnaroch was but a distant, fading place to which she'd be happy never to return. But then she spotted something strange.

Something coming towards her.

Lily's hands started to shake uncontrollably. She glanced

around for somewhere to hide, but she was surrounded by flat, bleak moorland.

He was coming for her, she knew it deep in her heart. And there was nothing she could do, nowhere she could go.

She was trapped.

Chapter Seven

L ily squinted through the gathering drizzle as the hazy shape came closer and closer. Instinctively, she leapt backwards, tripping over an unseen boulder. She clattered to the ground with a thud and cried out as her ankle twisted painfully beneath her.

She scrambled away from the road, dragging her throbbing ankle along the ground before crouching awkwardly in a pathetic patch of heather. All she could do was lie there half-hidden whilst her assailant grew ever closer.

The sound of hooves echoed through the air. After the sinister gold-robed man from Ardnaroch, a highwayman was about the worst possible thing she could encounter. This had to be more than bad luck; she had been followed.

The hooves stumbled to a stop.

She rubbed the rain out of her eyes and peered upwards. She was met by the sight of a huge, sleek chestnut horse with a pale cream mane and bright, intelligent eyes. It had no rider. There was no highwayman.

She was safe.

The horse was cantering back and forth on the road in front of Lily, whinnying and snorting with impatience. Steam danced upwards from its hulking muscles, giving it a sparkling, magical air of otherworldliness. The steed's chestnut coat rippled like flickering flames; it looked fit for the mightiest warrior, ready to charge headlong and fearlessly into battle. Lily couldn't believe her luck.

She clambered to her feet and took a tentative step towards the horse, careful not to put weight on her ankle. She held out a shaky hand and let the horse come to her. The huge beast trotted forwards and nuzzled its nose into Lily's hand and then turned so that she was faced with its flank. There was a beautiful, supple leather saddle already sitting perfectly on the horse's back, with 'Morrigan' carved around the curved edge.

'Morrigan,' Lily whispered to herself, tracing the intricate letters with her finger. The horse gave a satisfied whinny and nestled its nose into Lily's neck. 'That's your name? Morrigan?' Lily took the subsequent grunt as a yes.

In the pocket of the saddle, Lily noticed a small corner of white sticking out awkwardly, contrasted against the honey-brown of the leather. She tugged on the corner and it came free. It was a torn-off piece of paper with rough edges and deep folds. Unfurling it, Lily read the six short words that would give her the first tangible hope she'd felt since she left Uncle Alf and Alder Vale behind:

The sign you seek is here.

Lily glanced around again, wondering whether this horse had simply bolted and left its poor rider behind, but there wasn't a soul to be seen. Lily remembered what the apothecary had said just before she left. *When you see a sign ... take it.*

This had to be it. Morrigan was here for *her*. Lily spared herself the agony of fixating on the details, of the how and the why. Morrigan could help her reach Alice in half the time. *And*, she mused, *at least now I'm not alone anymore.*

Reaching into her pack, Lily withdrew one of the apples she'd packed for her journey. As an offering of kinship, she held it out on a flat palm for the horse. Morrigan didn't hesitate to gobble it straight out of Lily's hand, and nuzzled her once more in thanks.

'I guess we're to be friends then, you and I?' Lily stroked the bridge of Morrigan's nose, which inspired another satisfied whinny from the horse.

Lily slung her pack over Morrigan and attached it with one of the saddle's many brass buckles. She had always felt an affinity with animals, with the natural world, and this was no different. Morrigan was here to help her, yes, but she would give Morrigan the love, care, and attention she deserved, too. It was only fair.

'Will you help me find Alice?' Lily whispered, her voice catching in her throat. A final whinny and gentle butt of the head told her that Morrigan was growing impatient.

'Point taken,' she said. 'Let's get going, shall we?'

With a struggle, she climbed up on Morrigan's broad

back, almost slipping off the other side of the saddle. Her knuckles were bright white as she clung to the reins and took deep, steady breaths. She had ridden horses several times throughout her childhood, but she'd never travelled any real distance on one. But something about Morrigan's presence calmed her. She had forgotten just how much she missed the feeling of being connected to another creature and for the first time since she had set off, she felt a courage that grew from having the horse to accompany her. A new friend to help in the search for an old one.

Lily grasped the reins, clicked her tongue and instructed Morrigan to start down the winding road that stretched ahead, disappearing into the creeping fog in the distance.

Everything ached. It was like each of Lily's muscles was crying out in pain with every one of Morrigan's steps. They had been riding for hours. The novelty of rediscovering the joy of being on a horse had worn off shortly after she had to convince Morrigan to squelch through a thick, peaty bog that smelled so strongly of rotting eggs that Lily's head had felt it might burst with the fumes. The poor horse had trudged along without complaint or long periods of rest for the entire day and Lily felt she had little right to complain when all she had to do was sit there and guide her.

The landscape around them was strangely unchanging. It almost felt like she was trotting on the spot, for the miles upon miles of open moorland remained consistent throughout that day. At first, the sight of the heather still blooming, the open road, the undulating rolling hills had brought comfort to her. She had always surrounded herself with nature and she had been quietly gratified that this journey kept her amongst the wild things.

After a few more hours though, it had become maddening, disorientating. Even glaring at the map, she couldn't pick out one feature in the landscape from another. She felt heavy on the poor horse's back and pitied Morrigan's bad luck for ending up with her on this wretched journey.

They stopped to drink water and eat some simple food – bread and cheese for Lily and water and oats for Morrigan – when things got too much to bear. They lingered there together on the mossy ground and let their muscles rest while Lily pored over the map and Alf's instructions. She absentmindedly stroked the horse's soft mane for comfort, but something prickled on the back of her neck. She hadn't been able to shake the feeling of unease for a while, and it was growing.

Morrigan whinnied. If Lily hadn't already been nervous, she would have shaken off the concern that was laced through such a simple, natural noise for the horse. But Lily was nervous, and Morrigan seemed to be too.

Lily jumped, her stomach experiencing an uncomfortable swoop as the horse suddenly shot up. She stood directly in front of Lily, glaring down at her, her hooves scraping into the dirt like she wanted to run.

They were still surrounded by damp fog and the shadows of the setting sun cast strange shapes both up ahead and back in the direction from which they had come.

More than once, Lily had been sure she'd seen someone out there, following at a near-invisible distance. She had shaken it off as worry shrouded in the immense tiredness that coursed through her body. Still, the twisting, clenching ache in the pit of her stomach was enough to keep her glancing behind her every few moments, sure that she would see a figure materialise from the fog.

She tried, unsuccessfully, to calm the horse, but Morrigan wouldn't settle.

'What's got into you?' Lily whispered, trying to keep her voice confident and calm. She realised there was no use fighting the stubborn mare. Reluctantly, Lily clambered back into Morrigan's saddle and dug her heels into the horse's sides, encouraging the tired creature to keep on moving. The faster they reached the coaching inn, the sooner they could both rest their aching limbs. She kept picturing the azure flicker of the sea on the horizon, searching for some kind of confirmation that she hadn't strayed too far from the road, that she was still travelling towards Kelseth, towards Alice.

They had barely moved a few strides before a violet strike of lightning spiked across the sky, briefly illuminating the world around them. Rain started to hammer from above, and within moments she was soaked to the skin and shivering ferociously. Her horse continued to canter forwards, seemingly unabated by the brutal weather, and Lily was thankful all over again for the company and strength Morrigan provided. What would she have done without her? Lightning flashed through the sky again, but this time, Lily saw something else.

Something strange.

The prickling feeling on the back of her neck returned as she saw a hooded figure on a horse in the distance. The figure seemed to notice her at the same time; they locked eyes across the heath and then he was charging towards her, flying like a person possessed. With a shout, Lily commanded Morrigan to run, urging the horse to go as fast as she possibly could, away from their pursuer.

Rain blinded Lily and stung her skin as it slapped against her frozen face. Breath broke from her lungs in gasps and Morrigan panted heavily beneath her from the exertion. She didn't waver though, and she didn't stumble. She valiantly carried Lily onwards, away from the shadow on their tail.

'Leave me alone,' Lily whispered. 'Please leave me alone.' Fear rumbled through her. She felt like she might drown in it. She willed the rider to give up, to realise she wasn't the person he was seeking. Scrunching her eyes closed, she begged and pleaded to the rainclouds to drive him away.

Summoning her courage, she glanced behind her. How close was he now?

Her heart swooped. There was nothing there. Lily slowed Morrigan and stretched her neck around, trying to squint through the rain and the darkness to identify their moorland stalker, but they were alone.

Entirely alone.

Chapter Eight

'She's important, that's all Winter said. She doesn't want her harmed. We'll have to think of an excuse for her bruised face, 'cause I don't know about you but I don't much fancy ending up on Winter's bad side.'

Alice had regained consciousness but was careful not to open her eyes. She was sure that she was the subject of interest for whomever it was that was talking. If she stayed still and quiet, pretending to be lifeless, she might be able to garner some information on where she was going and why she had been kidnapped.

Everything still felt woolly, as if the whole world was wrapped in furs, muffling everything. Every sound, every emotion, every feeling. But she was sure now that the woollen bag over her head had been removed, and that the woolly-feeling stemmed from the pain that pulsed through her head.

She had to make a concerted effort to focus on the voices. Alice almost flinched when she felt a dampness pressed to her forehead, perilously close to the throbbing pain in her temple where she had been knocked unconscious. Had that happened earlier that day or had she been out cold for longer than that? The empty feeling in her stomach told her that she hadn't eaten in a long time, but she couldn't be sure how long.

The dampness on her head returned but this time it was gentle. Alice realised that someone was mopping her forehead, keeping her cool, making sure she didn't catch a fever. That person spoke next:

'She's young, though,' the voice said. It was a deep, strong voice, but Alice couldn't pinpoint from where the accent originated. 'She must be the same age as me, or a year or so younger. Why did we have to take her by force? I'm sure she would have come willingly...' The voice stumbled and petered out.

'Don't go getting sentimental about her. Just because you're a Protector doesn't mean you have to protect everyone. Don't waste your energy.'

'But what if I could convince the priestess to let me care for her? At least until she gets a bit stronger, and then maybe I could train with her. I could help her find the strength to get through this.' The girl mopping Alice's head continued, 'I got through it, didn't I? I may not have been training to use magic, but Protector training is just as brutal, if not more so.'

'Don't start,' the other voice warned. The first speaker sighed and Alice felt the breath brush her cheek. The conversation seemed to be over and a silence fell. Alice could still feel the rumbling of the wheels beneath her and tried to focus on the rhythmic beat of the horse's hooves to keep her present. She had learned very little from the conversation, but what she *did* learn was that she was needed for something. Something important and something for which she needed to train.

She could fight unconsciousness no longer. Oblivion slipped over her like fire over kindling.

Chapter Nine

L ily and Morrigan had covered an impossible distance
while pursued by the hooded figure. Lily couldn't
settle, could barely breathe still, even after they had
cantered on for hours after they lost sight of him. Her hands
were frozen over the reins, her knuckles so strained that it
looked like they were trying to break through her skin. The
rain had calmed into an annoyingly constant drizzle that
meant she hadn't been able to dry off at all since their
ordeal. She just shivered incessantly, goosebumps covering
her body.

As they rounded a corner, the most welcome sight came
into view. A coaching inn. It was the only building or sign
of human habitation she had seen since Ardnaroch. There
were no farms or grazing animals around and the landscape
was completely barren in the darkness, aside from the
endless bracken and heather.

Lily struggled to understand why someone, years ago,
had decided to drag all the materials here to build such a

rickety building. Coaching inns were required on busy byways and through-roads, but the track Lily was riding down was barely even visible through the tall grass and marshy moorland. It was almost as if this inn had fallen from the sky one day and its owners had clawed their way up from their nameless graves beneath the heath to run it.

As she drew closer, Morrigan slowed instinctively, and both Lily and her horse gazed up at the huge stone building. Parallel to the heavy oak front door, a tall signboard stood at a crooked angle, rusting in the damp evening air. The sign announced that Lily had arrived at The Old Silent Inn. The sign was painted in muted colours, depicting a ghostly ship with silver sails, illuminated by the light of a delicate crescent moon and several twinkling stars. The illustration had probably once been breathtaking, a real testament to the artist's skill, but now, with its peeling paint, the sign only intensified the ramshackle, soul-stirring atmosphere of the inn itself. With each gust of wind, the rusty metal hinges that held the sign to its post sounded like a woman's pained cry and it echoed across the gathering darkness.

There was a soft, warm glow coming from the grubby windows – a tell-tale sign of the candles and roaring fire that would surely be waiting inside. She shook off her childish fears, dismounted, and led Morrigan around the side of the inn to where there was a covered stable. There were no other horses, so Lily tied up her horse in the nearest, most sheltered stall and patted her on the side affectionately.

Morrigan had been her companion for just a day, but it

felt like the shared exhaustion of the journey had forged an unbreakable bond between them. *From now on*, she decided, *wherever I go, Morrigan goes.* Just before she left the horse, Lily took Morrigan's muzzle in her hands and kissed her gently on the nose. 'I'll be back with some water and some oats just as soon as I've sorted a room out for the night. Rest now, sweet girl.' Morrigan snorted with gratitude.

Lily calmed herself with a deep breath, trying to ignore the rattling heart threatening to leap out of her chest, held her head high, and feigned enough confidence to walk into the inn. She had never, in her entire life, entered a place like this without Uncle Alf in tow. With him by her side, she became invisible. He always did the talking, sorted out their rooms, ordered the food, made sure they had a seat by the fire, and allowed Lily to simply enjoy the peace of a little break away from the village. They tended to use inns and coaching houses whenever they needed to take a longer trip to collect ingredients for remedies that weren't easily harvestable from their local hedgerows.

Every few months, Alf would close the shop up early on a Friday afternoon and he would take Lily on an adventure for a few days. Sometimes they would travel north, venturing over the glens to collect mosses with special healing properties. Other times they would travel west to the coastline to harvest seaweed and see if they could spot a mermaid or a selkie if they were lucky. Lily was used to a little bit of travel, but she had always had Alf to guide her, to protect her, to lean on. Those adventures had never required bravery or strength. This adventure required every ounce of courage that Lily possessed.

The problem with being a lone female traveller in these parts, especially late in the evening, was that Lily drew attention to herself simply by existing. Women didn't travel alone. Especially young women. Lily was already bound to attract suspicious glances, but that, combined with her scared-rabbit eyes, short stature, freckled skin, and easily-flushed cheeks, meant she gave out an air of being considerably younger than she was. As she stepped over the threshold into the inn, she tried to ignore every face in the room that turned towards her.

The room had low, dark painted beams and a long bar which was dotted with men who seemed to prefer to stand there rather than find themselves a comfortable seat elsewhere. The inn was filled with a cacophony of heady scents that Lily found quite pleasant: there was the hoppy smell of ale, which was overflowing out of every cask. There was also a warming, spiced scent that seemed to dance through the air, reminding Lily of how hungry she was. Despite the intimidating clientele, Lily relaxed into the character of a confident traveller. Her body ached and she needed nourishment and rest if she was to continue on another long day's trek with Morrigan in the morning.

Lily stood tall, lifted her chin, and approached the bar. She caught the eye of a plump, friendly-looking woman who could only be the landlady. She had a round, welcoming face and a wide smile. Behind the jolly exterior though, Lily could sense a questioning curiosity, a level of concern that radiated from the woman's heavy-lidded eyes.

'Can I help you, love?' the landlady asked. Her gaze flicked behind Lily, following something. A hooded man passed into Lily's peripheral vision as he sauntered up to the bar and plonked himself down atop a barrel, waiting to be served. They met eyes briefly and she noticed a glinting, golden pendant hanging from his neck, visible beneath his hefty cloak – the same pendant that had been fastened around the neck of the golden man in Ardnaroch. This couldn't be a coincidence. Something in his face made Lily feel queasy.

'Yes please.' Lily exhaled, turning to the landlady, concentrating on keeping her voice steady. 'I'm looking for a room for the night, some food, and also I'd like to pay for the stable space I've used for my horse. Is that possible?' The woman seemed trustworthy enough, or at least she was inviting and unintimidating.

'Of course, dear. I'll show you up to one of our best rooms and we can discuss everything up there. Shall we?' She gestured to Lily to lead the way up the staircase on the left wall of the room. Once they ascended the stairs, the landlady led the way along a creaky corridor, opening a door at the end with a heavy iron key. With a firm flourish of her wrist, she gestured for Lily to walk inside.

'Now then, have a seat, will you?' Lily unfastened her sopping travelling cloak from around her neck and removed the heavy material from her shoulders, before perching on the edge of the bed, conscious that the rain had soaked through all of her layers. The landlady carefully closed the wooden door and then whirled around. 'You're being followed, did you know?'

'What?'

'That man, at the bar, he deliberately chose the spot next

to you. I watched him seek you out before he committed to coming inside properly.'

Lily's head was filled with hornets. She felt dizzy, panic rising in her throat. 'I knew it. I was followed all the way here. He chased me, me and my horse, across the moors. It was...' Lily's voice caught in her throat. 'It was horrible.'

'Do you want to tell me why a young girl like you is travelling this far out, in the night, alone?' The kindness had left her eyes, but she didn't seem threatening – only concerned and suspicious. Perhaps the stories of the Shadow Sect had reached this area too, and she was simply checking that Lily wasn't deceptively dangerous.

Lily frowned, unsure of how much to reveal. Before she had time to reply, however, the landlady shook her head and sat next to Lily on the bed. 'I'm sorry, dear. Where are my manners? You're here looking for sanctuary and I interrogate you. Let's start again.' She held out a hand, which Lily shook, gripping the hand tightly and demonstrating that she wasn't weak or vulnerable (even if she felt it). 'My name is Lorenna. This is my inn. I hardly have a right to judge you for being on your own when here I am, an *old maid*,' she rolled her eyes, 'with a business to run and a level of respect to maintain. I'll have that man turned out, don't worry. You do need to be careful though...'

Lily smiled gratefully. 'My name is Lily. And to tell you the truth, I'm feeling a bit out of my depth.' She sighed, and continued, 'I'm travelling to Kelseth. I'm seeking out a friend there, but that man unsettled me. That and the horrendous storm. It's not been the easiest journey.' She laughed meekly.

'Well, first things first, you and your poor horse need some proper food. Get yourself freshened up and then come down and we can sort everything out, all right? Don't worry about paying just now, and don't worry about that man – for this evening, at least. You're safe here.' Lorenna stood and brushed down her dress. 'Anyway, I have just the thing to distract you; we're having a folklore reading by the fire tonight. You're more than welcome to join.' With a kind half-smile, she left, closing the door behind her and leaving Lily alone with her thoughts.

After splashing her face with the water in the bowl on her windowsill, Lily reached into her bag, hoping that her spare dress had survived the relentless rainfall. She pulled out the heavy wool dress and, thankfully, it was bone dry. She changed quickly, stretched, and flopped down onto the creaky bed, aching. She caught a glimpse of her face in the tall mirror at the other end of the room, and immediately wished she hadn't.

Had it really only been yesterday that she was lying under her oak tree, carefree and bare-legged, looking forward to spending time with her best friend? It felt like a lifetime ago. Her eyes that had once shone with the joy of being free from worry were now circled with the charcoal shade that only tiredness could provide. She looked pale, paler than normal; her skin was practically translucent, almost grey. Her wild hair circled her head like a fiery halo, only making her appearance even more dishevelled. She felt her old self fading away. In her place was a feral, half-broken young woman with a tiredness that mere rest and food couldn't chase away. *But,* she thought, *perhaps I need to be feral to fight these people. Sometimes, a little wildness is key.*

She dampened her hands and attempted to flatten the hurricane of curls, but to no avail. Lily sighed and ventured back downstairs, heading out into the cold to make sure Morrigan was well-fed and comfortable. The horse was lying down, having demolished a bucket of oats, and was dozing, so Lily tiptoed away, careful not to disturb the poor, exhausted creature.

When Lorenna saw Lily reappear, she gestured for her to take a large, wing-backed leather chair by the fire. Lily glanced around, seeking out the oppressive gaze of the strange man, but couldn't see him. She dropped down into the chair feeling relieved and, positioning herself sideways, she flung her legs over one of the chair arms, too tired to bother about keeping up appearances. She had no intention of sitting like a normal person after hours of aching in the saddle.

Shortly after the chill had started to leave the tips of Lily's fingers, Lorenna appeared holding a bowl of steaming soup with a wooden spoon and a hunk of bread slathered in dripping. Lily's stomach growled with appreciation and she thanked Lorenna multiple times in between mouthfuls.

'He's gone. I told him we didn't have any spare rooms for this evening. Before he left, he asked me something strange... He asked me if I'd heard about the Lightkeepers. Is that anything to do with you?'

Lily frowned and spluttered through a mouth full of

bread, 'No, no, I don't know anything about any lightkeepers.'

'Odd.' Lorenna shrugged. 'He wasn't happy, but I watched him ride away. You're safe.'

Lily just nodded and smiled gratefully, still shovelling food into her mouth.

'I'm telling my tale very shortly. You shouldn't have to move though, just pull your chair around a little and you'll have an acceptable view. Finish your soup and then I'll get started.'

Chapter Ten

Lorenna stood on a stumpy barrel that was covered in animal furs and, lifting her fingers to her lips, let out an ear-piercing whistle. Silence blanketed the room. A few people glanced around, confused, but the majority of the guests simply sat and stared.

'Now gentlemen,' she cleared her throat and her eyes paused on Lily for a second, 'and lady,' she smirked not unkindly, 'I have a tale to tell. For some of you, this will not be the first time hearing it. But I must implore you – because I have reason to believe that they have returned – to pay attention to everything I'm about to tell you. This is the story of the notorious demons that are stalking the land once more: the Shadow Sect, or, as they are sometimes called, the Sisters of Shadow.'

Lily gasped, her hand covering her mouth.

The Sisters of Shadow?

Surely Lorenna must be mistaken. That was the name Alice had given their friendship, years ago. They'd sworn their friendship in the name of the Sisters of Shadow; it was who they were. Could she have known about this connection?

Lorenna must have heard Lily's gasp and she paused. But Lily nodded to her, encouraging her to continue, even though her mind was racing.

'Once, long ago,' Lorenna began, a hushed silence falling once again over the room, 'there was a child who discovered she was cursed. By the age of eight, she could command objects to move and bend at her will. She would often dream about what it would feel like to join the birds in the trees, and then find herself sitting on the highest branch of the tallest tree, amongst the birds of which she had been dreaming. But she had little control over her powers; she was reckless, careless, dangerous. Now, this little girl was also sweet and kind and, generally, innocuous. But her mother was terrified that she would be taken away or persecuted.

'A few days after the little girl's birthday, her mother woke her in the dead of night, helped her pack a few bags, and the two of them set off with the intention of hiding themselves away from whispering and gossip. The plan was to return to an old, long-abandoned lighthouse to which they travelled on occasion. They had always spoken about moving there forever, and it seemed to the child that her mother had just decided that it was time for them to make that move.

'What she didn't know was that her mother had been warned late in the evening that her daughter had been seen floating up into the trees by a man. A man who recognised her curse as evil and demonic. The man had rushed to meet with his companions, and together they had decided that the safest and best thing to do for this child would be to forcibly remove the demon from her body. The child would surely die, but the demon would perish with her, and that was a sacrifice they were willing to make, for the greater good of the people, *of us all*.

'When the child's mother heard of what they were planning, she took her daughter and they ran like cowards, intending to lie low in the lighthouse for a few weeks and then catch a boat across the seas to start a new life somewhere far away from those trying to save them from themselves. What she didn't prepare for was that there was someone watching their household every single hour until the time came for them to take the child and rid her of her demon possessor.

'On that fateful night, when they left under the oppressive darkness of a starless sky, they didn't notice the hooded figure that followed them across the moors from their village home. He didn't call to his comrades for aid, believing that if he caught the girl and the demon-harbouring woman who called herself the girl's mother, he would be a hero. He was doing it for the Brotherhood, but he was also doing it to save us all. This was his chance to shine, and he took it. For a while, the girl and her mother hurried over the well-worn stone path that led to the coast. They had walked this route so many times that it was ingrained in their memory and they needed neither map nor candle to find their way.

'When they were far enough away from the village and

still too far away from the lighthouse and the little town on the mainland that was nearby, the man pounced. He leaped from an outcropping of stone just above their heads, knife in hand, and the girl's mother took the full brunt of his weight, collapsing on her back, momentarily winded. The child stood in shocked, horrified silence. There was a struggle, and between the flying limbs, the screaming, and the tearing of hair, the mother managed to break free long enough to shriek for her daughter to run. She barely got five steps away when she heard a strained gurgling and glanced behind her back, just long enough to see her mother's lifeless body, throat-slit, with terror still etched upon her features. And then she ran. She ran and ran and ran. She screamed as she ran, her body overflowing with grief and rage. They say that something snapped in the child that night and, although she escaped from the man trying to save her from the demon, she never truly escaped the fear. In a way, his work should have been done; she was forever changed.

'The girl made it to the lighthouse and wasn't heard from for years. The Brotherhood congratulated their hero, for he had rid the world of a potential threat. But, many years after the horrific murder on the moors, something resembling a woman began to stalk the countryside. Blood, devastation, loss, famine, failed crops, sinking ships … all of these things followed in her wake. This was exactly what the Brotherhood had been trying to protect us from. Some said it was a ghost, the mother, who was seen walking aimlessly, weeping. Others knew it was that same child, a darker, more ruthless version of the once innocent girl.

'A witch.

'Twisted and mangled with hatred and grief. But one thing was guaranteed: whenever there was a sighting, someone would go missing soon afterwards. And then suddenly the witch was seen in two different places at the same time, and then three, and then four, and then the local people realised that she had been recruiting. There was more than one witch quietly terrorising their lives, terrorising the countryside and all who dwelled there. It was whispered that they resided in the old lighthouse, where the girl had been heading when her mother was murdered, and soon the folklore around that lighthouse and its hauntings terrified even the bravest of villagers: no one dared go anywhere near it. Then, one day, it all stopped. It was as if she had grown tired of her reign of terror. There were no more sightings, no more deaths, no more failed crops. The only trace that was left was a note, nailed to the front door of a member of the Brotherhood who resided in Kelseth, that read:

'I will never forgive, and I will never forget, but we are going from this cursèd place. We will return, but we will come in a different form.
'Be ready.
'Hecate Winter.

'Now, I have reason to believe that the Shadow Sect, as I am reliably informed they now call themselves, have returned. Their ever-evolving names are a ploy to remain anonymous, no doubt, to cause confusion and stir up fear.

The Brotherhood must be supported to protect us from the oncoming evil.

'They have grown in number. In sophistication. In power. I have heard of multiple sightings of them all over our moors, and I have heard of at least one case of an innocent victim being stolen away. So, my friends, be vigilant. Be aware. I wish you a very good evening.'

Lorenna stood down from her makeshift stage and disappeared behind the bar, seemingly unaware of the effect her story had had on the remaining guests. There was a muttering that filled the air as the guests tried to ascertain whether the tale was simply folklore made to sound factual, or whether they had just heard the true origins of a terrifying woman who really was stealing and murdering their children.

Lily was warm and comfortable by the fire with her belly still full, soothed by the bowl of soup, but the hairs on her arms and the back of her neck were standing on end and her hands were clammy and shaking. If Lorenna was correct and this story of a growing army of vindictive witches was true, then these were the very people she would have to face. And they were led by the woman who had written to Alice.

With a large gulp, she finished the flagon of beer that she had been sipping intermittently throughout the evening. She regretted eating so much, as the contents of her stomach were threatening to reappear. She rushed up the stairs to her room, determined to hide herself from the other guests of the inn, so that they couldn't see quite how much Lorenna's story had affected her.

Who was this Brotherhood she spoke of? Perhaps it was their help she should try and gain before marching headlong towards the lighthouse. But ... she had already wasted so much time. She couldn't bear the thought of wasting any more searching for another mysterious, creepy-sounding group. No, she would stay alone. She was more inconspicuous that way.

As she entered her room, Lily remembered the heavy book her uncle had given her just before she left the apothecary. He had instructed her to read it when she was alone and, sitting in her silent room, she decided that now was the time to gather whatever wisdom she could from within its dusty pages. She retrieved it from her carpet bag, turned to the page he had recommended, and read aloud in whispered tones:

'Sisters of Shadow: A Tale of Witches.'

There it was again, another reference to the light-hearted, harmless nickname Alice had given the pair of them years ago. She read on:

'Once upon a time, in a land just like ours, there was a girl who discovered she had magical powers...'

Frowning, Lily skim-read the next few paragraphs. This story was exactly the same one that Lorenna had told downstairs.

She felt as though she was dangling on the edge of a precipice, and the only way to discover the root of all this horror, all of these stories and tales and fears, was to let go and fall into a world far more terrifying than she ever imagined could exist.

She now had two sources that pointed to the lighthouse in Kelseth Bay, even if nothing else made sense. If her best friend was with these people, and these people were at the lighthouse, then to the lighthouse she would go.

She couldn't stand the thought of Alice – her dear, kind, vulnerable friend – being indoctrinated by murderers and witches. A day ago, she hadn't even known witches were real. Did she even believe it now?

It didn't matter what she believed, she realised, not really.

Tomorrow she would meet with the Sisters of Shadow.

Tomorrow she would rescue Alice.

Or she would die trying.

Chapter Eleven

A lice came round to consciousness slowly, like a cloud
passing across a starry sky. Trying to decipher reality
from dream, she racked her brains to work out where she
was, and who could have kidnapped her.

She could still feel the gentle, damp pressure on her
head of the girl who was keeping her cool, refusing to let
her fall back into a dangerous fever. Human contact made
Alice feel prickly at the best of times; she wasn't used to
anyone she didn't know being within three strides of her.
And here she was, allowing a total stranger to nurse her, to
care for her.

What was it the other woman had called the girl who so
dearly wanted to help Alice? A *Protector*. That sounded like
someone she wanted to keep on her side. Which was
strange, she realised, since this girl was still culpable. She
was still contributing to Alice's captivity. But who knows
what she'd need to be protected from?

Alice heard a pair of heavy boots get up, walk a few

steps, and exchange short, sharp words with the driver of the cart. The footsteps reverberated through the floor and made Alice's bones rattle.

She was almost sure that it was just her and the Protector girl now.

In the quiet, she tried to relax. On one or two occasions, the Protector accidentally brushed the wound on her temple with the damp cloth, and Alice involuntarily flinched and then held her breath, hoping that the girl hadn't noticed. Her hopes were dashed after the wound was caught for a third time and she flinched, hard.

She felt the girl shift her weight and then she lifted Alice's head so that it was supported. Alice realised that her head was now comfortably in the girl's lap. She flickered her eyelids, about to open them, but something made her stop.

With open eyes, she would have to face the frightening situation she was in; unconscious, she was bound to be left alone.

'Shh,' the girl whispered, and it took Alice a few seconds to realise she was talking to her. 'Don't open your eyes. I know you can hear me, but they must think you're still unconscious or they'll put that awful bag over your head again.' Alice twitched her eyebrows a tiny bit, hoping that the girl would interpret her curious frown well enough to continue talking. She clearly got the message because she continued in hushed tones. 'I convinced them that it was pointless to keep you covered up when you were passed out anyway. You were getting so hot and feverish, so I told them that I'd keep watch over you and make sure you stayed unconscious. They'd kill me if they found out I'd let you wake, but it just doesn't feel right, treating you like this. I had to do something.'

The girl moved a little, rearranging her seating position so that Alice would be more comfortable, and when she took Alice's hand to help her lie on her side, Alice took the opportunity to squeeze it gently. She hoped that would be enough to show her gratitude for now. Having an ally couldn't be a bad thing, and as strange as Alice felt, she knew the Protector was on her side. That could be key in escaping later.

The pain still seared through her head and the Protector had fallen into a peaceful silence, still dabbing Alice's head with the damp cloth. The gentle swaying of the cart sent Alice into a fevered sleep once more.

Chapter Twelve

S creams cut through the air like a knife through flesh.
Lily awoke with a start, her forehead damp with sweat and her heart racing. Another horrified scream broke the early morning silence and she leapt out of bed, realising that the screaming wasn't an echo of a nightmare, but was coming from just underneath her window, out in the stable yard.

She stumbled across the room to grab her leather boots and threw her heavy green cape on over her night-clothes. She was too terrified to bother about public perception. She had to discover the source of those awful, ear-splitting screams.

Lily ran out into the yard. It was still early and the sun was just starting to rise. The moorland was covered in a thin layer of gossamer mist that was glittering and swirling around the inn. As she hurried towards the stables, the first thing she saw was the crowd. Everyone else, too, must've been roused by the screams and had come together to investigate, all crowded into the small patch of cobbled yard facing the stable. A couple of women were clutching each other and one of them had her face hidden, as if she couldn't bear to look at whatever had captivated everyone else. As Lily grew closer, the crowd seemed to sense her and parted, though she had no idea why.

Until she saw the source of the commotion.

A horse lay in the stable, the hay surrounding it soaked with crimson blood. The horse itself was covered in fatal wounds and had been dead for some hours. The wounds were no longer bleeding and the blood surrounding it looked tacky, rather than wet and glistening. Lily wretched. She was bent double, attempting to catch her breath when she caught the scent of death and retched again.

No. Lily's mind was reeling, trying to make sense of the horror before her eyes. *No, it can't be... It can't...*

Her head was spinning, her eyes stinging with the threat of tears. Bile rose in her throat and it felt like her legs were thigh-deep in a marshy bog; every movement was slow and strained and painfully sluggish.

No, no, no, please don't let this be true. It can't be... It can't. I won't let it. It's not real. It's not true...

It was. It was Morrigan.

Her Morrigan.

The loyal steed who had faithfully carried her across the moors and through the marshes only yesterday. Today, she was dead.

Nauseous, Lily stumbled forward to the horse's body. She sobbed until her throat rasped and closed up, panicked flutters coursing through her body. Underneath Morrigan's head, a piece of paper had been left behind. Lily pulled it and the blood-soaked paper came free. On it, there was a strange symbol; it was crudely drawn but looked like a tree encircled by the sun. Beneath the sketch, two words were written in scarlet ink.

Stay Away

It was a warning. A threat to force Lily to abandon the rescue mission. Without her horse she was not only distraught, distracted, but also vulnerable and slow. Painfully slow. Morrigan had been the sole reason they had been able to escape their pursuer; now, Lily realised, if he caught up with her again, she had no chance of outrunning him. Not to mention that she still had to cover the rest of the miles between The Old Silent Inn and Kelseth, and now she had to do it on foot.

Lily couldn't shake the earth-rattling guilt that seeped into her bones. She had been tasked to care for this poor creature; Morrigan was her responsibility alone, and now ... she was dead. It was her fault.

She heard moaning and screaming in the distance, only to realise that it was her own voice. The grief was an echo chamber. Dazed, she floated above the crowd, above the pain, and watched as Lorenna placed a motherly arm around her shoulder and attempted to lead her away from the scene.

Lorenna shook Lily gently and she jolted back to her body, looking up at the woman's face through tear-streaked eyes. 'Come on, love,' Lorenna pleaded. 'Come inside and have a warm drink. It'll be all right. Come on.'

Lily clung to Morrigan's lifeless frame, sobs still bursting from her throat. Her white nightgown was painted scarlet and blood was caked into her unruly curls. She was a girl possessed, eyes streaming.

'Whoever did this wanted to stop me,' she spat, venom flying from her mouth. 'But they're fools. Now I know they're scared. Now I am alone and I am fearless.' She paused to gasp a raspy breath. 'I'm fearless and I have nothing left to lose.' She turned to Lorenna, flinching away as the older woman tried to take her hand. 'It was him, wasn't it? The man, from last night.'

'No, love. I doubt that very much.'

Lily was too terrified, too angry to listen.

She stormed inside the inn, tears flowing freely from her eyes, and collapsed onto the floor of her room. *How could this happen?*

She rubbed her eyes, sending stars flickering behind her eyelids. *Life was so easy*, she thought, *before all of this. Alice needs help, but at what cost?*

Is she even worth all of this pain and misery?

Lily stopped herself. Thoughts like that wouldn't get her very far. Thoughts like that let them win. *If they can put so much effort into scaring me away*, she realised, *how much effort are they putting into keeping Alice captive?*

Alice was everything to her. She was strong, resilient, unflappable. Lily tried to embody the strength of spirit that Alice had to personify every single day, living out in the woods, alone and exiled. Lily imagined what Alice would have done if the roles had been reversed, if it had been Lily taken and Alice were the rescuer.

It didn't take much imagination. Alice was far better suited to heroics than Lily was.

But something has awoken inside me. Lily clenched her fists and screwed up her eyes. *Something terrifying, something wild.*

The weight of the grief crushed her body into the ground. But underneath it all, there was a burning fury coursing through her. She couldn't let this destroy her: they wanted her unbalanced, stranded, weak.

Their confidence that murdering her horse would stop her was horrifying, but it had unhinged something within Lily that terrified her. She wanted to track down Alice's kidnappers – Morrigan's murderers – and she wanted to make them pay. Never in her life had she had violent or angry thoughts. She was a peaceful person, quiet, thoughtful. But now something else, deep within, was emerging.

Her fingers tingled and flames licked at her throat. She struggled to her feet, wiped her tear-stained cheeks, and took a few deep breaths. The strength seeped back into her legs and her tired eyes were suddenly alive with purpose.

She threw off the blood-soaked nightgown and it pooled, scarlet and ruined, on the floor. The dress that had been soaked through only yesterday had warmed and dried by the open fire, and she held it in her hands for a few moments, allowing the heavy weight of the wool to ground her, bringing her back to earth.

The dress felt like a companion in itself as she pulled it

over her bruised bones. It was familiar; it felt like home. Like her, it was soft and feminine, but also impervious to damage, impossibly strong, robust through the most dreadful of days.

Lily took up her mantle and wrapped it tightly around her shoulders, the material falling in thick, draping folds. It gave her strength, protection, the ability to throw up her hood and disappear into the inky shadows. Yesterday it had been simply a cloak, but today it was her armour.

She still had blood caked beneath her fingernails and streaked through her curls, but glancing in the mirror, she rather enjoyed the fierceness it lent her appearance. She looked like someone she wouldn't want to cross.

As she flung herself from her room, bag slung over her shoulder, she looked again at the blood that had soaked into the soft skin of her fingers

Lily had a strange feeling she'd be covered in blood again before the day was out. But this time, it wouldn't be her blood, or the blood of someone she loved. No. That wasn't going to happen ever again.

She started out into the early morning on foot, leaving behind a note and payment for Lorenna, and headed straight towards the coastline. The fire in her belly burned with relentless abandon, and she didn't look back.

Not once.

Chapter Thirteen

Lily pushed on, on, on. Towards the lighthouse. Towards Alice.

She drove forwards with relentless fury, terrified that if she stopped to let deep breaths into her stinging lungs, if she stopped forcing her muscles to breaking point, she would feel a worse pain. The pain that was threatening to crush her.

She had lost Alice, she had left her home without any real idea of when she would see her uncle or her beloved apothecary again, and now she had lost the one companion she had on her journey.

Morrigan's death had affected her to an unexpected depth; on their short journey together, they had relied on each other to continue. They had connected through mutual pain and exhaustion and she'd felt that she had found a friend. Lily didn't believe in fellow creatures being 'just animals'; she could never understand how anyone could slaughter or even eat another living soul. Morrigan wasn't just an animal, she was a companion, a kindred spirit.

Desperate to ignore the deep aching pain in her heart, she walked and walked towards the pale blue horizon. The sky was finally clear, and the further she walked, the clearer the day became. After a few hours of relentless slogging, Lily was rewarded with a magical sight.

The sea.

Flat as glass, and a deeper, richer blue than the beautiful, wide-open sky.

Lily was sure she had never seen anything quite as lovely. After the most horrendous of traumas, the sight was a tonic for her aching heart.

The cobbled road on which she had set out from The Old Silent Inn soon fell away and became little more than a mucky dirt track and Lily suddenly understood why the stagecoach driver had refused to come this far. It was treacherous, even on foot. The ground was slippery with mud and filled with hidden holes, only noticeable once you'd lost your foot in them. Even if Kelseth itself didn't have a troubled reputation, she imagined that the coach drivers rarely needed an excuse to refuse to travel this way.

It remained treacherous for mile upon mile, until she couldn't remember what it was like to walk on flat ground. Her legs were half-coated in thick, treacly mud, her hem was soaked through, and her thighs screamed from yesterday's battering on the back of Morrigan, worsened now by the grief and the strain to stay upright through the quagmire.

Traipsing ever onwards, the path finally peaked and

started to head downwards, towards the edge of a crumbling cliff. Then, the path dropped off violently and Lily was rewarded with a sweeping view over the bay, down onto the village of Kelseth.

She took a few moments to rest at the peak of the cliff, no longer caring that the mud would soak through her dress. Dangling her legs over the edge, she breathed in the welcome scent of the sea. The salty air was restorative. She reached into her bag and pulled out a hunk of bread, finding herself suddenly ravenous.

She sat for a while, silently devouring her measly meal, taking sips of water from a leather flagon in between mouthfuls. She felt the wind whip through her hair and lift the cares from her shoulders. They hung in the air for a moment, before a rogue seagull plummeted from the sky to catch them and carry them far away, until she could feel them no longer. A single tear rolled down her flushed cheek.

At the end of this path, on the crumbling rocks, was a lighthouse. And at that lighthouse, this nightmare would end, one way or another.

She inhaled once more, ready to face whatever lay ahead, and clambered back onto her feet.

Chapter Fourteen

T hrough the mud and moss, Lily spotted another path snaking its way down the steep edge of the cliff. Several sections of it had already fallen away, leaving a precarious track of rumbling rocks, damp, sticky-looking dirt, and scree. Lily felt a morbid sense of relief that Morrigan wasn't here; guiding the heavy and powerful horse down such a treacherous slope would have been almost impossible. *No*, she thought, *for this one occasion I am glad I am alone.*

She reached down and picked up the hem of her checked woollen dress, ringing out the muddy water that clung to it before tucking it into the thick leather belt she wore tightly around her waist. This way, she had free movement of her legs and her feet and didn't have to add flowing skirts onto her list of potential trip hazards as she traversed the cliff-edge. She rolled the sleeves of her dress up to her elbows and pushed her cloak behind her. If she fell, at least the heavy folds of material would soften the fall a little.

She stepped down the first part of the slope, one hand poised against the edge of the cliff wall to guide her and the other left free so that she could catch herself if necessary. With precarious steps, Lily made her way down, her eyes flicking between the glimmering lamp of the lighthouse that was her target, and the ground, which was the complication that lay between her and her destination.

Halfway down the cliff, Lily started to feel confident. She was a child of the land; she had always been short and sturdy, and her legs were strong with thick muscle, which meant they kept her upright and balanced. She felt so appreciative of all that time she had spent climbing trees and hiking the moorland, leaping from stone to stone to cross the river.

With quiet joy, she recalled chasing Alice through the forest, the two of them unconsciously building stamina with all of their playing and running. For the first time in her life she felt solid, capable, powerful, when before she had only valued her logic and her cleverness, and thought of herself as stocky and unadventurous. She found it hard to believe that just a few days ago she had been that person. *Alice will barely recognise me*, she thought, pride bubbling through her chest.

It didn't occur to Lily that she might not recognise Alice.

Halfway down the crumbling track, Lily's breath became laboured and her thigh muscles cried out from the continuous tension she had to maintain in order to stay upright. A gust of wind took advantage of her momentary lapse of concentration and she stumbled, the rocks and mud beneath her feet sliding and taking Lily along with them.

She was helpless to their movement; she couldn't resist, couldn't hold on to anything. The rock face was suddenly devoid of handholds, and all she could do was attempt to stay upright as the sliding debris gained momentum. She was careering towards the very edge of the cliff, seconds away from being pitched over the edge. There was still a huge drop to the level of the village, and alongside the inevitable fear, Lily also felt a strange frustration that this was how she was going to die.

Here, now, on a stupid cliff, after days of relentless travel, just a few miles away from where her best friend was being kept, this was where she was going to die.

Would Alice even find out that Lily had tried to find her?

She was gathering speed. Her balance was failing and she screwed her eyes closed, holding her breath in an attempt to brace herself for the fall. She covered her face with her hands and screamed 'Stop!' in her wild, panicked, near-death state. Almost as swiftly as the rocky avalanche had started, the entire sliding path stopped. She had ordered it to halt and it had listened.

Lily pitched forwards, landing with a thud on the ground. She opened her eyes and gazed down at the village that was still so far beneath her. Miraculously, she had fallen in such a manner that her head was suspended over the edge of the cliff, but the weight of her body kept her firmly on the ground. Through the folds of hair that fell down around her face, she felt her blood pounding in her ears.

She had no interest in looking down at the ground a moment longer.

All she could imagine was a picture of herself in a crumpled and bloody heap amongst the little buildings and outhouses. Death had been watching, close by. She had felt him, felt the flicker of his skeletal hand at her throat, seen the light glimmer on the edge of his scythe. He had been ready to send her over the edge, and she felt sure that in some other world, she had fallen to her death there and then. But somehow, she had cheated him. Lily felt sure that she heard his frustrated cry as she rolled over and sat up, heart racing but very much alive.

She let out a crazed laugh of disbelief. Lily couldn't work out how or why the falling rocks had simply stopped in their tracks, but she was too appreciative to focus too heavily on the details. If she believed in magic, which she most definitely did not, she might have believed that something otherworldly had saved her in that moment.

She expelled a breath, brushed the dirt and grit from her dress as well as she could, threw her hair up into a messy knot on top of her head, and secured her carpet bag over her shoulder before attempting to continue down the cliff path. She walked with slow, deliberate steps, acutely aware of every rock, every piece of gravel, every patch of mud beneath her feet.

After what felt like a thousand steps, she finally reached the bottom and felt a wave of relief wash over her. Then she looked ahead and her heart sank. The sun was beginning to set, but instead of casting a warm glow over the world, there was a bitter and eerie fog rolling in off the sea.

Chapter Fifteen

When Alice woke again, the first thing she noticed was the lack of movement. It seemed that they had finally reached whatever destination they were heading for, which brought her more fear than comfort. She knew she couldn't hide from these people any longer by sleeping.

Glancing about, Alice found herself alone in a dimly lit room. It was deathly cold and there was a draught that grasped at her bare ankles and sent chills through her body. She sat up, rubbing her hands together, trying to shake off the icy stiffness that had settled in her bones, and looked around. In the flickering torchlight, she could make out the walls of a small, cramped space. One wall, the one directly in front of her, was made from thick metal bars, and the three other stone walls and floor were damp. There was the sound of dripping water on stone in the distance that echoed through the hollow room and the passageways beyond.

This is not a room, she realised. *It's a cell.*

She felt around in the dimness for her cloak and her travelling bag. If she crouched beneath one of the torches, she might be able to find out some information from her tarot cards. Her stomach dropped when she realised that she had none of her possessions in the cell with her, and her cloak was missing too. She heaved a helpless sigh, her breath swirling into the cold air in tendrils of white.

Just as she was beginning to believe that she had been left down in the cell to freeze to death, she heard hurried footsteps coming closer. She pushed herself back to the darkest corner of the cell, hoping to hide from whoever was coming for her. The dragging and clanking of the chains that froze her ankles were a definite giveaway that revealed her return to consciousness. The figure came closer and Alice saw that it was hooded, tall, and carrying a large bag. Keys jangled in the lock and the wall of metal bars creaked open with an ominous groan. To Alice's surprise, the figure bolted forward and fell onto her knees in front of Alice, removing the hood and throwing her cloak around Alice's shivering shoulders.

'Are you all right? How are you feeling? Honestly, I told them … I bloody told them, it isn't necessary to keep you locked up down here, but they insisted. They said that until they know how dangerous you are, you need to be kept here. Ridiculous, if you ask me—'

'Hold on,' Alice interrupted, completely overwhelmed with this girl's chatter. 'Where am I? What on earth is going on?'

'Ah, shit. Sorry! You have no idea who I am.' She held out her hand, but Alice didn't shake it. The girl let it drop to her side, shrugging. 'It's me who's been making sure you're safe and comfortable on our journey. Things will all make sense soon, I promise.'

'You're the one who got that bag off my head, right?'

'I certainly am.' The girl winked.

'Then you can tell me how to escape then, yes?'

'Well, I … I… That won't be possible. I wanted to escape once too, when I first came here. But … you'll get used to it. It's good to be amongst others, others like us. We're able to be our true selves here and once you get used to that, there's no going back to life before.'

'No offence, but you're talking nonsense. I'm cold, I'm tired, and I'd like to leave. I'd like to leave right now. I'm expected in Kelseth and I have to be there.' She tried to move, but the manacles were deceptively heavy and dug painfully into the thin skin of her wrists and ankles.

'Ah. No one is waiting for you in Kelseth… You're with the Shadow Sect now. We aren't allowed to take people directly from their houses on principle, so we sent the letter to force you out of your safe space. I know it sounds problematic, but I need you to trust me.'

'Problemat— Yes it sounds problematic! How can I trust you when you won't tell me anything? You kidnapped me! Not to mention the fact that I'm chained up in a damp cell with no explanation. But it's fine because everything will make sense soon, right? No, I won't stand for this.' Alice tried to stand, but the chains tripped her before she could. She was sent flailing forwards, clattering onto her hands and knees. The force of the fall and the pain in her limbs made her cry out, and once she'd found her voice, she cried out again, shouting for help, demanding that she be set free.

The girl yanked her back into the shadows and covered Alice's mouth with her hand. Alice struggled for a moment, looking around with panicked eyes. She twisted her neck to see a frown contorting the face of her captor; she appeared to be in deep concentration. A few seconds later, Alice heard steps approaching the cell. The girl grasped Alice's hand and she felt herself growing lethargic but the girl remained still, focusing hard on something beyond Alice's understanding. The footsteps stopped in their tracks and turned around, the sounds echoing away into the distance.

'Please,' she looked up at Alice, 'don't do that again. I am here to help you. I had a really hard time when I arrived here and I want to make sure that new people don't have the same experience. So please, let me help you.'

'Did you just do magic?' Alice asked, ignoring the girl's ramblings. She was annoying, but she seemed harmless enough. And maybe it was a good idea to try to be a little nicer to her; she could be useful. But Alice couldn't trust her, not yet. Not here.

'We did magic, yes.'

'We?'

'I don't have powers myself – I'm what's called a Protector. Witches have the magic, but I'm able to channel power through you to use as my own, to protect us both. I'd normally ask your permission or we'd have some kind of mutual agreement but you were too busy trying to get us both killed.' She glared at Alice, and Alice couldn't hold her gaze. 'However...' She sighed. 'I shouldn't have taken your energy without asking, and I'm sorry.' Alice recognised genuine sincerity in her gaze, even in the low light. 'It was necessary though. As soon as they hear that you're awake, you'll be dragged up there to be inspected. They'll decide then and there whether you're worth spending time on. If you are, you won't have to come back down here again.'

'And if I'm not?' Alice snapped.

'It's not worth thinking about. You're going to need your strength and your wits about you, though. I'm going to try and delay that knowledge reaching the priestess until at least tonight. You need food and warmth before you can even consider attempting to face them. Now ... please may I use some of your magic to conjure up some food?'

Alice nodded, still dumbfounded. 'I didn't even know I had magic...'

'You wouldn't be here if you didn't, believe me.' The girl held out one hand and placed it on Alice's shoulder, concentrated for a moment, and then in her other outstretched hand a bowl of steaming soup appeared, right before Alice's eyes. She had a feeling that this was going to take a lot of getting used to, but her hunger had overtaken any other instincts. She grabbed the bowl from the girl and lifted it to her lips, her stomach growling.

The sensation of warm, spiced soup lining her empty stomach was euphoric. She had no idea when she had last eaten. The girl sat back, crossed her legs, and watched Alice like a proud mother bear watching her cub demolish a fresh kill. Alice's joints immediately felt less stiff and she sensed strength rising through her body. Her fingertips tingled with a powerful energy she'd never felt before. While Alice drank the rest of the soup, the girl rested a hand gently on each of her ankles.

'May I?' the girl asked.

Alice just shrugged, gulping heartily from the bowl that was still lifted to her mouth.

The girl nodded and the shackles on her legs disappeared, but the grazes and sores remained. Alice finished the soup and handed the bowl back to her companion, who emptied it with a flick of her wrist, and then handed it back to Alice, filled with steaming water.

'Hold this for me. I'll help you get those cuts and bruises cleaned up,' she instructed.

Now that the warming, healing powers of the soup had passed, she felt the keen and raw throbbing of her injuries. She raised a hand to her temple and found it tender and crusty with dried blood. Her hair, too, was hanging in clumps around her shoulders. The dried blood from her head injuries had coagulated until her hair was a greasy, brittle bird's nest. Alice became self-conscious all of a sudden.

The warmth of the water in the bowl seeped into her arms with a comforting glow, and the girl soaked a strip of cloth and took great care while she dabbed and cleaned each of Alice's many seeping wounds. She started with her face and head, letting the warm water run through Alice's hair. She was painstaking in her attention to detail, and she took her time, washing away the blood from Alice's neck and collarbones. She moved further down to clean the mud and the raw skin on Alice's wrists and then finally ended by cleaning the dirt and the blood from Alice's ankles and feet.

Alice started to shiver; the dampness from the cloth combined with the chill in the air was uncomfortable. With a flick of a wrist, the girl eliminated the residual water and a warm breeze chased away the shivers.

Alice was overflowing with confused and conflicted emotions. She hated being kept in the dark, literally and figuratively. She was angry, she had been betrayed, and all she wanted was to be home with her best friend, with everything back to how it was.

Up until now, she had had to force thoughts of Lily to the back of her head because it was too painful to imagine Lily's reaction when she found out Alice was gone. Would she be upset that she'd left without saying goodbye? Would she be angry, or heartbroken? Alice recalled the argument they had had the last time they spoke and felt bile rise in her throat at the thought of her own despicable behaviour.

Then she looked at the girl sat in front of her, who'd spent her own valuable time keeping Alice safe, tending to her wounds, and sitting in a dingy cell just to keep her company. But how could she warm to her when she was a part of the Shadow Sect?

When she was one of the people who had captured her, chained her up, and locked her in a cell.

This girl was her enemy.

Chapter Sixteen

L ily shivered. The temperature had been gradually dropping until her whole body tremored with the chill. In the distance, she could hear the pained whimpering of the wooden boats tied up in the harbour. It sounded like they were tugging with desperation at their ropes, trying to get free and escape the horrible fate of staying there, in that place, at night. Lily understood those boats. Kelseth was an unnerving place.

The path she had just joined sliced through the village, winding around the houses, the taverns, and the shops in a brutal, jagged line. Looking up at the buildings, it was as if a giant had passed this way, wielding an axe to hack a path through the crooked structures. Most of the buildings were unfinished, or they had fallen into disrepair many years ago and the rot had crawled through the wooden beams. The path was lit by flickering streetlamps and, up ahead, she noticed a hunched lamplighter with his long stick, lighting the streetlamps further along the way.

Lily was thankful that she had the light to guide her as the fog began to creep and curl around her legs, but she couldn't shake the unease she felt deep within herself. It would only be a matter of time until her vision was obscured by the gathering mass of dampness.

Lily noticed the absence of light in the windows of all of the buildings she walked past, and she kept her pace swift, not wanting to be caught loitering. She knew at some point she would have to ask someone for directions to the lighthouse, but the lamplighter had disappeared into the mist. There was no one else around other than the occasional woman lurking in shadowy alleyways and she wasn't feeling brave enough to knock on any doors. She pushed onwards in the cold and oppressive violet hour, hoping that she would be able to find her own way.

She followed the distant sounds of the boats in the harbour, making her way over the stone cobbles. The echo of Lily's footfall from her heavy leather boots bounced and refracted off the contorted buildings that frowned down upon her, and she found a strange comfort in the knowledge that if her footsteps were so loud, then at least no one would be able to sneak up on her.

Every movement, every rustle of a skirt, every footstep was audible. She felt the hairs on the back of her neck prickle, and she was unsure whether the goosebumps raised on her arms were from the chill in the air or from the strange, surreal feeling that she was being watched by a hundred little faces staring out of the grimy windows. With that thought, she focused straight ahead with even more intent, refusing to glance upwards.

She hurried, hands buried deep in the pockets of her cloak, her hair falling from its knot and billowing around her shoulders. She was acutely aware that her curls were still streaked with the dried crimson of Morrigan's blood, so she flicked her hood up, hiding herself from any prying eyes.

She stayed in the light of the lamps, skipping from one skulking patch of fog to the next, avoiding the shadows, until she rounded a corner and the walkway opened up into the harbour.

There it was.

Shining intermittently in the gloom was the lighthouse. The fog was so thick now that only the very top of the tower was visible, its gleaming light a ghostly moon in the darkness. Its purpose was to warn ships away from the coastline, but Lily felt it warning her, too, to stay away, to turn back. The sense of being pushed back was visceral; she felt the instinct take over her whole body. The entire scene before her seemed to cry out, 'No! Do not go on! Turn back while you still can!' and it took every fibre of Lily's strength and courage to push forwards, through the boundary of fear.

She had been so preoccupied with the strange juxtaposition of relief and terror that she hadn't noticed the figure in the shadows. The sound of a thick chain being dragged over the clanking wood of a boat brought her out of her fevered imagination and she whipped around towards the source of the noise.

A hooded man stooped to gather the chains in his hands and Lily felt immediately threatened. She knew she couldn't run and she knew that she had to find a way to get over to the lighthouse. It stood, mocking her, far out in the bay. There was no bridge or walkway that she could make out in the darkness.

'E-excuse me, sir?' she asked, as calmly as she could.

'Who goes there? Wha'd'ya want?' To Lily's surprise, he sounded as terrified as she felt. She remembered the stories of the murders, the coven stalking the land, the witch originating here in this very village. She hadn't spared a single thought for the villagers who lived here still, who had to deal with the fear every single night that the witch might return, that she *had* returned. They were all at her mercy. No wonder this man was frightened at the sight of a lone woman in the fog.

'I'm not here to hurt you, I promise,' Lily began, trying to ensure that her voice sounded non-threatening. 'I'm just wondering if you might help me find a way out to the lighthouse?'

'You don't want to go there if you've got any sense. There's all sorts o' bad stuff that goes on over there. It's a bad place. Haunted, see. What's your business there?'

'My business is my own, but I must get over there. Tonight, if possible. Please...' Lily crossed her fingers in her cloak pocket.

'I'm not happy about it, but if you really mean to get across, there's plenty o' boats here you can take. Most o' the owners upped and left years ago; no one would notice if you took one o' them out onto the water. Mind you choose one wi' strong oars though – the current's rough out there at this time o' day and your visibility won't be great with all this fog.'

'But ... I don't know how to row a boat. Is there anyone who could take me over there? Could you?'

'Not a chance. If you insist on goin', I'll show you which boats you can take but you're on your own. I told you, no one goes out there because it 'ent right.' He gestured to the boat he was standing by and she edged closer. His face was obscured by a wide-brimmed hat under a heavy hood and his coat was pulled right up to his chin. He gave off such an unwelcoming atmosphere that she would have got in that boat and rowed away as fast as she could just to get away from him, had she known how.

She couldn't put her finger on the source of her discomfort, but being near him made her skin crawl. She climbed into the boat he was standing next to and placed the strap of her bag across her body so the dampness of the floor couldn't seep into her belongings. She grabbed the oars, attempting to look confident when in fact she felt like the entire contents of her stomach were about to reappear in the bottom of the boat.

The man unchained the vessel from its mooring post and pushed hard. Lily kept the oars in at her sides until she had floated past the other boats that hugged the harbour and then dropped them into the inky water. Her first few attempts to find a rhythm failed and she flailed, trying to get a strong hold on the wooden handles.

She soaked herself to the skin with icy water trying to turn the boat around but, gritting her teeth through the chill that was already threatening to immobilise her bare, freezing hands, she finally found a rhythm. The boat rocked and swayed as Lily discovered a certain power and strength in her arms. The ceaseless, relentless rowing sapped her energy but she felt strong; she knew that she was near her friend and that this ordeal was almost over.

She fell into the rhythm and lost herself in her thoughts. The fog was clearing now that she was away from the shoreline and she could see the twinkling lamplights of Kelseth slowly ebbing into the distance. Lily barely noticed the wind whipping her bare face, the same wind that was whipping up waves that were growing and growing in size and ferocity.

Her concentration wavered when a huge crack of lightning illuminated the dark sky. She had shut out her fearful thoughts, her terror at being alone on the open water with only a rowboat separating her from being swallowed by the waves.

The next strike of lightning broke open the casket in which she stored her fears and she was suddenly nose to nose with her darkest nightmares.

In the flash of lightning, she saw that she was surrounded by huge, white-tipped waves and she felt nausea rise from her stomach and clutch at her throat. She fumbled and the rhythm she had worked hard to maintain slipped away as she lost her grip on her left oar. In slow-motion, she watched as it slid out of its metal rigging and disappeared into the sea, floating away, away, away, her hopes of reaching dry land floating away alongside it.

She let out a cry of frustration, of panic, of helplessness. At that moment, a wave crashed into the side of the little rowboat and knocked it sideways, capsizing it. Lily's mouth was still open from her wails of fear and she barely had a chance to gasp in a lungful of air before she plunged headfirst into the black water, her mouth and nose filling with the stinging salt.

She was weighed down by her heavy woollen dress and cloak, and her bag that was still hooked over her body. She was pulled this way and that by the violent current and she soon lost all orientation. Lily had no sense of which way the sky was, and which was the bottom of the sea. She couldn't swim, she couldn't breathe, she couldn't see. All she could do was feel, and it was excruciating. Her lungs seemed to be full of rocks, her eyes burned, her chest felt as though it was being crushed in a vice, and her head was pounding.

Then the pain faded.

Lily felt her consciousness floating away with the waves and she no longer felt the urge to struggle or panic or fight for her life. For the second time that day, she was seconds away from death, and this time, this time he was laughing. He knew she couldn't evade him again. Lily felt death take her arm in a strong grip and pull her down, down, down, into the thick coal-black darkness. It was peaceful, and she let herself be taken away.

And then she broke the surface of the waves.

In the darkness she could just make out a figure holding onto her in the water, but as she tried to gasp for air, another wave crashed into her face, filling her lungs with even more water.

Before she could choke, she lost consciousness.

Chapter Seventeen

Alice felt like a fuse had been lit deep in the pit of her stomach, and that one day soon all of this emotion and pain and confusion would cause an explosion that she wasn't sure she'd be able to contain. In an attempt to distract herself from the violent pain bubbling inside her, she turned her thoughts to her companion, who was slumped against the wall. She looked exhausted. *What could she possibly do all day to make her this tired?*

The girl's hair hung in a curtain just above her shoulders. Even in the flickering torchlight, Alice could see that her hair was thick as treacle and a warm chocolate-brown colour. It wasn't straight as the horizon like Alice's own hair, but it wasn't quite curly either. It fell in waves past her jaw and the light from the torches made it shimmer, the flecks of red within it glowing like dying embers. She had high, strong cheekbones and large eyes that gave her a fierce intensity when she spoke. She also had a silvery, jagged scar that creeped over her left eyebrow and ended at the top of her cheekbone. It looked like an old wound, but a brutal one.

From what Alice could gather, this was a girl with a generous heart and a penchant for trouble. Why else would she be risking everything to help Alice? Sitting in her company, even in silence, Alice felt herself exhale a little of the tension she'd been holding on to. But she was still angry – bitterly, painfully angry. The girl's kindness in this damp and terrifying place was like a thin bandage over an amputation; it could barely stop the bleeding.

The girl looked up, still half asleep, and their eyes met. Alice's stomach gave an involuntary lurch and she was suddenly paranoid that the girl had noticed her staring.

'Who are you?' Alice asked, her voice a little more venomous than she had intended.

The girl smiled. 'I'm Grace. I don't know if that's my real name, but it's the one I chose. My brother and I were washed ashore not far from a grotty little fishing village years ago, when we were just a couple of kids. I had sustained a pretty serious head injury'—she gestured to her scar—'so I recall absolutely nothing before we moved into the lighthouse that we made our home. He said we had to find new names, names that would help us blend in if anyone came asking questions. I couldn't remember our names anyway, so I became Grace.

'It took us ages to choose... We just rifled through a bunch of old books hidden away in the lighthouse's library until we found some that we liked. I chose a book about a swashbuckling pirate queen called Grace, and it stuck. My brother used to laugh, as I'm probably the least graceful person you could meet.' Grace paused to clear her throat. Her voice had taken on a gravelly quality, as though she were fighting against a lump in her throat. 'Sorry, I haven't thought about him for a while. It's easier to block out the memories than to face what you've lost – you'll learn that. But hiding from grief makes the dagger of pain that much sharper when you do face it.'

Alice thought about reaching out to hold Grace's hand, as Grace had done for her in the back of the cart, but something stopped her. The sound of scraping metal and heavy footsteps shattered the silence, and they jumped in unison. Grace gestured for Alice to be quiet.

'They're coming.'

Chapter Eighteen

B right light streamed through the open windows. Lily scrunched up her eyes and found them stinging and raw. She came around to consciousness slowly. In her mind, she could see waves and darkness; she had felt death pull at her arm. But ... it mustn't have been death, because here she was.

She had cheated him. Again.

Lily opened her eyes in a panic and shot upright, realising she was in an unfamiliar bed. The warmth, the softness, it all felt wrong. The blood rushed to her head and dizziness overcame her, nausea washing over her like the waves that had wanted to drown her. She tried to gasp and call for help; she had a million questions, most of them along the lines of, *where the hell am I?* and, *how am I alive?*

But her voice was gone, and the only noise that escaped her lips came out as a painful croak. The inhalation of saltwater must have ripped apart her throat because each breath felt like raw flesh dragging across sandpaper. Tears leaked from her eyes, partly with the intensity of the pain, partly because she was terrified and confused, and partly because she'd been dreaming of her sweet, innocent Morrigan.

Lily attempted to push through the pain and focused on inhaling and exhaling with deliberate slowness, a method she'd learned long ago when panic would course through her body with such violence that she'd be confined to her bed for days. Even through the pain in her throat, she felt her heart rate slow to a more manageable pace and she could finally hear herself think over the relentless drumming in her ears.

Spinning herself so her legs dangled over the side of the bed, Lily looked around the room for some kind of clue as to her location. She figured that she must be in the lighthouse, but the room didn't feel like it would belong inside a haunted lighthouse that was home to a coven of murderous witches.

It was small and round, and the walls were painted a warm, bright white that was almost cheerful; there was a large circular window directly across from where she sat, through which tendrils of sunlight shone and dust motes danced like midsummer fairies in the rays. Lily could hear the calm lapping of the waves outside and the cry of seabirds circling ahead. She forced the remaining grogginess from her brain. In that moment, once she had shaken the sleep from her eyes, she realised that she had been tucked into a bed covered in layers of thick, warm knitted blankets, and instead of her woollen dress, she wore a long white nightgown.

Her heart jolted.

Someone had pulled her from the water and saved her life, yes, but they had also stripped her of her clothes and undergarments, washed her, dressed her, and put her to bed, all while she was unconscious and unable to defend herself. She felt vulnerable and exposed. The drumming in her ears started up again, only so much louder this time.

Lily threw herself off the bed, goosebumps raised on her arms, her stomach churning. The coolness of the air was a welcome sensation after the stifling press of the blankets, and the weight of the realisations that were threatening to crush her. The comfortable warmth of the bed felt unclean, and she knew she needed to find clothing as soon as possible. The familiar material of her dress and her belongings, at least, would be a small comfort.

Underneath the window there was a wooden rocking chair with a pile of clothes laid out on it. Her heart sank as she realised her own things were nowhere to be seen. She glanced at the door and then pulled the nightgown up over her head, grabbed the first garment on the pile of clothes – a linen shirt – and wriggled into it. Her muscles cried with every stretch and in her half-nakedness, she caught sight of the black, blue, purple, and green flecks that covered most of her body.

Lily then picked up a heavy skirt and was just about to climb into it when she realised with abject horror that it wasn't a skirt at all. It was a pair of trousers. Frowning, she grabbed at the dresser drawer and yanked it open, presuming there must have been a mistake. The dresser was empty. If she wanted to go and find out where she was and who had taken her, she was going to have to swallow her vanity and ... *wear trousers.*

Grimacing, Lily pulled them on. To her surprise, although her legs were short and stocky, they were not lost in the fabric. In fact, they fit her perfectly. The trousers fastened with an ivory button around her waist, leaving her more than enough room to breathe. They could've been made for her. And on the plus side, she reminded herself, she may be in trousers, but at least there were no corsets to be seen. Underneath where the trousers had sat on the wicker chair, there was a brown leather belt with a weighty bronze buckle that matched her favourite boots perfectly. She fastened this around the waistband of the thick trousers, which were a dark brown colour and made from a sturdy flecked wool, and tucked in the shirt.

The last item on the chair was a soft, crocheted cowl which she wrapped around her shoulders, crossed over her chest and fastened into a knot behind her back. She took another deep breath, her throat still throbbing, and looked at herself in the tall mirror that stood by the side of the bed. Lily gasped. She still looked like herself, with her mane of unruly curls, but she had regained the colour in her cheeks that had been drained from the relentless travel.

The effect of the trousers was shocking. If she ignored the bruises, she looked like a version of Lily who could run and fight and jump on and off a horse without effort. The trousers allowed her to move freely without having to hitch up heavy skirts, and although they weren't exactly what she was used to, she understood that perhaps she would benefit from their practicality.

There was a knock on the door.

Lily jumped, moving far away from the mirror and standing in a position that she thought, or rather hoped, would make her seem strong and intimidating. Her muscles still ached but she found that if she stretched and tensed as she stood, the pain gradually lessened.

'Who's there?' she croaked, her feeble voice eliminating any air of intimidation she might have been able to create.

'I am a friend. I am here to help you. May I come in?' The voice was unmistakably male, and Lily felt a strange mixture of relief and fear. If the person who had brought her here was male, then he couldn't be a part of the Shadow Sect, which meant that she was safe from their powers whilst she was still in recovery from her incident. But then, that also meant that this person was unpredictable, unknown, and thus potentially even more dangerous than those she was tracking. What if he was the man who had chased her across the moors? The man who had killed Morrigan?

Lily clenched her fists and raised them in front of her, poised to defend herself.

'Enter,' she croaked again, wincing.

The door opened slowly and silhouetted in the doorway was a tall, slender figure. The man took a step into the room, holding his hands up in a gesture of surrender. As he stepped into the light, Lily realised that he wasn't a man at all. He was a boy, of a similar age to her. The way he carried himself created the illusion of age: he stood straight and his shirt sleeves were rolled carelessly, showing his strong arms that rippled with muscle. He had brown skin and dark russet hair that fell in a thick curtain past his shoulders. He had a kind but weary face; he looked like he had the weight of the world on his shoulders, but he was more than happy to carry it.

A smile tugged at his lips when he saw Lily's fearsome stance.

'Woah, woah, I told you, I'm a friend, I promise,' he said, hands still up, in a feigned attempt to show her that he wasn't a threat. In one of his clenched hands, Lily noticed, was a crumpled brown paper bag.

Lily relaxed a little but didn't move from her spot at the back of the room.

'Who are you?' she asked. 'Where am I?'

'It's all right. We will get on to all of those things very soon, but first I need to inquire after your health.' Seeing her frown, he continued. 'You had quite the ordeal last night, and you were lucky that the light from the tower illuminated your boat just as it capsized. I ran down to the beach as soon as I could but you had already swallowed an awful lot of water.'

'That ... that was you?' Lily croaked, suddenly aware that she was facing the person who had risked his own life to save hers. A total stranger. She sat on the bed, brow furrowed. She had been convinced that it really had been death pulling her away, holding her under the water. It hadn't occurred to her for one moment that someone else had saved her from drowning.

The boy smiled humbly, crow's feet appearing around his sea-glass eyes. 'It was, and you were very nearly dead when I dragged you onto the beach. Before I ask you questions about why exactly you chose the middle of a storm to row a boat out here, and before I allow you to bombard me with the questions that I can see are threatening to burst out of you at any moment, there are just a few more checks I need to do. If you'll allow...' He stepped closer to where she sat and knelt in front of her, so that their faces were at the same level. He popped the paper bag down beside her and gestured for her to open it. Hesitantly she lifted one edge and saw that there was a thick slice of bread, some cheese, and an apple inside it. Her stomach grumbled involuntarily. 'Help yourself, once I've checked you over.'

The boy reached out a hand to lift her arm and inspect the bruises. Lily felt an overwhelming awkwardness and she flinched, cringing away from him. For a reason she couldn't quite understand, she was unable to meet his gaze. He withdrew his hand and gave her what she thought might have been his attempt at a reassuring smile.

He was competent and swift with his inspections of her eyes, her throat and the bruises that covered her arms, chest, and jaw. He sat back on his heels and nodded, apparently satisfied that she wasn't about to keel over and die any time soon.

'Right, well, other than a few nasty bruises and a rather angry-looking throat, I think you're pretty much unscathed. Which is, quite frankly, miraculous. I'll see if we can rustle up some kind of honey-drink to soothe your throat and I think I have some leftover salves for those bruises. You'll be fighting fit in no time. Now, I believe you had a few questions?' He sat where he was, on the floor, and gazed at her with wide, patient eyes.

'Firstly, where am I?' Lily croaked. She reached tentatively into the paper bag and pulled out a very soft, cloudlike slice of bread. The crust she thought might be too risky for her throat, so she started deconstructing the edges while the boy answered.

'I thought that would've been obvious,' he remarked, but then he caught sight of Lily glaring at him, without mercy, and continued. 'We are in Kelseth lighthouse. And no, it isn't haunted, but don't let anyone else hear you say that. We rely on the lore around here to keep us safe.'

'We? Us?' Lily spluttered with a mouth full of the delicious bread.

'Yes, we. There are several people here in this lighthouse, but we'll get onto that in a minute. Next question!' The boy appeared to be enjoying himself, but Lily did not return his kind and easy smiles. She had not yet decided if he was to be trusted. She had read all about men who take advantage of women; those who are easily trusted can turn out to be the greatest deceivers. This boy, with his kind eyes and happy, easy manners, might not be all he seemed. She was hungry though, and her lack of trust didn't stop her from continuing to devour the food he had provided.

'What's your name?' She felt like she probably should've started with that and inwardly cursed herself for being awkward.

'My name is Jameson Rafferty, but everyone calls me

Jem. There are no formalities here. I'm just plain old Jem.'
He held his hand out for her to shake. 'And you are?'

Lily shook his hand, taking care to grip it tightly to make
sure he didn't fall into the habit of underestimating her. 'I'm
Lily Knight. And I was in that ridiculous boat last night
because I was told by numerous sources that this lighthouse
belongs to the coven that kidnapped my best friend. I am
going to make an assumption now and say, I presume, that
you are not a member of, nor the leader of, said coven?'

"Fraid not,' Jem replied, a sympathetic look on his face.
'However, I do know who you mean, and I know why you
were told that they were here. There is an awful lot you
most likely do not know, and you are fortunate that it was
us that discovered you, and not Hecate Winter.'

'You know about her?' Lily asked, her intrigue taking
over her reserve.

'I do. Like I said, we rely on local lore to keep us safe
here. I will explain all downstairs, but you're going to have
to tell me everything you know.'

Lily looked at him, frowning.

'What makes you think I'm going to tell you anything?
Look,' she cleared her painful throat and stood, acutely
aware of how exposed and vulnerable she felt, alone with a
boy she didn't know, wearing trousers, bruised and aching,
'I'm very appreciative that you saved me and stopped me
from drowning and gave me warm clothes and a bed and
all of that, but I'm not sure you understand. They have my
best friend and I need to go and help her. Time is precious
and she needs me. So, if you don't mind, I'd like to borrow
a boat so I can go back to the mainland and find out where

the hell the Shadow Sect are, because obviously it's not here.'

Lily was flustered and her breath was thick and heavy. She stared at the ground, still unable to meet his eye, and tucked a curl behind her ear. She could feel her face growing hot and itchy; it wasn't often she lost her temper, but his inability to understand the time-sensitive nature of her situation got the better of her.

Jem looked affronted and stood to face her. Lily knew she'd been rude and that she should probably have been thanking Jem over and over again for saving her life, and looking after her, but she also couldn't stand being here, warm and comfortable in her clean clothes and her sheltered room, when she didn't know where Alice was or what had been done to her. Guilt had settled within the cracks of her heart and only now did she realise that was what was making her feel so sick, so uncomfortable.

'Look, I'm not forcing you to stay. However, if you're serious about tracking down your friend—'

'Alice.'

'Alice, then you have, albeit accidentally, come to exactly the right place.'

'The right place? Are you trying to tell me that she's here?' Lily was fraught and her head was pounding. Everything ached and her eyes were heavy and kept pleading with her to close them. She was sick of being in the dark.

'No, she isn't here. But I have an inkling as to where she is. I track them, you see. The Shadow Sect, which is a new name, I think. I knew them as the Sisters of Shadow, but they've had other names. "The Lightkeepers", for example, is the one we particularly enjoy taking advantage of.

'Anyway, I've been tracking them for just under a year now, and I think I've finally got the bastards.' He spoke the last line with such a mixture of anticipation and malice that his entire face changed. Lily was taken aback to see his features morph into pure hatred. Whatever reason he had to want to track down the Shadow Sect, it had made him hate them with a clear and visible passion. 'If I'm going to help you track them down, I'm going to need all the information you have, in exchange for all the information I have, and,' he paused to clear his throat, catching her eye with an intensity that made her shiver, 'you are going to have to trust me. Do you think you can do that?'

Lily paused. If this boy knew anything that could help her find Alice, then she'd do anything to help him. It was Alice above anything. Above her own safety.

She met his gaze for the first time since he'd entered the room, and nodded. 'What do I need to do?'

'First, you need to come with me and meet everyone else. Second, you need to eat. Third,' he paused, smiling at her with a warmth that was contagious, 'you need to lose those worried eyebrows. We will find her. You're not alone anymore, Lily. You're not alone.'

Chapter Nineteen

Grace leapt up and stood in a protective stance in front of Alice who was still sitting on the damp floor, shivering and unnerved. The open and kind girl that Alice had come to know over the past few hours had disappeared. In her place was a fierce and powerful Protector. Alice couldn't see very much because of Grace's position in front of her, but she could hear several pairs of boots now, coming closer at an alarming speed.

'Grace, I believe you were under strict instructions to check the consciousness of our guest and return to us immediately. Which part of those instructions did you not understand?' The voice was harsh, croaky. Alice didn't have to see the woman who spoke to know that she was cruel and toad-like.

'She was injured. Had I not stayed down here to tend to Alice's wounds, she would've been dead by now and all the effort you put into organising her capture would have been wasted. So, you're welcome.' Grace was defiant. Alice wondered how this ferocious woman would exist inside the talkative and tender person she had so far shown herself to be. Alice couldn't decide which Grace she liked more.

'Insolent child,' the woman croaked. 'Get out of my way.'

'No. She's not ready.' Grace stood even taller, blocking Alice from the interlopers.

'I don't care what you think, child,' the woman sneered and then Grace disappeared from in front of Alice, crashing into a wall at the side of the cell. She landed in a crumpled heap and groaned. 'Now, what have we here? You're awake then, girl?'

Alice looked up into the wretched face of the woman who had cast Grace aside and felt a rage burning inside her. Rage that overcame her fear, her confusion, and her need for answers. She fought against the pain of her stiff joints and muscles and pulled herself to her feet.

I don't know who you are, or why you need me, but you hurt her again and I will make you pay! was what Alice desperately wanted to say, if she could channel even an ounce of Grace's courage. Instead, she avoided the woman's eyes and stayed silent.

The woman cackled and croaked, and her companions, whom Alice could now see clearly, also exchanged amused smirks. 'We've got a talkative one. Brilliant,' the woman replied, condescension clear in her tone. 'Unless you want to stay down here for another week, I'd advise you to get a grip of yourself and follow me.'

'I-I demand that Grace accompany me,' Alice squawked.

Her stutter negated any self-confidence she had hoped her demand might convey.

'You are in no position to be making demands, little girl. No, Grace will join us later and only if she behaves. For now, you will come alone.'

Alice's wrists flew together, and the cold pressing of metal manacles appeared out of the darkness to attach them together. The icy gaze of the toad-faced woman confirmed to Alice that she would have to follow them, willingly or not, but she felt like it would probably be less painful if she just followed, leaving Grace behind to regain consciousness. It was less painful on her body perhaps, but her heart ached to walk away from Grace's crumpled body and the protection she promised.

They left the damp cells behind and went up a dimly lit staircase, then walked down dark corridors, twisting and turning. The walls turned from damp stone to polished oak, which wasn't any less oppressive, but it was at least a warmer atmosphere. The manacles felt like glacial ice around her wrists, so any change in atmospheric temperature was welcomed. The winding walkways felt like a rabbit warren, with passages and corridors and doors snaking in different directions. Alice knew if she lost sight of the people leading her, she would never find her way back to Grace, let alone to wherever they were going. After what felt like an age of walking, Alice felt the strength return to her limbs and her aching muscles were grateful for the movement and the opportunity to stretch and strengthen. She felt an ounce of her courage and a beacon of hope beginning to glow in her chest. With her strength returned, she might be able to figure out a way to escape. She was careful, however, to keep herself limp, to drag herself along as if she were half-dead. If they underestimated her, she would have a greater chance of overpowering them.

They passed through a towering door made from a single monstrous slab of stone and Alice found herself in an open, cavernous room. There was a large altar at the far end and a roaring fire in a hearth along the wall to her right. On the walls, on the weapons, even around the necks of the women escorting Alice, a symbol was repeated over and over again. It seemed that the Shadow Sect, or the High Priestess herself, had an emblem: a crooked tree pierced by a lightning bolt, all encircled in a golden ring of pale light.

The room itself could have been comfortable, almost cosy. Yet, the presence of a woman, reclining with her endless legs hanging off the edge of the wooden altar table on which she was perched, made Alice's blood run cold. She was willowy and tall, with a fiery halo of deep-red hair that fell to her waist in delicate, soft waves. From this distance, Alice was both compelled and repulsed by this woman. She looked no more than twenty, maybe thirty, years older than Alice, but her eyes told a different story. Her eyes were clandestine, inscrutable; they were the eyes of someone who had lived through centuries, perhaps even millennia. Alice could feel the power pulsating from her.

'Alice, my dear girl, welcome!' called the woman, as Alice was forced to move closer. The woman's voice was smooth and lyrical, like treacle flowing over polished granite. The woman pushed herself off the table with an elegant leap and sauntered forwards. She wore a corseted black dress and a heavy hooded cloak. Her wrists were covered by hammered bronze cuffs and her hands were weighed down with a variety of gemstone-encrusted rings.

'Oh dear.' She frowned as she grew closer, eventually stopping directly in front of Alice, so close that Alice, out of pure instinct, took a step back to widen the gap. 'I do believe we have treated you rather poorly. Look at the state of you!' The woman brushed her hand over Alice's crusty hair and then lifted her chin so that Alice was looking directly into her eyes. 'I think we're going to be good friends, you and I. After all, you're the mirror image of your dear mother. How could we be anything *but* friends?'

Alice's heart was hammering a tattoo in her chest and her stomach clenched and knotted. How did the woman know her mother? Alice herself barely remembered her mother, and they'd lived far away, hidden.

The woman was effortless and charming, otherworldly in her beauty, and yet there was also something rotten and degenerate about her. Alice could sense the mould and decay in the woman's core and her physical beauty did little to hide the putrid soul within. Alice was confident that she'd rather spend a week locked in a cell with toad-face than spend five minutes alone with this woman.

Amused by Alice's unease, the woman stepped back and smiled, a wicked glint shining in her eyes. She held out a hand.

'My name is Hecate Winter, and it is I who invited you here, and it is I who will train you to be one of the most powerful witches this mortal world has ever seen.'

Alice shook her hand, feeling every ounce of courage and defiance slip away. Hecate then turned her back on Alice and walked away, which Alice took as a dismissal and she turned to leave. Hecate paused and then turned back to her. 'Follow Blayne to your living quarters and be ready to start training first thing tomorrow. Do not let me down.'

Blayne, the toad-faced woman from earlier, waddled over to Alice, grasped her by the wrist and dragged her from the room. After even more confusing serpentine passages, they finally reached Alice's living quarters, which were at the end of a long corridor. Before leaving her, Blayne squawked, 'Your dinner will be brought up soon. Don't leave this room until morning. You've been warned.' And then she spun on her heels and disappeared, slamming the door behind her.

Alice gazed around the room in awe. It was the complete opposite of the cell she had just left. There was a fire in the grate, furs covering the bed, a wardrobe stocked full of beautiful, hand-embroidered dresses and a shelf overflowing with books. She was relieved to find her travelling bag and her cloak were on a chair underneath the window. It was a cosy and comfortable living space, but there was still a tiny voice in the back of her head wondering, *why did they capture me, tie me up, and leave me to rot in a dungeon, only to bring me here and make me comfortable?*

What was it that Grace had said? If they thought I was worth spending time on, I wouldn't have to return to the cells. Spending time on? Time doing what?

Alice flopped backwards onto the fur-covered bed and closed her eyes, trying to contain the well of emotions that was threatening to overflow. She was confused and she still didn't know what fate awaited her in the morning. She kept seeing Lily's panicked, hurt face as if it were permanently etched on the backs of her eyelids. Her thoughts also strayed to Grace's courage, and Alice tried to focus on that image, rather than on the one of her in a crumpled unconscious heap in a dingy cell. She secretly hoped that Grace would return in the morning, and with that hope in her mind, she drifted into a lifeless sleep, her exhaustion finally catching up with her.

Chapter Twenty

Lily's eyes filled with tears.

The lighthouse, Jem, the accident, Morrigan. It was all so overwhelming. She didn't know whether she was angry or grieving, or both. But here was a boy who actually seemed to want to help her. She didn't have to face this fight alone anymore. The weight that perched in her chest with claws clinging to her heart flapped its wings slightly, making space for a little hope.

'I'm sorry.' Lily looked up at him now they were standing side by side, about to leave her room. 'For being so unappreciative. I'm just scared. For Alice, for myself.'

'You don't have to explain.' He gestured with his arm for her to leave the room ahead of him. She still felt exposed in the trousers and kept pulling at them, flattening the material, adjusting the belt. She stuffed her hands in her pockets and shook her head. There were more important things to worry about.

Outside of her bedroom, a dark stone staircase wound

around in an endless spiral. She leaned forwards but couldn't spy the bottom. Lily started the descent, each muscle and bone in her legs screaming with the strain of movement after their relentless pummelling the day before. She stopped a few times when the pain was unbearable and glanced behind her at Jem, who just stood there watching, quiet and patient. Something about his stance made her think that he was poised to catch her if she fell. She smirked and rolled her eyes.

When they reached the bottom, she went through a door opposite the staircase, expecting another room or a corridor, but instead found herself outside in a large cobbled courtyard. The morning sunshine had hidden behind heavy, darkening clouds and it had started to rain. Thunder rolled in the distance and the air was charged with energy. Lily didn't have much time to look around properly, but she did notice a few things that intrigued her. The courtyard was pentagonal, rather than square, with single-story buildings that were all connected by small walkways. All of the rooms had huge, clear windows that sat in the shadow of the vast and hulking lighthouse.

Jem took Lily's arm gently and guided her to a door directly across the courtyard. As they entered, Jem leading the way, Lily became flushed with self-conscious apprehension. Who was she about to meet? Did she need to earn their respect before they'd help her? What if Jem was actually just a way to gain her trust before they kidnapped her like Alice had been kidnapped? She tried to keep her face neutral and calm but her heart hammered against her ribcage like a hummingbird threatening to break free. She stuffed her hands back in her trouser pockets to hide their shaking.

Jem walked down a corridor and stopped outside a door on the right. He ran a hand through his long, dark hair and Lily could have sworn there was a nervousness there, behind his eyes, that she hadn't noticed before. 'Ready?' he asked, but he pushed open the door before she had a chance to reply.

He stepped over the threshold and immediately melted into his natural habitat. The room was warm and cosy, not bright like her room, but beautiful, shadowy, and comfortable. It was oak-panelled and there was a roaring fire in the grate. There were a few old, tired leather sofas dotted around and books piled everywhere: on shelves, on the mantelpiece, on the mahogany desk that dominated one wall and which was illuminated by the light of one of the huge windows she had seen from outside. After she had taken in the general splendour of this cosy hideaway, she noticed the small figures dotted about the room.

Jem cleared his throat.

'Everybody!' He moved to a spot in the middle of the room and all eyes fell upon him. 'I'd like you to meet our guest and newest member, Lily Knight.' He gestured for Lily to join him and, limping towards the middle of the room, she felt several pairs of little eyes follow her. From her position by Jem's side, she could see five children of varying ages. She didn't know who exactly she had imagined she was about to meet, but a group of children definitely wasn't on the top of her list of expectations. 'Now, what do we say?' he asked them, with the authority of a schoolmaster but the affection of a big brother.

'Hello, Lily,' the children chorused with robotic obedience. Lily glanced at each of them in turn, trying to figure out their ages. Two of them, who sat side by side on the largest sofa by the fire, looked about fifteen. Two others, who looked the same age as one another, were definitely under ten, although it was hard to pin exact ages on them. And the last, a watery-eyed boy, could've been sixteen or he could've been nine. His pursed, shy face was freckled and his wide eyes gave him an air of innocence.

'Hello, how do you do?' Lily asked, in what she hoped was her kindest voice. She smiled, trying not to show her anxiety, and then glanced at Jem who gave her an encouraging nod.

'Take a seat, Lily, and I'll introduce everyone. Like I said, it's nothing formal. You'll fit in just fine here.'

Lily sat, feeling awkward, on a rug by the fire. Jem wandered over to a table and collected teacups, saucers, and a couple of tins that she presumed held tea of some sort. He reached over and unhooked a cast-iron kettle that had been boiling above the fire and poured steaming water into several of the mismatched cups. He passed them around to each of the children, and then handed the largest one to Lily after he'd poured a thick amber liquid into it first. She was thankful for something to hold to keep her from picking at the skin around her fingers. 'There's some honey in that,' he explained. 'It should ease the pain in your throat a little.' He then dropped down beside her on the rug, crossing his legs and resting his elbows on his knees with the ease of a child.

'Introductions!' Jem clapped his hands together, enthusiasm glowing from his face. 'I'll start. I'm Jem Rafferty, I'm eighteen years old, and I don't know where I'm from. This is my home now.' He looked to his left, which Lily took as a sign that it was her turn.

'I'm Lily, I'm also eighteen, and I'm from a little village a long way from here called Alder Vale. I'm in search of my best friend who has gone missing, and before that, I worked as an apothecary with my uncle.' She gulped, and was glad when all of the eyes in the room moved on to the next person.

The girl on the sofa to Lily's left, one of the older children, introduced herself as Morven. She was fifteen, exactly as Lily had guessed. She was tall and broad with paper-white, almost translucent skin. Her mousy hair was tied in a braid that fell down over her shoulder, stopping just above her waist. She looked sensible, like she wouldn't put up with any nonsense.

Next to Morven was a freckled auburn-haired skinny boy of the same age who called himself Cass. They held hands, and Lily wondered how long it had been that they had relied on each other. Cass looked at Jem with a kind of admiration that Lily had never seen before in the face of a boy or a man, not even Alf, who had always been the most affectionate fellow in Alder Vale. She wondered, for a moment, what it might mean.

Next were the two girls sitting opposite the fire, both of them squeezed onto a single leather armchair. They were small and identical, both with dark skin and heads bursting with bushy ebony curls. They were currently staring, unblinking, at each other, trying to convince the other to speak first. After a few moments of silence, Jem had to intervene.

'Maeve, you go first please.'

The girl on the left spun her head around to glare at Jem, mortified to have been singled out. Her twin also glared at Jem, looking hurt not to have been chosen. They both looked at each other again, nodded, folded their arms and didn't say a word. They sat there in protesting silence, until Jem had to give up and turned to Lily. 'The one on our left, that's Maeve. On the right is her twin sister, Brenna. They're seven years old and they're headstrong and independent, though they may not seem it yet. They will stop being so quiet and shy soon, I promise.' Jem cast one glance back at them, their frowning faces already having softened. The one on the left, Maeve, caught Lily's eye and winked. In reply, Lily stuck her tongue out at the girls, who burst into quiet giggles.

Last, there was the other boy that Lily had noticed earlier. He was sitting on the last sofa with his knees pulled up to his chest and his arms wrapped around them. He had hair the colour of sea-soaked sand and sunken, blood-shot eyes. He also looked on the verge of tears. Jem looked to him and smiled with silent encouragement. 'H-hello,' the boy stuttered, trying and failing to meet Lily's gaze. 'I'm Glenn. I'm eleven.' He looked down at his knees, clearly reluctant to talk anymore.

Jem wasn't perturbed by Glenn's quietness; instead he

looked proud. Jem turned to Lily, who had just drained her teacup, glancing at the tea leaves that had formed shapes in the bottom. Alice had always snatched her teacup from her whenever she finished drinking and then would predict something from the myriad patterns. The memory caused an uncomfortable lurch in Lily's chest, as if her heart had tried to give up beating. Jem must have noticed that Lily had drifted away momentarily, because he placed a light hand on her shoulder. She flinched and immediately regretted it as she felt Jem withdraw his hand, holding it instead in his lap.

'I'll show you around now, if you like? Then we can go to my study and start to forge a plan of attack.'

He stood and pushed up his shirt sleeves which had unrolled slightly, then ran a hand through his hair. Lily noticed that he did this involuntarily every time he needed to speak, or whenever he was aware that he was being watched. It didn't seem to be a vanity habit, more like a twitch of acute self-consciousness.

'Everyone else: can you make sure this is all cleaned up and we have some warm food to eat in a couple of hours? There should be everything you need to make a stew in the pantry. Cass,' he turned to the boy, 'I'm putting you in charge.' The boy puffed up his chest. 'Shout us when dinner is ready, all right?' Cass nodded, and then Jem led Lily back out of the warm light of the main room and into the cold corridor beyond.

They walked in silence for a few steps. Lily was bursting with questions, but something about his aura made her hold back. He struck up a casual conversation, perhaps sensing Lily's quizzical gaze.

'That wasn't so bad, was it?'

Lily took a deep breath and sighed, noticing the difference the honey had made to her raw throat.

'No,' she answered, 'not *too* bad.' She smiled at him as they walked out into the courtyard. He was a full head and shoulders taller than her, and in the dim light, looking up at him made her head spin. The conversation had died completely and neither of them tried to start it up again. They both had deep questions to ask, information to gather, yet Lily didn't feel like the moment was right.

Silence fell between them.

Chapter Twenty-One

A lice jolted awake. It was still the dead of night, but something had disturbed her exhausted slumber. She sat up, listening in the darkness. Every creak, every gust of wind was deafening. Alice sat there, as still as a statue, for what seemed like an eternity. Just as she was about to shake her weary head and put the noise down to a vivid dream, Alice heard it again. A quiet but unmistakable knocking sound.

There was someone at her door.

She took a deep breath and went over to the oak vestibule, too groggy to be worried about her safety and too curious to try and sleep without discovering the source of the knocking. After yesterday, there were very few things she could actually muster up the energy to be fearful of.

She pulled open the door and her heart gave an involuntary leap. Grace was leaning against the doorframe, smirking. She was holding a tray that was piled with food, a couple of mugs, and a large steaming teapot.

'Midnight feast?' Grace winked.

Alice managed a half-smile and the exhaustion that had been weighing her eyelids down floated away the instant she smelled the food. Alice waved Grace into the room and invited her to place the tray down and sit on the bed. Alice joined her and they sat across from each other, cross-legged.

Alice wasn't sure what to say. It felt more nerve-wracking to be alone with Grace in a normal environment where they could talk as equals, rather than as the captured and the sympathiser. Talking to strangers had never been her strong point. She liked to be alone. She liked the solitude and lack of judgement that came from a reclusive life. Letting Lily behind the barriers of her heart had been hard enough... Could she find the strength, the courage, to let someone else in?

'How did it go with Hecate? From what I heard, she seems to like the look of you, so that's a good start.'

'I ... I didn't really know what to make of the whole situation. I couldn't even find my voice to speak. And there's something about her that makes me feel strange.' She shivered, recalling Hecate's ancient eyes.

'Hey.' Grace leant forward and took Alice's hand in hers. Alice flinched. 'I'll help you through this.' She removed her hand and poured hot, fragrant tea into the mugs, passing one to Alice. 'Now, let's not talk about where we are – it's boring and stressful. Tell me about something that makes you happy. What did you used to do, back home? I want to see if there is anything I can do that will bring you a little bit of calm.'

Alice was touched by Grace's thoughtfulness, although

she wasn't sure how to take it. She didn't know how to trust. She couldn't help but be suspicious of every kind gesture. What if Hecate had put Grace up to this? And why was Grace making her feel so strange, so … different?

Alice shook her head. The only other person who had ever been kind to her was Lily, but this felt different. Lily's friendship was like a beacon in the night, constantly guiding Alice through life, supporting her hopes and dreams. Lily and Alice were two sides of the same coin. So completely different and yet utterly perfect companions for each other. In Lily's company, Alice felt safe and warm. Here, sitting in front of Grace, Alice felt like she was burning, feverish. Her hands shook and her stomach churned. Every time Grace looked at her, her heart jolted.

'I-I…' she stuttered. 'My home made me happy. Being there, reading my cards, my tea leaves, my grimoire.' She blushed, avoiding Grace's eyes. 'I like my own company. I like the company of people who don't drain my energy, and I've only ever met one person who I could spend any length of time with. We used to sit for hours and hours by the fire in my cabin. Or sometimes we'd go for walks in the meadows, or we'd get lost in the foggy forests that surrounded my home. Sometimes, at the end of the day, my tummy would hurt from all the laughing.' Alice smiled, lost in the memory. Grace was watching her, unblinking.

'Do you love him?'

'What?' Alice was taken aback. 'Do I love who?'

'The boy … that you were talking about…?'

'Oh!' Alice chuckled. 'No, I'm talking about my friend, Lily. But I can't think about her without remembering the fact that I left after we argued and I never got the chance to apologise.'

'What did you argue about?' asked Grace.

'Silly things. I was upset about something and I couldn't get her to understand why. I ran off when she tried to help and that was the last time I saw her. She's probably worried sick. Ugh, I feel awful.' Alice brought her legs up in front of her and rested her chin on her knees, still clutching the comforting warmth of the mug of herbal tea. 'It's a very *me* thing to get angry and hot-headed and then regret it. I've never been able to hold my temper.'

'I'm sure you'll see her again one day, if you really want to. But … there are so many things we need to do here first. You'll discover things about yourself that you never even knew existed. It might be scary, but it's worth it, I promise you. You're going to shine, Alice Blackwell. I can sense it. You're going to shine and shimmer like a full moon on the waves of the stormiest sea.'

Chapter Twenty-Two

Lily felt like she had known Jem for much longer than just an hour and yet, when his easy chatter wasn't there, he transformed into the tall, muscular boy with an intimidating frown and an intensity that infuriated her. He was already making what should have been a simple linear route to Alice into something far more complicated and long-winded. Quite frankly, she still wished she could fly away on the breeze and continue on her journey. But, if Jem had knowledge to share, she knew it would be illogical to leave before hearing it.

Instead of opening one of the doors off the courtyard, they passed through a gap in the wall and carried on walking, away from the main cluster of buildings. They circled around the lighthouse tower itself and then headed to the right, making their way along a little rocky outcropping. There was a small building, hidden from view of the main buildings, in the shadow of the lighthouse. It was to this building that they headed, and Jem pulled an iron key out of his breast pocket. He unlocked the heavy door and invited Lily inside.

All of a sudden, everything felt much more intimate. She was aware that, before today, she had never actually been alone anywhere with a boy her own age. It made her stomach twist.

The door opened into a large square room that seemed to double as a study and living quarters. The wall opposite the entrance was made entirely of glass, in the style of the rest of the buildings she'd seen, but this room looked out onto the raging sea. The weather had really closed in: black clouds stretched far beyond the horizon, white-tipped foamy waves crashed on the shoreline, and the pouring rain danced a jig on the window panes.

In front of the window was a desk, covered in books, papers, and maps. Lily felt sure that, like her old workbench at the apothecary, the mess and the apparent disorganisation was actually precise in its construction; she was sure Jem would know exactly where every single piece of paper or newspaper cutting was on that desk. It was easy to spot that Jem was a kindred spirit, now she could see him in his natural habitat. That didn't exactly calm her jitters though. She had never needed a chaperone in Alder Vale; she had always just stuck with Alice or with Uncle Alf. She wondered for a painful moment how he was coping without her.

Jem had gone over to the fireplace that dominated the wall left of the door and knelt down, building a fire to take the chill out of the room. To the right was an iron-framed bed with a variety of mismatched blankets and quilts strewn over it, and there was a book that lay open on his pillow. There were also novels, guides, and encyclopaedias stacked up next to his bed, creating a makeshift nightstand with a precarious brass candle holder perched on the top.

Lily couldn't help but feel comforted by the plethora of tomes scattered about the room. She could hear their voices chattering away, telling tales of adventure and mystery and romance. It was hard to feel uneasy in the presence of books.

Lily plonked herself down on an old, moth-eaten sofa in front of the fire and sank into the blankets and cushions that covered its surface. The whole room had an aura of comfort and profound cosiness and she let a little of her anxiety burn away into the warmth of the room.

Lily lost herself gazing into the fire that Jem was still stoking, noticing the smell of oak, honey, and saltwater, the softness of the woollen blankets, the aching still thrumming in her muscles. She was pulled out of her reverie as Jem stood, the fire finally beginning to catch. He looked shy. Lily realised he must have watched her take in the details of the room, and as she looked up at him, he seemed keen to know her opinion, perhaps even to impress her, but also apprehensive. The room was a direct reflection of him, a window into his soul.

'It's...' She paused, looking for the right word. 'It's magical in here. It really is. For somewhere I've never been before, it feels remarkably like home.'

'Ah, it's all right,' Jem answered with a modest shrug. 'It is home though. I've built my life here. Every scroll, every book, every map, every piece of furniture. I couldn't survive without this little sanctuary.' He fell silent and let his tense shoulders drop as he soaked up the comfort of his hideaway.

He seemed to snap out of his nervousness then because he straightened and the look of nostalgia vanished from his face, an easy smile replacing it. Lily was left wondering which side of him was the real Jem: the relaxed, talkative boy with the kind eyes and the welcoming smile, or the boy who occasionally broke through that veneer, the thoughtful, forlorn, quiet, maybe even shy boy who looked so much older and more strained.

She was sure she already knew the answer.

Chapter Twenty-Three

Alice started to receive visits from Grace most evenings. It had become a habit to spend their quiet hours of rest together. Alice's days were filled with strange, intense training. She would be forced to run miles and miles around the edges of cavernous training rooms, all in her heavy overdress and boots. Building stamina was important, apparently, before she trained in witchcraft. She'd also been taught to handle a bow and arrow and to fight with a sword, and was warned that the easiest path to defeat was to rely on her magic. The food Grace brought to her room each night was the only thing that stopped her from shrinking too much, although her dress still hung awkwardly on her bony figure.

Along with the food, Grace also brought company. Alice hated to admit it, but she had warmed to her companion. She had fallen into a comfortable routine around Grace and her friendship was a welcome distraction from the fear that lay on the other side of her bedroom door.

'You'd love it there, I feel sure of it,' Grace told Alice one evening. 'At the top of the tower, in the lantern room where the lamp is, all you can see is the wide, open sea. The glass curves around you, almost like the sky is trying to embrace you. On a clear day, you can see dolphins dancing in the waves. I used to sit up there at night with my sketchbook and draw the everchanging shapes of the water. I even saw a selkie once, I'm sure of it.'

Alice raised her eyebrows and gestured for Grace to keep talking. This was the quiet agreement between the two of them; Grace always had so much to say and Alice was at her happiest just listening with her eyes closed, picturing the places of which Grace spoke.

'One night,' Grace continued with a glassy-eyed smile, 'I couldn't get the lamp to light and it's still a working lighthouse. I was terrified that there would be a wreck when I woke up in the morning and I couldn't settle. I couldn't even entertain the idea of trying to sleep.

'I couldn't think of a better plan, so I pulled on my boots and one of my brother's huge woollen overcoats and I walked right out onto the rocky outcropping just beyond the base of the lighthouse tower. I stood there, clutching the biggest lantern I could find, being whipped and beaten by the crashing waves and the vicious, cutting winds. I stood there all night. As the sun started to rise, I extinguished the lantern and perched on one of the rocks for a while. I don't know if I saved any lives that night, but I like to think that maybe I did.

'You see, the sea is an unpredictable, fearsome creature. Like a wild animal, it's beautiful to watch, but it's dangerous to get too close. I realised, sitting there, that I wasn't scared of the sea at all and I couldn't imagine how anyone could be. The sea birthed me, in a way. It created Grace as you see her now. I washed up on a stony beach, choking on sea water, soaked through and shivering, and became who I am.'

'I hope I can see it one day. Feel the cool water on my skin and the salt on my lips. I imagine it's such a beautiful thing to see.'

'You've never seen the sea?'

'I've only seen my village, my forests, my moorland. I've never ventured much further, but I always dreamed of escaping. I guess they're right when they say you should be careful what you wish for.'

Grace half smiled. There was a forlorn distance in her eyes.

'Well...' Alice lifted her mug, unsure how to handle Grace when she wasn't chirpy and optimistic. 'Here's to new adventures?'

Grace lifted hers in response, and they both took hearty gulps.

At some point in the early hours of the morning, when the fire had died in the grate, Grace shivered. Alice budged up onto one side of the bed and invited Grace to sit by her, under the warmth of the thick duvet and furs. Grace clambered in beside her, clearly grateful for the comforting temperature. The conversation began to fade as the two girls succumbed to their mutual exhaustion. Grace's head lolled to one side, coming to rest on Alice's shoulder.

'Alice,' Grace whispered, only just audible in her sleepy

voice. 'I'm glad you're here...' Her breaths became deeper then, and she drifted into a peaceful sleep. Alice let out a heavy sigh, trying to ignore the little voice in her head that reminded her not to let her guard down, not to grow comfortable in this place of evil and witches who kidnapped and tortured and imprisoned. But lying there, with Grace asleep on her shoulder, she felt a warmth flow through her that had nothing to do with the layers of blankets that covered them both.

For the first time since this ordeal began, she felt content.

Chapter Twenty-Four

J em invited Lily to sit in an armchair by the fire and he chose for himself the chair across from her. He sat with one leg underneath him and the other bent up in front of his body. He rested an arm on his knee and leant his head on the back of his hand. He suddenly looked years younger. The flickering warm light of the fire made his skin glow like the late afternoon sun that shone over the fields surrounding Alder Vale in the autumn. He looked up at her through heavy, tired lids and smirked.

'I thought you had questions?'

Lily nodded, sat up straighter in her chair, and explained, 'I think I need to tell you what's happened first, and what I already know, and then I can frame my questions in that context. Does that make sense?' The words tumbled out of her in a blur. Jem smiled and nodded.

She talked him through everything that had happened, from the moment she found the letter, to stumbling into Kelseth. 'And then I got in that boat and started rowing, absolutely convinced that it was them that I was going to find here. I still don't know what I was planning to do when I got to the shore, but I was so angry and scared – I still am angry and scared – that I thought I could at least try. I felt so conflicted this morning when I woke up comfortable and warm because as thankful as I was to still be alive, I knew I hadn't found her and that she still didn't know I was coming for her. I felt guilt like I've never known.'

Lily had always been a comfortably caged being, happy to be restricted by routine and logic and life. She had discovered a strange, new purpose in this expedition to find and recover Alice, and something about the company of someone who sympathised, who perhaps even understood, was helping her to heal a little. 'So now you can tell me everything. What do you know? Why have you been tracking them?' The questions spilled out with uncontrollable fervour, like a waterfall of terrified curiosity.

Jem laughed. 'This is going to take a lot longer to explain than just tonight!'

'But we don't have time. *I* don't have time.' She was growing tired of his know-it-all nature. Why couldn't he just give her a straight answer for once?

He made eye contact with Lily and gave her a reassuring smile. 'I had, or rather, have, plans in place to attack when the moon comes to the end of its waning gibbous phase. I am going to explain everything you need to know over the course of the next few days and give you all the information you will need to join me in beating them. You've come this far. Are you ready?'

With a deep, nervous exhale, her throat still burning, Lily nodded. *All right, so maybe he's going to be useful.*

'As you know, there is a legend surrounding this lighthouse that we call our humble home – that it is haunted. We rely on that to keep us safe. With Kelseth and the surrounding villages convinced that this place houses a group of bloodthirsty killers hellbent on revenge, they feel like it is riskier to provoke the Lightkeepers than it is to fight us. All we have to do is keep the legend alive, and we can live here without persecution. We're safe.'

'There was a man ... at The Old Silent Inn... He, and the other strange man in Ardnaroch, they had a strange symbol hanging around their necks. Could they be connected somehow?'

Jem shrugged, frowning. 'I haven't heard much about men. I don't think the Shadow Sect even recruit men... What did you say the symbol was?'

Lily scrambled across to the desk and tore off a small piece of paper. She dipped the nib of a pen in a bottle of ink, and drew the strange, crooked tree encircled in gold metal that she'd seen the men wearing. She handed it to Jem.

His eyes narrowed and he scratched his head. One finger traced the circle Lily had drawn. A look of realisation passed over his face and he dashed over to the pile of books by the side of his bed. He flicked through several until he found the one he was looking for. He let it drop open, and pulled out a piece of paper hidden inside.

'This'—he handed it to Lily—'this is the only symbol I could find related to the Shadow Sect. I couldn't uncover the relevance of it and it wasn't helping me progress, so I hid it away, intending to come back to it another time. But look.' He pointed and Lily looked properly at the parchment. On it was a crude sketch of an encircled tree, but this one was split by a huge lightning bolt, cutting the tree almost in half.

'This can't be a coincidence…'

'Did the men say who they were or where they were from?'

'No … no, but the apothecary in Ardnaroch called one of them "Brother", and not in a friendly familial way. More like it was his title, or something.'

'Brother… That rings a bell, but I can't put my finger on why…' Jem was distracted, lost in a trail of thought.

'Maybe things will become clearer with more research.' Lily was keen to get things back on track. They didn't have time to be dallying over the men, not right now. 'What I don't understand is this: how is the legend of the Lightkeepers connected to the Shadow Sect? I know that the girl in the story, the witch, was headed here when her mother died, but I don't understand how the story of her stalking the lands, gaining followers and so on translates to the current fear of you now. People know that the Shadow Sect move around, from place to place. My uncle said that they hadn't been in these parts for years.'

'Ah, very clever,' he commented, and Lily rolled her eyes, unsure whether his patronising was deliberate or just a by-product of being around younger children all the time. 'Sorry, no offence meant. But it is clever that you picked up on that. Long story short, when we arrived here, I was almost immediately warned away from the lighthouse by everyone I met in Kelseth. There's a fairy tale, a sort of poem, that's told to children as a ghoulish bedtime tale but apparently the grown-up residents haven't grown out of their fears of this place. Hang on.' He leaped up from his chair once more, rushed over to his desk, shuffled through a few of the papers, and then returned, clutching another tattered piece of parchment in his hands.

'You know, you really ought to have some sort of organisation system around here. All these torn-off corners of paper are a nightmare.'

Jem tutted and dropped back into his chair, ignoring her comment. 'Here it is. I think it was folded into local lore years ago and it's haunted the residents ever since.' He handed the parchment to Lily, who read it aloud:

'Beware the lighthouse keepers,
For they will hear you weep,
Beware those wretched lighthouse keepers,
Who'll steal you in your sleep.
Beware the lighthouse keepers,
Armed with swords and knives,
Beware those deadly lighthouse keepers,
They've stolen many lives.
Beware the lighthouse keepers,
Who stalk the streets at night,
Beware those wicked lighthouse keepers,
And run when they blacken their light.
Beware the lighthouse keepers,
They've taken many before,
Beware those thieving lighthouse keepers,

They'll leave you drowned upon the shore.
Beware the lighthouse keepers,
For they need to have their fill,
Beware those evil lighthouse keepers,
For tonight it's your blood they'll spill.'

Lily shuddered. 'No wonder no one comes here.'

Jem nodded in agreement. 'I was overconfident and had very little to lose. I needed to find shelter for my sister and I, and the lighthouse just made so much sense. There was no one here, even back then. It was abandoned and dusty, but not quite dilapidated. No one had been here for years. I think Hecate Winter manipulated the story of the Lightkeepers that you know and used it to her advantage. I think we can probably agree that she is the "girl" in your story; it seems too coincidental otherwise. In every town or village that she's passed through, there is lore attached to a building nearby, a poem similar to our own. My theory is that she needs to keep these buildings empty of inhabitants, so if she ever does need to use them for sanctuary, they are free from prying eyes.

'All I had to do when I moved in here was make it habitable and then keep the lore alive. I needed to make sure that my sister and I were protected, especially when I had to leave the lighthouse for one reason or another. I needed the security of knowing that no one would dare to come here, so I began to add to the lore. I had to steal livestock and grain to feed us, and...' He paused. 'I'm sorry if this is a bit gruesome, but I carried around a little jam jar filled with animal blood. Whenever I took a sheep or a pig, I left splatters of blood on the walls of the pens and the stables, so it looked like something violent and horrific had occurred.

'I'd sometimes even leave warnings written in a scruffy hand, pinned to doors or fences, or handwritten on the walls with blood. I needed to make sure that I found a balance between taking enough to scare them, but not taking too much. I didn't want to push them or encourage a revolt or an attack or something similarly devastating.

'My sister and I began to build a little life here. As she grew more confident and surer of herself, she would go out some of the evenings to collect food.'

'By "collect", you mean steal, don't you?'

'Well, yes ... but we rarely had other options. We don't have an income; neither of us can get work without being discovered. She wanted to help and she couldn't stand being without purpose. We took it in turns – one of us would cook and build up the fires and the other would go out foraging and scavenging.'

'How did you get hold of food?'

Jem shrugged. 'I'm sure my sister had her own methods. I, for one, would break into places like the bakery or the butcher's, especially when we'd already taken too many animals. It was easy. I got really good at lockpicking. I crept in, took what we needed, and left again. Late at night, when we returned, we'd share a hot cocoa and talk for a while, or we'd just sit and stare at the fire.' Jem swallowed and his voice had become deep and husky with repressed emotion. He rubbed his eyes and, with a sharp exhale, he stood.

Lily remembered all of the evenings she and Alice had

sat staring into the flames, clutching warm drinks in a comfortable silence. Her throat closed up, the fist of grief closing around her neck.

'Speaking of hot cocoa, would you like one? I feel like I should at least offer you some sweet relief while you listen to me ramble.'

Lily smiled and nodded in agreement. 'What was her name? Your sister.'

'Grace. It always made me smile as she's the least graceful person I've ever known; she's all muscle and strength. She's about as graceful as you were, trying to row that bloody boat in the middle of a storm.' He grinned and then turned away in pursuit of the warm drinks he'd promised.

She struggled to admit it, but she was enjoying herself... Even if the tale made her heart ache for Alice, not to mention how difficult it was to behold Jem's evident anguish. His story was intriguing, but something about that glimpse of emotion made her want to reach out and hold his hand, to reassure him, like he had reassured her, that he was not alone.

Jem reappeared holding two steaming mugs. Lily noticed that his hair must have been bothering him, for he had tied it back into a careless bun at the back of his head, a few strands refusing to conform and falling over his face. The room was filled with a cacophony of calming scents, from the wood-burning of the fire to the sweet, bitterness of the chocolate. Lily felt sure that, had his story not been so interesting, she'd have been long asleep by now.

After he seated himself across from her again, crossing

his legs and clutching his hot cocoa, Lily stifled a yawn and encouraged him to go on.

Jem nodded, inhaled, and continued. 'One night, when Grace had gone out and I was busy preparing dinner, the rain started to pour. It was the worst storm I'd seen since we moved in here. Even though Grace was a strong and competent rower, I always felt anxious at the thought of her out there, alone in the dark, fighting with the high winds and the relentless waves. You yourself have discovered how perilous that can be. I knew she wouldn't be away too long, so instead of fretting over the stove, I decided to go and watch from the window of the lantern room to see if I could see her. When I looked out, there was the little rowboat, battling through the storm. But then I realised that it wasn't Grace. It couldn't be. There were three people in the boat.

'I panicked. Every single possibility ran through my head, most of them revolving around the awful prospect that Grace had been caught and that these people were coming to get me as well. I ran down the stairs and grabbed a knife and my overcoat, hoping that it might give me a little bit of protection if these men came armed with weapons as well as fury. I stood there, poised and terrified, sword in hand, as the door was flung open and the storm blew in the three figures. They were soaked to the skin and considerably smaller than I was expecting.

'The tallest one looked up through her rain-drenched hair, took in my terrified battle stance and burst out laughing. It was Grace. I could see that once the cloud of terror had passed, but it still didn't explain the two small figures she had with her. I think she noticed the stony look on my face, because as her big brother and the only guide she had, she'd seen that face many times, and she stopped laughing.

'I told her to come in and explain herself. It was then that I realised, as they removed their coats, that Grace had brought with her two children.' Jem seemed to notice the mix of shocked confusion and strange understanding on Lily's face.

'Grace looked from their terrified little faces to mine and back again. I could tell that she was worried about what I would say, but I also saw defiance in her eyes. In that moment I knew that she must have a reasonable explanation, so I decided to hear her story. She encouraged the two girls to sit by the fire, wrapped them in blankets, and gave them warm drinks to fight off the chill. They seemed exhausted and terrified by the entire situation. It was then that Grace explained what had happened.

'She had been on her usual route, walking anti-clockwise around Kelseth, staying in the shadows, when she heard crying. She knew she should have ignored it and moved on, but for some reason the desperation in the sobs moved her and she decided to seek out the source of the crying. Crouched behind one of those horrible, crooked buildings were the two girls; one of them was crying and the other was trying to quieten her, to calm her down.

'When they saw Grace approaching, they backed even further into the shadows and it took a lot of coaxing and persuading to get them to talk. Fortunately though, Grace w-was,' he stuttered, '*is* one of those people who gives off an aura of calm. It's so easy to trust her. The girls just about managed to whisper their names and explained that their mother had died and their stepfather was cruel and he had kicked them out into the cold to punish them. They each were covered in tiny little bruises and Grace put two and two together. She decided there and then that we would look after them, whatever the cost.

'I was angry with her, for a while. But seeing those two tiny figures who were underfed, bruised, cold, but still somehow optimistic and bright-eyed, I couldn't help but sympathise. With begrudging acceptance, I agreed, and they've been with us ever since.'

'Maeve and Brenna?' Lily asked.

Jem nodded slowly. 'That's right. Since then, Grace and I have always kept an eye out for children who needed our help. Most of them don't stay longer than a month or two. Once they've eaten a few good meals and we've taught them a few skills for surviving out in the world, they willingly leave and go in search of their futures. Maeve and Brenna have been with us two years now.'

'Surely people notice they go missing though?'

'Of course, but their disappearances play into our hands quite nicely. Maeve and Brenna's stepfather is convinced that they were murdered by the Shadow Sect. I couldn't stand the thought of him taking them back so I used a few of the tricks I've picked up along the way and found a way to protect them.

'Grace and I, we became obsessed with the purpose we had been given. We care for these lost souls, clothe them, feed them, teach them valuable skills; it's good, wholesome work and it keeps us occupied so we barely notice the isolation of living out here...' Jem tailed off, approaching a part of the story that seemed to cause him some distress.

'Jem?' Lily leaned forward in her chair, pulling her legs up in front of her and wrapping her arms around them. Fear stoked in her heart and her voice shook as she spoke: 'If you don't mind me asking ... what happened to Grace?'

Chapter Twenty-Five

When Alice awoke, she felt more rested than she had in a long time. Blinking the sleep from her eyes, she looked around the room and noticed that Grace had already left. Alice frowned and dropped back onto her pillow. She hoped she hadn't done anything to offend her new friend, because she had come to rely on her. Especially as she was sure things were about to get much more frightening.

Alice crawled out of bed, her neck stiff from sleeping in an awkward position. She opened the dresser and pulled out a long black dress made from heavy lace. It was more beautiful and expensive than anything Alice had ever owned. She pulled it on and fought with the fastenings, trying to get herself into the complex garment with all of its buttons and ties. It had a high lace neck, and an emerald-coloured stone was set into the material that rested in the notch between her collarbones. The dress itself was heavily structured and a bone frame was fitted into the lining which made her corset obsolete.

After several attempts to reach behind her back to fasten the final few clasps at the nape of her neck, made nearly impossible by her stiff joints and anxious shaking hands, she decided that she'd just have to throw a shawl over her shoulders to cover the gaping hole at the top of her dress. As she rifled through the drawers in search of a shawl or a wrap, there was a quiet knocking at the door.

'Come in,' Alice muttered. She still felt thorny around anyone in the Sect except Grace, and hated the thought of having to speak to any of them.

'Good morning,' said a familiar voice, smooth as satin and as comforting as a warm apple crumble.

Alice spun around, paranoid that Grace would laugh, or worse, judge her, for her inability to fasten her dress. 'Grace, um … hello.' Alice smiled awkwardly, but she couldn't ignore the writhing feeling in her stomach, as if there were a thousand tiny creatures living in there, trying to free themselves. She hoped Grace wouldn't notice the tremor in her voice.

'Having a few dress issues, are we?' Grace asked, smiling at Alice without a touch of judgement or amusement – but with, perhaps, a hint of playfulness.

'Oh, it doesn't matter. I'll just find a shawl to wrap around my shoulders and no one will notice. I hope...' Alice trailed off, embarrassed.

'No, don't be silly, I'll help!' Grace strode across the room, clearly confident in her dress fastening skills, even if she herself was dressed in a linen shirt with rolled up sleeves and loose-fitting slacks. She led Alice by the hand until they both faced the full-length mirror. Alice shivered as Grace, with her gentle and delicate hands, swept Alice's curtain of raven hair over her shoulder, out of the way of the fastenings. 'Now, I have to admit,' Grace began, and Alice was thankful that she was making the effort to create casual conversation, 'I've had much more experience undoing dresses from this angle, but I'm sure it's just as easy to fasten them.'

Alice's eyes widened in shock and her breath caught in her throat. She glanced at Grace in the mirror, but she was busying herself with the fastenings and hadn't looked up. Alice then caught sight of her own face, which had turned a particularly concentrated shade of beetroot. Just as she was wracking her brains for a witty response to cover up her embarrassment, Grace patted her back.

'All done!' She smiled as Alice turned around, apparently unaware of Alice's embarrassment. 'Right, I'll help you get yourself ready and then I'll come down with you. Your witchcraft training begins today and I'm loath to leave you alone.'

The moment to be witty had passed, and Alice was left with an uncomfortable, dry mouth and a heartbeat that refused to calm. Had Grace been joking when she had suggested that she was in the habit of undressing girls? Did she mean that she just helped out girls here with their undressing out of politeness, or did she mean something else? Did she mean that she, Grace, frequently undressed girls for a reason *other* than courtesy?

For a long time, Alice had been at war with herself over

her feelings and her emotions. She remembered Lily having crushes on the village boys, of her going all giggly if one of them looked at her or came into the apothecary to talk to her. Alice, at first, didn't spare a thought for the fact that she had never once felt giggly or breathless around a boy. In fact, she had never felt anything of the sort with anyone and she had simply presumed that there were other routes laid out for her in life, away from men and marriage and children. And she had been more than happy about that.

However, one night when she was fifteen or sixteen, she'd had a dream that had upended her previous notions of love. She had dreamed that a girl from the village had come to visit her in her cabin, a girl who was not Lily. The girl had invited herself into Alice's home and, after a few minutes of conversation, she had kissed Alice.

She had woken up with a shock, her entire body covered in tiny fizzing jolts and her stomach bursting with butterflies. It had been as if a curtain had been dragged away from a window Alice didn't even know existed, and suddenly the world was clearer; it had shone with the clarity of understanding. She had not realised – still did not understand – that it was possible for a girl to love another girl that way; it wasn't something she had ever seen before. But now she knew the love she felt for Lily and the feelings that had been awoken by the dream were as different as the forest and the moor.

After the initial shock had worn off, Alice had decided that it was probably best not to share this part of herself with the world, and had learnt to live with it locked away in a dark, quiet corner of her heart. The last few days, in

Grace's company, she had felt a gentle tugging at those caged feelings, and now she was very aware that there was a high chance those feelings were about to burst out like a swarm of bees from an agitated hive and there was nothing she could do about it.

'Alice?' Concern was etched on Grace's face.

Alice forced a smile and tried to swallow, but it felt like there was a ball of dry, rough sand sitting at the back of her throat. 'Yes, yes of course, I really appreciate your help.' She managed to speak but the words sounded forced. She was panicking. She hadn't thought about these feelings for such a long time and now, in this terrifying place, surrounded by danger, she was being forced to face them.

She was acutely aware that she needed a level head, and she was worried that if Grace held her hand again, or visited in the night, she would be forced to face the fact that these niggling feelings were real and it was Grace who was causing them.

Alice shook her head and tried to busy herself, but she didn't know what she needed or how she was supposed to prepare for the day. Her breathing was panicked, laboured, and she dashed from one side of the room to the other, muttering to herself. She felt hot and uncomfortable, the high collar of her dress was irritating her neck, and hives started to appear on her skin.

'Alice, sit down.' Grace had noticed that Alice was unsettled and behaving in an unusual manner. 'I'll get everything sorted for you, all right? Take some deep breaths; I promise you'll be all right.'

Alice forced a smile and sat. One of her legs was

bouncing up and down uncontrollably. She was thankful for Grace, of course, but why did everything feel so complicated and terrifying all of a sudden?

Grace pottered around the room, her leather boots clicking a tuneless melody on the unwaxed floorboards as she walked. Alice sat and watched her work, trying to regulate her breathing.

She found that she was both alarmed and excited by the feelings that were growing, that were unfurling like a flower to the sun in her heart. She wanted to run as far away from Grace as she could, but she also wanted to run full pelt towards her. She wanted to be far away with Lily again in her cabin, but she found that she couldn't cope with the thought of being more than ten feet away from Grace.

What is happening to me? Her brain felt like it had melted in her head; she couldn't string two coherent thoughts together.

Grace knelt down in front of Alice and held her hands in a tight, unfailing grip. She was still concerned. 'You can do this, Alice. I promise you. You are strong, you are brave, you are capable. You've just got to show them that you're worth their time and their energy.'

'But...' Alice shook her head. *I need to concentrate on this stupid training and less on the girl kneeling in front of me, damn it, brain.* 'What are we training for? What's the point of all this?'

'Honestly? I'm not even sure. Hecate has something planned, something important, but she won't divulge the details until everything is organised and she has enough witches and Protectors. Until then, it's a mystery. So relax, you won't be charging into battle any time soon.' Grace nudged Alice.

Grace was very persuasive and Alice was happy to hide her real feelings beneath the shade of fear for her future in this place. Grace stood and offered Alice a helping hand.

She pulled the scarlet wrap from around her own shoulders and placed it around Alice's. It smelled faintly of cinnamon and the ocean: a warm, crisp, comforting smell. It smelled of Grace. 'Hold onto this; it is my soul cape and it will give you strength if you begin to waiver. It means that I will always be with you in spirit, even if I have to be elsewhere during the testing.'

'Soul cape?'

'It's a garment gifted to every Protector once they've reached a certain point of their training. We all have different colours, based on the colour of the magic we can protect the best.'

'Hang on ... magic has colours?'

Grace nodded.

'Each person is different, each witch is different, and so the magic presents itself in different ways. I presume you know about elemental magic, or at least of the elements?'

'Yes, like fire, water, earth, air?'

'Exactly. So the colour in the soul capes, and in the magic, is based upon the element for which the witch has an affinity. So my soul cape is red, for the fire element, which also means that I can only be assigned to a fire witch.'

'But ... I haven't even started training. Will it still protect me?'

'I've gifted it to you, as a sign of appreciation, of trust. The cape senses that; it will do its job.'

Alice felt a wave of gratitude. She pulled the soft mantle around her, unable to speak her thanks; the gesture had left her utterly without words.

'But, hey,' Grace took her hand, 'it would be really useful if you could visualise some flames for me in training and unlock your fire magic, because it would be pretty awkward if I couldn't be assigned your Protector now. You know too much.' She winked and nudged Alice.

Alice smiled for the first time all morning. She looked herself up and down in the mirror, breathing in and out in an attempt to calm her hammering heart. With this cape's protection, with Grace's protection, she felt almost confident.

Eventually, Grace squeezed Alice's hand. 'Come on, they'll be expecting you in an hour. I'll show you where the kitchens are and you can get some breakfast. Then we'll go and see the priestess.' She kept hold of Alice's hand and they walked together to begin Alice's journey to becoming a true Sister of Shadow.

Chapter Twenty-Six

J em sighed, his shoulders slumped and his eyes
glistening in the firelight. Lily knew talking about
Grace was hard for him, but she was keen to hear his
sister's story. Perhaps it would make her feel closer to Alice,
somehow.

His voice grew husky again, but he continued. 'Morven
and Cass joined us around the last winter solstice. They
were originally from a place I don't know, beyond the
Shadow Lands. They told us once how differently we live
our lives here compared to where they came from. They
fight, not with swords or bows, but with things far more
deadly; Cass said he once saw a man die, killed by an
assailant with a weapon twenty strides away. I asked him
how a man could fight with a sword the length of twenty
strides, but Cass said they don't have swords there, not
anymore. After the wars, apparently they laughed at us for
staying "stuck in our ways" while they advanced and grew

their cities. You should ask him about it, when he's in a good mood. He has some fascinating stories.

'Anyway, they found themselves in a poor house in a village called Barley. They were treated dreadfully, forced to work in awful conditions, and barely given enough food to survive. They escaped, thankfully, and I found them drifting around the backstreets of Kelseth, stealing discarded corners of bread from behind the bakery. Glenn had only been with us a few weeks as well, although his story isn't mine to tell.

'They're getting ready to leave at the moment. They've grown in confidence so much, especially Glenn; he wouldn't talk at all when he first arrived.'

Lily could tell Jem was stalling, trying to find the words to tell Grace's story properly. He stared into the fire and Lily worried he'd never start back up again, but all of a sudden, he inhaled deeply and continued.

'One night, it was Grace's turn to go out and gather supplies, and Cass was desperate to go with her, to "protect" her. He has always been the paternal type; he is fiercely protective over all of us, and he was so angry at me for not letting him go. But I couldn't risk him being seen so soon after he had come to us because his "death", along with Morven's, was still a talking point in the town and I couldn't bear to imagine the consequences of someone seeing him.

'Anyway, Cass was sulking and Grace promised him that she would return within the hour and that he wouldn't even miss her. That seemed to pacify him, and we were all mostly in good spirits when she left.

'The hour came and went, and there was no sign of Grace. After two hours, I started to worry, but I didn't tell the children. After four hours, I knew I had to go and look for her. I woke Cass and told him that he had to look after the rest of them for the next few hours and I could see him battling between pride and fear. The thought of something bad happening to Grace filled us all with terror.

'I set out in the boat and, even at that early hour of the morning, there were people in the streets, crying and panicked. Something was wrong. So wrong that it had dragged the village folk from their beds at an unearthly hour and set them wandering and wailing. Mooring my boat as quietly as I could, I pulled my hat brim down and my scarf up over my mouth, hoping that it would keep me unknown, unnoticed. It was then that I started listening in to the mutterings and the theories.

'What I heard was that the Shadow Sect had returned. That night, screaming had woken the village folk. As people had come out onto the streets to see what was happening, they discovered that two young women from the town had been taken, and a note had been pinned to the village noticeboard outside the crumbling church. The Sect apparently had a new method to torment the families of those taken, because the victims had been forced to sign their own names before they had been swept away. I still have the notice, if you want to read it?'

Lily nodded, even though she felt like she was going to throw up. She knew that this story couldn't possibly end well and she was dreading reading the notice that Jem had just placed before her. With shaking hands, she picked it up.

She couldn't help but notice the similarities between Alice's letter and this notice. It was the same hand, the same authoritative tone, and it, too, carved through her heart with an icy sword.

Residents of Kelseth Village,

We have returned, like we always said we would. We are building our ranks and it would be unwise to resist us if we come for you or any of your family members. There is no way to escape us. We will steal you from your beds; we will follow you if you walk after dark. We will take you when the lighthouse light is blackened. It is useless to resist. We have taken three of your number tonight and there will be more.

For the families' sakes, we have very kindly asked our new recruits to sign their names below.

Ailsa Merryck
Rowenna Arasgain
Grace Rafferty

You will never see your girls again, but never fear: if they have potential, they will be trained and cared for.

Be warned,

Hecate Winter
High Priestess of The Shadow Sect

It was penned in a neat, careful script. It was emotionless but was clearly intended to terrorise the village, to prevent the residents from living carefree lives, to force them inside their homes.

Now Lily understood why Jem had taken her in without a second thought. She understood why he was willing to help. They both had loved and lost someone to the Shadow Sect. And they were both willing to do anything to get them back. Lily looked up from the paper in her shaking hand.

'I have a letter, too. Hecate Winter wrote it to Alice and told her to meet them here. I wonder if Hecate is her real name?'

'Probably not. "Hecate" is a mythological figure from beyond the Shadow Lands; few of their legends reach our shores but I stumbled across the tale in an ancient book in this lighthouse. She's the goddess of witchcraft, amongst other things. It seems too coincidental that the High Priestess, leading a coven of witches, just happens to be named Hecate. It's probably a ploy to remain anonymous. Plus, Hecate sounds much more fantastical and foreboding; with a name like that, people are automatically frightened of her.'

Lily nodded, deep in thought.

'But now you know. You know why I'm here and who the children are and why I am ready to take down those who call themselves the Shadow Sect. They have my sister, and they have Alice, and they have so many other families' loved ones. I feel like now, more than ever, it is our responsibility to do something about it. To stop the fear, to stop the death and the kidnappings and the torment. Now you know everything there is to know, are you willing to stay here and help me?' He looked up at her, a strand of dark hair falling over his face, his eyes shimmering with tears.

Lily swallowed the lump that had formed in her throat and choked out an acquiescence. 'Of course. Of course I'll help. With our combined knowledge, we can do this. Jem, we can take them down.'

Lily felt stronger than she'd ever felt before. She felt a confidence in her cause, in her abilities, in this newfound team. Things were still terrifying; she couldn't remember the last time she had crawled into bed without an anxious, uncomfortable knot in her stomach. But, with Jem and the others, she finally didn't feel alone. She was glad that she was the one who had come all the way out here to face this evil. And she was glad that Alf, at least, was safe, far away and tucked up in his bed, in peaceful, quiet Alder Vale. That gave her the peace and the hope she needed to succeed and to get herself back home one day.

Jem and Lily's eyes met across the dimly lit room. While Jem had shared his story, the sun had disappeared and the moon was attempting to break through the heavily clouded sky. They had been gone far longer than either of them had expected.

In that little room, in the shadow of the great and hulking lighthouse, an alliance had been forged. Without having to utter the words, both Lily and Jem knew that they would put every ounce of their strength and their power and their love into retrieving Alice and Grace. Each of them felt strength in the companionship of the other. It didn't seem to matter that they had only just met one another, because they had a shared cause. A shared trauma. Lily trusted that Jem would get her to Alice, but she also knew that this beautiful boy with a shadowy but selfless heart needed help too, and she felt compelled to join him.

This wasn't just about Alice anymore. It had grown into a purpose so much larger than she could have ever imagined when she had set out in the beginning. She felt herself drifting away, the flickering of the fire disappearing as her eyes closed involuntarily. Just as the wave of sleep was crashing over her, she heard Jem stand and she shook herself awake.

'It's been a long day for you; it's probably time for us to have some dinner and get some rest,' Jem said, offering her a calloused hand to help her out of the chair into which she had sunken. She took his hand and stood, her bones aching and her throat still sore. She tried to ignore how nice his hand felt in hers.

They walked together out of the room and back around to the lighthouse entrance. Jem accompanied Lily up the stairs, clearly still worried about her strength. When they reached her door, she opened it and entered the room before turning around. There were so many words that she wanted to say, feelings she wanted to convey, but seeing him standing there, illuminated by the moonlight, leaning against the doorframe with his messy hair and his tired eyes, she found that the words left her. 'I—' she began, and then stopped, unsure of what to say.

'Get yourself settled, Lily,' he said. 'I'll send Cass up with a tray of food now, but I'm sure you've got a lot to think about and then you need to try and sleep. If you're anything like me, you'll know that people are draining. New people are even worse. Rest will help, I promise.'

Lily managed a half-smile. Her rumbling belly was warring with her mind's desperation to let her slip into oblivion.

'Come down in the morning whenever you wake and there'll be food left out. When you're ready, I'll be in my study. We can start then. Sleep well.' He smiled, and then disappeared like a forlorn ghost back down the stairs, leaving questions still hanging on the end of Lily's tongue, unsaid and unanswerable.

'Goodnight, then,' she said to the vacant space where Jem had stood. As she closed the door and gazed across the quiet room to the window overlooking the rolling sea, she felt his absence.

And it scared her.

Chapter Twenty-Seven

L ily and Jem were both seated around the large oak table in his study. The others were busying themselves and were happy to let Jem take on the role of getting Lily up to speed. They would be joining in for the rest of the training in the latter stages of the week, when they felt they could really be useful.

Lily had recovered her battered carpet bag that she'd lost after the storm. Jem had found it washed up on the shore with its contents soaked but intact. She held it now, the only true attachment to her old life, and clutched it with white-knuckled hands. The documents and the old folklore book from Uncle Alf were damaged, but not beyond repair. Lily rooted around in the bag until she found the book and papers, and then handed them to Jem, who placed them with care onto the table.

The oak table had been cleared of its usual debris, but was now strewn with old, faded maps, books on local lore, compasses, and notebooks. Jem had been showing his research to Lily and together they had narrowed down the Shadow Sect's location to two possibilities. Lily was uncomfortable looking at the locations because they both seemed inhospitable, mysterious, threatening. Every time they found themselves close to an answer, an image of Alice, cold and tortured, would flash through Lily's mind. She knew it was her guilt-ridden conscience playing tricks on her, but it made her feel uncomfortable all the same.

'My sister will be with her.'

Lily looked up. Had Jem read her mind?

'I promise you, if Grace is'—he swallowed—'still alive, she will be caring for anyone she sees as vulnerable or in need of a friend. It's in her nature to take people under her wing.' Jem ran a hand through his hair and sighed. Lily had momentarily forgotten that he, too, was experiencing the same pain that she felt at the loss of Alice. 'Look,' a flicker of a smile lit up his face for a brief second, 'we've just got to hope that they've found each other, like we have.' Their eyes met across the messy desk and Lily felt a real sense of comfort, knowing that she didn't have to face the Shadow Sect alone.

Whoever 'they' really were.

Jem and Lily fell into a comfortable silence, sorting through the documents in front of them, making notes, in the hope that they could give themselves the best possible chance.

'That book you got from your uncle, can I see it?' Jem was munching on a sticky-looking bun that smelled like honey, and spoke through a full mouth.

Lily passed the book over the desk, open on the story

that Alf had recommended. It was illustrated beautifully, but the golden edges of the pages had faded with the water damage.

'Strange...'

'What is?'

'That your uncle knew so much, but you'd never heard any of it. Why would he keep that from you?'

'I guess he never thought it was relevant. It's hardly a casual conversation starter.'

'Hmm...' Jem popped the last bite of bun into his mouth and wiped his hands on his trousers. He tentatively flicked through the pages, careful not to transfer any crumbs onto the book. 'You don't suppose he knew more than he let on, do you?'

'I was in a rush to leave Alder Vale, and he made it clear that he could only tell me the few things I really needed to know. I'm sure he'll explain when I get back.'

'Just ... this story. The men in it ... they're a bit odd, don't you think?'

Lily frowned. 'Odd?'

'Why is it acceptable, in a book full of tales probably meant for children, to depict a man brutally murdering a woman whilst trying to capture an innocent child? I know she's supposed to be haunted or possessed or whatever, but still. It doesn't make sense.'

Before they could further ponder the story's inclusion, the door of the study burst open with a violent crash. Morven flew into the room, a ghost with terror etched upon her face, her eyes wild and panicked.

'Jem, you've got to come quickly!' Morven was frenzied.

'It's Glenn and Cass – they're fighting again and it's really bad. Please, Jem, now!' Morven disappeared back through the door and Jem leaped out of his seat, papers flying everywhere. Lily followed, running to catch up with Jem who had already disappeared into the main building.

Lily wondered what Morven had meant by 'again' as she ran. The panicked look on Morven's face had been mirrored on Jem's when he saw her. Something made Lily think that maybe these fights were not infrequent and could be serious. When she arrived outside the main living room of the lighthouse, the door was already open, swinging on its hinges. She passed over the threshold and Brenna and Maeve ran directly at her, grabbing at her skirts and hiding their faces. They were shaking. Lily put her arms around them both and walked towards the centre of the room. Her line of sight was partly obscured by one of the large leather sofas, but there were scuffling noises, grunts, shouts, and growls filling the room, bouncing off the wooden walls, amplifying the sound in a series of cacophonous echoes.

Jem was wrestling with Cass, trying to calm the boy down. As Lily drew closer, she noticed a figure haloed with sticky red liquid. Blood. Glenn was on the floor, battered and shaking, curled up like an earthworm who'd spent too long in the sun. She knelt down to face Maeve and Brenna.

'Girls, I need you to do something for me, all right? Maeve,' she turned to the wide-eyed little girl on her left, 'I need you to go and get me a big bowl of hot water. Careful not to burn yourself. Brenna,' she said, turning to the other girl, 'I need lots and lots of cloths. Can you both do that for me?' The two little girls puffed up their chests and nodded, proud that they had been given such important tasks. The fear in their statures dissipated with this newfound responsibility. They ran together out of the room, holding hands.

Lily didn't stand around to watch the girls disappear; she was too keen to inspect the state of Glenn. She dashed forwards and knelt by Glenn's head, lifting it so it was elevated and resting it on her lap. Morven joined her.

'Can I do anything?' she asked. Lily recognised the look in her eyes as a desperation to be useful. Lily herself had felt like that every time Uncle Alf was called out to help someone with an injury. She hated to sit by, idle, when someone was suffering.

'Yes, if you would. Go up to Jem's study and go into my bag. There should be a brown bottle full of a thick liquid, and also a metal tin labelled Wolf's Bane Salve and a box labelled White Willow Bark which I really hope hasn't been ruined by the water. Bring me those as quickly as you can, as well as some bandages if you can find any.' Morven nodded and disappeared.

Lily stroked Glenn's hair, attempting to soothe the boy. He was whimpering and there was blood painted in swirls and splatters across most of his face. His knuckles were grazed and raw. His breath was laboured as he tried to contain his cries of pain, and Lily watched as red and purple bruising formed on his neck – bruising that looked suspiciously finger-shaped. Cass had strangled him. She didn't know what had caused the fight, or who was to blame, but she felt an overwhelming urge to protect this poor, vulnerable boy. She laid a comforting hand over his chest as she looked up to see how Jem was progressing with Cass.

No longer fighting, Jem had managed to subdue Cass enough to sit him on one of the armchairs, as far away from Glenn as he could get the boy. Although, it looked like Jem didn't trust him enough not to lash out again, as he was kneeling in front of the chair, holding Cass's arms at his sides. Jem's back was to Lily, but she could tell that he was whispering to the boy, calming him down and attempting to extract some form of explanation. Lily had a suspicion that there was more to this than it seemed. Growing up in an apothecary, she'd learned much about how the human body changes and how the formative teenage years often trigger outbursts of emotion. She'd studied remedies and tinctures that could calm and soothe an anguished heart. But for some reason, she knew already that they'd be wasted on the shaking scarlet-faced Cass. Lily half expected steam to start pouring from his ears. This wasn't a petty fight. This was serious.

Lily couldn't help but be desperate to learn more about the complexities of this little family unit that Jem had built with his sister. His swift arrival at the scene of the fight confirmed to Lily that there was something darker at work here. This was a safe space for these children, yes, but it was clear that everyone was troubled in their own way. She decided that she'd ask Jem about it at a more opportune time, when he wasn't covered in blood and trying to patch up his wards.

Maeve and Brenna returned through the creaking oak door, carrying the hot water and the cloths. Worry was still etched across their faces but they seemed to calm a little once they realised the fighting was properly over. Lily thanked them and they sat by her, one on either side.

Lily set to work soaking the cloths in the water and wiping away the dried, crusty blood that covered Glenn's face and hair. Maeve and Brenna both took a handful of cloths each and, dampening them, they helped her clean his arms and chest while she focused on his face and neck, where the wounds were deeper, bloodier. As the three of them worked to clean Glenn, Jem stood and gestured for Cass to follow him. The boy struggled to his feet and Jem wrapped an arm around his waist, allowing Cass to lean his weight on him. They disappeared outside without another word.

Lily quietly hoped that Jem gave Cass the telling-off he deserved after brutalising Glenn so badly. Cass's injuries were minor in comparison to Glenn's, probably owing to the fact that Cass was twice his size, both in height and in muscle mass. Cass was built like a shire horse, slender but strong. It was no wonder he had so easily overpowered Glenn, who was a skinny, watery-eyed pine marten in both stature and appearance.

Just as Lily, Maeve, and Brenna had finished cleaning up Glenn's wounds, Morven arrived back, out of breath. She was carrying the ointments Lily had sent her away to fetch. She rushed over, dropped them on the floor by Lily and looked around with desperate wildness in her eyes.

'Where are Jem and Cass?'

'Jem took him away. I don't know where though. Why, what's the matter?'

Morven snarled, her entire face changing from concerned to venomous. 'I swear, if he hurts him... If he punishes him for this, I will never forgive him.' She turned on her heel and dashed back out of the room.

Lily frowned but tried to focus on tending to Glenn. She dabbed the wounds with the copper-coloured liquid out of the first bottle, then coated them in the thick salve, before covering the worst ones in thick, tightly wrapped bandages. She worked methodically, finding peace in the familiar routine of healing. Maeve and Brenna sat and stared, fascinated by the process. She found herself almost wishing that she had more time here amongst these interesting souls so she could learn their quirks, their routines, their habits. She decided that, if she did have more time, or if she ever returned once she had rescued Alice, she would take on Maeve and Brenna as apprentices, if they were interested. They were young still, but in a few years they would be ready to help with pulling together the remedies, and their quiet determination to assist her warmed her heart.

Lily took the bowl of bloody water and poured it out of the window. Her apron was covered in red streaks and she could feel beads of sweat running down her neck. What a strange, stressful turn of events. How often did Jem have to deal with this? And, more importantly, how did he manage it all?

As if summoned by her thoughts of him, Jem returned, alone. He looked exhausted and his eyes were red raw and puffy. A shimmer of tears was still just about visible on his eyelashes. There was a bruise the colour of midnight rising on his cheek bone and his hair had been yanked out of its usual knot so that it fell in a thick blanket around his face. The whole impression was one of hopelessness.

'Jem?'

He shook his head and lowered himself into the armchair, wincing. He closed his eyes and let his head rest on his palm. Brenna, who Lily had learnt was very sensitive to others' emotions, stood and went over to Jem. He looked up and managed to force a smile. Brenna proceeded to climb into Jem's lap and rested her head on his chest and he wrapped a protective arm around her. From the look on his face, Lily knew that Brenna's simple act of kindness meant more to him than the little girl knew. He needed confirmation that he was able to do right by these children, to care for them and protect them.

A single tear rolled down his bruised cheek.

Chapter Twenty-Eight

Lily managed to convince Glenn to walk, or rather limp, with her over to his room. She tucked him up in bed with fresh blankets after reapplying the salve and gave him strict instructions to rest and sleep.

'I'll bring some stew up for you in a few hours, all right? But rest now, Glenn.'

The boy smiled gratefully and then, with a wince, turned over onto his side to face her. 'Lily?' He rasped.

She paused in the doorway. 'Can I get you something, love?'

'C-company,' he stuttered, 'would be really nice.'

This was the most he'd spoken to her since she had arrived. She didn't know whether to be concerned or flattered that he had chosen her to keep him company, but she was pleased either way; if he was ready to talk, if she could help him at all, then she'd give him her full attention. She perched on the end of his bed and gave him what she hoped was a reassuring smile. 'Of course. But I don't want you to overexert yourself. We can talk a little while, and then you really must get some sleep.'

He nodded, but didn't speak. He bit his lip and suddenly couldn't meet her eye.

'Was there something specific you wanted to talk to me about, Glenn?'

He nodded again.

'Where were you, before you found your way here?' Lily hoped leading questions might help his shyness. Perhaps he didn't want to impose a subject on her, but if she could lead him towards what he wanted to talk about, perhaps it would lessen how stressed he felt.

'In between places. On the streets, mainly, but sometimes in the Barley poorhouse too.'

'The same place Morven and Cass escaped from?'

He nodded once. His face was growing paler and his eyes looked even more watery than normal.

'Did you know them from there?'

He nodded again. 'They weren't my friends; they never helped me, never stopped them.'

'Stopped who?'

'The others. And the wardens.'

Lily was careful with her word choice. He was opening up to her, but gradually. She didn't dare push him in case he dived back into his shell. 'What happened, Glenn?'

'I-I'd been living on the streets for as long as I could remember. My mother died when I was born, and my father couldn't bear to look at me. Called me her "bastard". He left me with a wet nurse in her cramped cottage in a tiny hamlet outside of Ardnaroch and returned to a city; I don't know its name, but it's beyond the Shadow Lands. He never came back for me, never wrote.'

'Oh Glenn, that's awful.'

He continued as if he hadn't heard her. His face had taken on a glassy expression, as if he was living through the memory, not just recounting it. Lily wondered when he'd last spoken openly about his life.

'My wet nurse, Pirra, she was nice, but she had nine of her own children. I was at the very bottom of the pile. Then, when I was seven, I think, or eight, she died. Right there in the middle of the kitchen.

'Well, the next thing we knew, we were in the back of a rickety cart, being taken to Barley poorhouse "for our own good". They said it would make us strong, so that one day we could work the fields and earn proper money.

'It was horrible. The work was mostly pointless, designed to make us exhausted and quiet more than it was to teach us anything. Those who cried got beaten. If you cried during a beating, you were taken away and never heard from again.' He shivered and wiped his nose on the back of his hand.

'Are you all right? You don't have to carry on, if you don't want to.'

'No, you're nice. You're kind. I think … if you know where I've come from, maybe you'll understand why I am as I am: rotten, unpleasant, everyone's least favourite.'

'I don't think you are those things though, Glenn. All I

know is that you're sweet, and maybe you've got a bit of a temper, but honestly, what young person with such a history wouldn't? I think you're far better than you give yourself credit for.' She reached out to hold his hand, but he flinched away, a tear escaping and rolling down his cheek.

'I tried to escape once. They caught me just as I made it outside, just as I'd begun to hope that I might be free. They dragged me inside and beat me in front of all the other children. That's when I first saw Morven. She couldn't look at me and she was crying. I thought to myself, "What's she crying for?" I couldn't understand. But then I saw Cass. He had a black eye and a bruised jaw, and yet he stood there with his arms folded, smirking down at me. Like he was somehow better.

'Anyway,' he continued, yawning, 'I managed to escape again, successfully this time. I flitted around the villages and towns and eventually ended up in Kelseth. Grace found me and brought me back here, and who was waiting for us as we walked through the door? Cass. To him I'm just a snivelling, conniving child whose sole purpose is to get in his way, so I've always borne the brunt of his pent-up frustrations. No one else will stand up to him, see. I know I don't look like much but after the poorhouse, I couldn't stand by and let people be cruel any longer. People need to pay for what they say and do.' Glenn coughed and then winced, clutching his bruised ribs.

'All right, all right.' Lily settled Glenn back down into bed, trying to ignore how uneasy his story had made her feel. She'd found Morven and Cass to be amiable, quick to help, generous with their time. The version that Glenn painted told a different story. 'Let's get you settled. We can carry on talking later, when you've had some rest. How does that sound?'

Glenn smiled weakly and exhaled. 'Thanks, Lily. You're just like Grace – kind.' He closed his eyes and his breathing very quickly turned heavy and rhythmic.

Lily felt satisfied that she had managed to help him, even a little bit, and left his room, closing his door quietly. What a complex, unusual boy, with such a horrendous history. *Could it all really be true?*

She took her time walking back to the main room, knowing that she wanted to coax some answers out of Jem, but unsure how she would manage it without upsetting him.

When she entered the room she found it eerily empty, embers still hissing in the grate. Bemused, Lily wandered back out the way she had come and headed into the courtyard. There was no sound but the crashing waves. Lily decided to try Jem's study, but on the way there, noticed a lone figure sitting out on the rocks. Her heart fluttered.

Jem.

She swallowed the lump that had formed in her throat, buried her hands in her pockets, and wandered over to him. She made sure to tread heavily and to clear her throat on approach; Lily figured that surprising him in this state would only make him harder to communicate with. He was sitting cross-legged on a large rock, wrapped in a dark checked woollen blanket, and his hair was still out of its usual bun; the wind was whipping it around his shoulders, but he didn't seem to mind. His arms were wrapped defensively around his knees, and when he heard Lily approaching, he glanced over his shoulder and gave her an almost-smile. It was unconvincing.

'How is he?' Jem sounded concerned, but not as concerned as he should. It was a polite concern, as if Glenn were a passing acquaintance, rather than a boy in his care.

'He's sleeping now. The salves I've treated his wounds with should quicken the healing process, and he's pretty well bandaged. I'll keep an eye on things, change his dressings, but I've every faith that he'll be right as rain in a few days. Surface wounds, that's all. Bad ones, I'll admit. But surface wounds, all the same.' Lily dropped down by Jem, not wanting to impose but craving the warmth of his blanket in the cold, salty air. 'Where's everyone else?'

'Maeve and Brenna have gone for a nap. I think they were more scared than they wanted to let on, and Brenna fell asleep on my chest almost instantly once things had calmed down.' He sighed. 'Morven and Cass are both in their rooms. Scheming, I expect.'

'Scheming?'

'Apparently there was more to that fight than I realised. I think you, too, have fallen into the trap of underestimating Glenn. He's so scrawny and limp and quiet, you'd think he wouldn't hurt a fly. And then there's Cass. He's always had an alpha streak in him, and I think he looks to me as a role model, which is fine, I guess.'

He definitely did not seem to find the idea fine. At all.

He was gazing out towards the horizon, unblinking, and cracking his knuckles absentmindedly.

'Anyway, that means he gets defensive and he thinks it's his responsibility to dish out punishments. He's very protective over everyone here, but he and Glenn have never seen eye to eye. I don't know if it's because he feels threatened by him or whether it goes deeper than that, but the two of them bicker and snap at each other all the time. Fights don't break out often though. According to Morven, Glenn had been saying something about Grace and me and it sounds like Cass took it pretty personally.'

'Wait, what was Glenn saying about you and Grace?'

'He is an ... unusual boy; I'm sure you will have noticed. He took it really badly when Grace didn't come back. Blamed me, I think. That anger has built up over the last few months, and then with you arriving, I think he thinks I'm trying to replace Grace. Morven said he just flipped out, started calling me awful names, and calling Grace names too, which is really odd because Grace was the only one who could ever really get through to him.' Jem sounded fraught and hurt. His voice cracked and he coughed, trying to clear it.

'How strange...' Lily thought back over everything Glenn had told her. 'I didn't think he seemed the type of boy to start a fight.'

'Well, you don't know him, do you?' Jem snapped.

'I just meant—'

'I know what you meant. Don't make assumptions. You don't know them, you don't know me, you don't know anything about us. You can't just saunter in here and presume you know exactly what's going on and you can't expect to understand either. I'm thankful that you helped Glenn but don't push it. All right?'

Lily was furious. How dare he speak to her like that? How dare he, after she had agreed to stay and help him, after she had nursed Glenn back from the brink?

She turned to him, ready to tell him exactly what she thought of him and his arrogant outburst. Jem was shaking, anger rippling through him like the waves that battered the shoreline, and Lily lost all of her fire. He looked pitiful. There was a huge part of her that was tempted to storm away and leave him to sulk. Something kept her there though. Sympathy perhaps, or curiosity.

There was an angry black cloud hovering just above his head and his face was dark, tragic, contorted. He looked younger than she had ever seen him, and it was then that she remembered that he was just a boy. Barely eighteen, without guardians to care for him, with his sister missing, and with these children who looked to him like a father. All of that responsibility, all of that worry and torment and pain. Her heart ached for him. Jem Rafferty, the hero to so many children. But who was there to look after him? Who was there to tell him that everything would be okay?

She moved herself closer to him and tentatively placed an arm around his shoulder. When he didn't shake it off, she pulled him closer, wrapping her arms protectively around him and pulling him into her chest like a child. That was when the tears started. Instead of fighting her like she expected him to, he buried his face in her hair and sobbed, his whole body wracked with raw emotion. Lily wondered when he had last allowed himself to cry, when someone had last held him.

'It's all right, it's all right,' she crooned softly, stroking his hair and encouraging him to cry every last tear from his eyes. She found herself crying too, and they both sat there, illuminated by the light of the setting sun, clutching each other like lost children.

Chapter Twenty-Nine

'Ah, so you've brought her to us eventually, have you, Grace?'

The priestess towered over them both. Just before they entered the room, Grace had let go of Alice's hand and now she felt the loss of her comforting strength. She tried to lift her chin to make herself look unwavering, steadfast, when on the inside she felt the same repulsion, the same urge to run as before. Alice had started to enjoy her physical training sessions; she had started to feel muscles beneath the lace of her gown and she no longer found herself out of breath after running a few strides. But she also knew that physical strength couldn't prepare her for whatever the priestess had planned.

'You can leave us now,' she said to Grace, and the girl nodded, glanced at Alice with her kind eyes, and swept out of the room. Alice's heart dropped to her feet. Why couldn't Grace stay?

'What do you want from me?' Alice asked in a tone that she hoped sounded curious and a little venomous.

'I want to make you strong, Alice Blackwell. I want to teach you about the powers that lie dormant inside of you. I want to tempt those powers to leave their hiding place. I know you have magic, because you are from a long line of witches.' The tall woman looked at Alice down the bridge of her straight nose. 'You may be confused. You may deny the existence of your magic. But...' she paused, thoughtful, as if trying to work out how much she should divulge, 'your mother was as powerful as they come. Almost as powerful as me. Not quite,' she smirked, 'but almost.'

'I don't understand...' Alice was reeling. How could her mother have allied herself with this woman?

'She was one of us. She ran away, of course, when she found out she was expecting you. When she realised I'd find out about how she betrayed me. I imagine she was trying to protect you and her revolting lover. He was a fallen member of the Brotherhood, just to really drive the dagger into my back. You were just a dreadful symptom. I could have perhaps forgiven her indiscretion had she grovelled on her hands and knees, but no. She left me for him, and that was the ultimate betrayal.' The priestess cackled. 'She put all that effort into hiding you away – she even got herself killed – and all for nothing! Because here you are, standing before me, the spitting image of your poor mother. You have to appreciate the irony, no?'

Alice felt tears burning behind her eyes. It felt like such an injustice that this woman, with her smirks and her callousness, had spent much more time with her mother than Alice ever had. 'You killed her, didn't you?' It wasn't a question, not really. It was a fact, and the gaps in Alice's personal history began to fill up with vague explanations.

'Killed her? Maybe. If you want to see it that way. I gave the order to have you all killed but we couldn't find you. They succeeded in squirreling you away for years. I'd almost forgotten about her. But magic leaves traces, and I couldn't really sit here, thinking about her living her life, carefree, with a scrawny little rat of a daughter to fawn over. No, the image itself made me squirm. So, a few years after Ailísh left, I decided I would take her by surprise, let's say. But she got the better of me for the last time. She and your disgusting father hid you away and ran. They abandoned you, Alice. But I knew I'd find you one day, so I had no qualms in dispatching your wretched parents the moment I heard they'd been caught.

'I've been searching for you ever since. To begin with, it was because I wanted you dead, just like your mother. I wanted to punish you for what she did to me. But after a while, I started to feel the loss of a powerful witch by my side and I decided that the closest I was ever going to get to a woman of Ailísh's power was her daughter, so I gave the order to find you, track you, and eventually steal you away as soon as you were old enough to join our ranks. We had no interest in raising a snivelling child, so when we found you, wide-eyed and defenceless, when you were probably eleven or twelve, we waited until you were grown, and then we snatched you in the night. It really was a faultless plan and I'm still impressed that it went so smoothly!' She paused, smirking, as if waiting for Alice to confirm that her plan had been, in fact, impeccably executed. 'Do you want to know how she died, your mother? I received a very detailed account from my—'

'Shut up.' Alice was shaking with rage.

'Apparently she was crying and screaming, begging like a common peasant. She was stripped of her powers so all she could do was plead for her life from the lowly witches that I sent to kill her. She wept, relentlessly: she cried for me, for what we'd had before she betrayed me. She even cried for her precious daughter that she knew she'd never see grow up. Well,' she paused, looking Alice up and down, ignoring the tears that were flowing down the girl's cheeks like blood from a wound. 'How disappointed she'd be that this is all you've amounted to in your seventeen years.'

'You're lying!' Alice's rage boiled over and she screamed, every single cell in her body howling with fury, her arms flung out wide. She felt something snap inside her chest and light flowed from her; she was a flaming star, burning, exploding, filling the room with a brilliant blood-red glow. She dropped to her knees and the scream turned to a cry. She collapsed, curling herself into a ball, trying to become tiny, invisible.

What just happened? Panicked thoughts ripped through her mind in confusing, scattered patterns.

She couldn't bear to understand. She couldn't bear to remember her mother, her mother's face, her mother's heartbreak. All she knew was the pain, the feeling of the flames licking at her arms, her legs, her face, her heart. Every single part of her was ablaze and scorched with the power that had been dormant all her life.

The priestess was clapping, deranged in her excitement, unharmed by the burst of magic that had poured from Alice. 'Brilliant, brilliant!' She laughed, ecstatic. 'That will do for today.' She gestured for two hooded women to remove Alice. 'She needs rest. We want more control from her tomorrow and she will need to have regained her strength before then. Take her away. Inform Rafferty she's to take her some food and watch over her tonight.' She paused. 'In fact, it's best if she's kept under constant surveillance at this stage. Take her to Rafferty's room.' They lifted Alice up and dragged her from the room. She lost consciousness with the agonising, hair-raising sound of the priestess' maniacal laughter reverberating in her ears.

Chapter Thirty

The next morning, the sun rose, bright and low. The days were getting shorter and shorter. They were running out of time. As Lily entered the kitchen, everyone was busying themselves to distract from the silence that sat in the room like a phantom.

'Morning, all!' She skipped over to the stove and poured some hot water into a mug from the kettle that sat on top. She refused to be a part of the negative energy. That didn't mean the others would join her in her positivity though, and it was only Jem who looked up from his book and sent a solemn nod in her general direction. 'Since you all seem to be in a wonderful mood, I have a plan that requires help from every single one of you today and it is of incredibly high importance. So,' she paused for dramatic effect, hoping that they were all listening and not just ignoring her, 'if you all don't mind, I'd appreciate it if you stopped being so moody and paid attention.' She looked up and saw a smirk tug at the corner of Jem's mouth, which she took as a good sign. Everyone else remained silent and unmoved. Lily felt frustrated. She hated being ignored.

'If any of you have any interest at all in rescuing our friends, Grace and Alice, then we need to concoct some remedies, tinctures, and salves, both for the journey that Jem and I will be embarking on, for any possible wounds that the girls may have, and, most importantly, I want to test out some new experiments I've been working on: offensive rather than defensive potions.'

This seemed to capture Morven's attention, who elbowed Cass in the ribs and gestured for him to pay attention. Brenna and Maeve both sat, arms linked, staring intently at her. Even bruised, sorry-looking Glenn gazed at her with watery eyes from the corner of the room. Jem stood and walked over to join her. 'We're listening,' he said, looking around the room to make sure everyone really was paying attention. Lily didn't need Jem to help her persuade the children, but his quiet support by her side gave her an extra dose of strength and confidence.

'By *offensive* potions, I mean things that Jem and I can arm ourselves with when we infiltrate their hiding place. I need ingredients for three different potions, and enough for two or three bottles of each. My plan is to send you out in small groups to gather enough supplies for the different potions, and then I will teach you how to make them. This is invaluable knowledge for you all, especially when you choose to leave here and go your own way. Knowing how to make these potions could save your life.

'Right. Morven, Cass, you're first up. My uncle Alf's great-grandmother collected this from a lost tribe that existed on an unknown uncharted island thousands of miles from here. When she returned, she adapted the recipe so that she could use local ingredients to create the same effect.' Morven's eyes lit up with fascination. Lily made a mental note to take more time to talk to Morven in the near future. Tales of adventure always made Morven's eyes glow and Lily was curious about the girl's beginnings, and where she wanted to head next.

Cass's chest was puffed out, a sign that Lily took to mean that he was feeling proud and protective. He was clearly honoured to be entrusted with this task. 'I need you to go out along the coastal path, the one that follows the shore and curves around the island cliffs. Collect seaweed, any type, some dry driftwood, and I'm going to need as much Common Scurvygrass as you can.'

'Common Scurvygrass?'

'It's the one with the kidney-shaped leaves and white flowers; you'll find it if you're looking near the rocky shoreline. It might not be blooming now though, this late in the season, so look out for its reddish-brown seedpods instead. I need you to bring me as much of that as you can carry. Understood?'

'Yes, ma'am,' Cass said, with a glint in his eye and a smirk tugging at his lips. Lily rolled her eyes and smiled at him, glad to find herself on the receiving end of his cheek. It felt like a very good omen.

'Right, well, finish off your breakfasts and then get yourselves gone. It's very important that we start brewing these potions tonight.' Lily tried her best to be authoritative and found herself awkwardly fitting into the role of guardian for these children, as Jem had. It was a huge responsibility on top of the already heavy burden of finding and rescuing Alice, but she was growing accustomed to the routine of the lighthouse children. 'Maeve, Brenna, can you come over here please?'

The two girls climbed down off their chairs and skipped over to her, pleased to have a purpose. Lily knelt down so she was at their height and placed one hand on each of their backs, a gesture she hoped would seem comforting and trusting. 'You two have the most important job of all.' Maeve and Brenna exchanged excited glances. 'I need you to collect a big bucket of sand, along with some of that water from the stream that runs orange. Do you know the one I mean?' They nodded. 'And some black paint. I think Jem might know where you can find that last one?'

They all turned to look up at Jem who had been gazing at them all with an expression of proud wonder on his face. Their attention brought him out of his reverie and he spluttered, 'Yes, yes of course, yes. Um … yes, I painted over the lines on the lighthouse just last month. I think I still have some.'

Lily mouthed an appreciative 'Thank you' to him, and turned back to the girls. 'This is a very, very important job and I wouldn't trust anyone else to do it. So, promise me you'll be very careful?' Maeve and Brenna both nodded enthusiastically. 'Good, go and finish eating then. Go on.' She gently pushed them back towards the table and stood. She turned to Jem.

'Do you think you'll be okay going out with Glenn

today, or do you think he's best staying in where its warm?' she asked under her breath.

'I think we'll stay in today. He's still feeling really tender and I don't want him to exert himself too much.'

'You're right, of course,' she whispered, before turning and going over to Glenn and seating herself beside him. 'How are you feeling today?'

'Tired… Sore…' He looked up at her through teary eyes. Huge black rings circled them, a tell-tale sign that he hadn't slept much the previous night.

'Are you all right to stay inside? You can get some more rest and you'll be feeling much better tonight, I promise. Then you can join in and help us all with the potion-making this evening.' He smiled and pushed away from the table, wincing with pain. 'Do you need any more medication?'

'I think I just need some more sleep,' he croaked.

'Of course. Look after yourself, love.' Lily squeezed his hand affectionately, and then he left the room, dragging his feet.

The room was filled with the sound of spoons scraping bowls as the children tried to finish up as quickly as they could so they could head out. They seemed excited to have a purpose and a task that was actually going to be useful. The air was filled with excitement and anticipation. All at once, it seemed, everyone got up and, chattering amongst themselves, left the kitchen. Only Lily and Jem remained.

'I think it's incredible, what you did just now,' Jem commented as he started to clean up the dishes from breakfast. It was a casual comment, but it felt like an acceptance. A proper invitation into the little household that he had built. She was no longer just a guest, helping to find Grace. A lost soul in search of her best friend. She was a part of them, as much as anyone else.

'Thank you. And thank you for supporting me. I don't want to impose or push in anywhere I'm not wanted but I just really felt like they needed that this morning. After last night...' She paused. Lily had been desperately attempting to edge around last night. Jem had been so vulnerable and she felt sure he would be embarrassed at the memory. She had no wish to make him uncomfortable, or ruin what they had built together.

'I'd appreciate it if you didn't mention last night to anyone.'

'I won't; I promise I won't. But, Jem ... if you need someone to talk to—'

'I don't,' he replied, with a tone that cut through Lily like a sword through flesh. The kindness that had been in his eyes only seconds earlier as he admired her for organising the children had left him. His walls had started to come down, though she thought by now he knew he didn't have to pretend to be all right and strong with her, like he did around the children. Lily had been sure that she had begun to get through to him but those hopes had been dashed on the rocks.

Then his features were masked once more with his easy, casual smile and he was Jem again, the Jem she had first met. The trouble was that now she knew that the real Jem, the one who was hiding under the façade, was hurting.

'Come on then, Lil. We need to draw up our final action plans today so we're ready to set off the day after tomorrow.

Can you head down to my study and I'll go and get that paint for Maeve and Brenna?'

'Of course.'

Lily hated the fact that she was upset by Jem's attitude, especially when she had more important things to worry about. Alice was still out there somewhere, suffering, and she was sitting around wasting her energy and her thoughts on worrying about Jem's wellbeing.

Chapter Thirty-One

Lily wandered slowly down the corridors and out into the courtyard. She caught a glimpse of Jem disappearing through a small door on the far side of the courtyard, scratching his head, in search of the elusive paint. She followed the well-trodden route to Jem's study, a walk she had done several times a day, every day since she arrived.

This practice usually lit a flame of excitement within her, but fear had settled in her heart. They had decided where they thought the Shadow Sect were *likely* to be hiding, but she couldn't find it in herself to be excited, or to feel accomplished. Instead, as she walked, she felt an overwhelming sense of hopelessness.

She wasn't sure whether it was the fatigue, the anxiety, or the absence of her best friend's wisdom, but Lily found herself growing irritable and increasingly low in mood. Presenting a positive, chirpy version of herself to the children was one thing, but embodying it was becoming harder and harder. She wanted to feel optimistic, she really did, but the doubts were creeping ever forwards and settling in the pit of her stomach.

What if they'd wasted too much time and Alice had already succumbed to their power? What if she didn't want to be saved? Or, what if Alice had already left this world, left Lily behind to find her way blindly through a life without the light of Alice's friendship?

She entered the study, a cloud of dejection and pessimism floating inches above her curls, threatening to crush her. For the first time in her eighteen years of living, she felt alone. She had left Alf to fend for himself, Alice had left her, the children only saw her as a temporary acquaintance, and Jem... She didn't know what to think about Jem. She thought she had found in him a kindred spirit, a friend. Perhaps in a normal world that wasn't full of witches and murder and kidnapping, perhaps he could have been something more. Lily knew it was a selfish thing to think about, to yearn for. But that evening on the shoreline they had spent together, vulnerable, raw, completely and utterly at peace with each other, holding on as if they were the last two people on earth, holding on for dear life ... that all felt real. Her chest had been ripped open and she had willingly scooped out her heart and placed it next to his, right there on the floor in front of them, and they had accepted each other – or so she'd thought. Now he was closed off and guarded again, as if it had never happened, as if he were ashamed.

Why hadn't someone written a book about this that she

could study, so that she might understand her own feelings and interpret everyone else's?

She tried to push the distracting thoughts out of her brain and focus on the task in hand. She decided that organising their maps and notes would be the best way for her to reengage with the material and with her own mind. Lily Knight was no witch, but she was certainly magic when it came to organisation.

She stood tall over the desk, examining each piece of information carefully, trying to work out the best way to structure the process. She eventually decided to group their research into stages: things to remember before setting out; things to keep in mind as they travelled; and things they would need to know upon finding the Shadow Sect. Once she had these headings in her mind, she set to work furiously arranging and rearranging the documents in order of importance. The process of creating order out of chaos helped to calm her mind and reinstate a little bit of confidence. Between them, she and Jem had managed to collate a wide variety of information.

By the time Jem came into the study, Lily was gazing at her handiwork, flushed with pride. He looked like a nervous puppy as he observed her from across the room. He was covered in splatterings of paint and his hair was messy – and Lily thought she'd never seen anyone lovelier in her whole life.

'I just wanted to apologise, first and foremost, Lil. I'm such an arsehole sometimes. I didn't mean—'

'Oh, shush yourself, Rafferty. We're both idiots, but

we're idiots with a job to do, so come over here and help me, will you?' She grinned.

Jem expelled a sigh of relief. 'What on earth have you done to our research?'

'I've organised it. Wipe that concern off your face; it's much easier to navigate now, see…?' She pointed at the piles in turn. 'We have three sections of information, and in each of them we have documents ordered by importance. This way we will be able to gather all the information we need to track them down, and all the information we need to stop them. By organising everything like this, we also reduce the risk of missing vital pieces of information. Also, I have removed every map except the one with our most recent annotations and routes written on it. Another way to reduce any issues or confusion.'

'You are a wonder, Lily Knight.'

'Well, I do try.' She tried to sound nonchalant, but she felt colour rise into her cheeks. 'Is there anything you think I've missed? Or anything that still needs solidifying? I want to make sure we have everything we need by dinner time, so tonight can be spent concocting the potions and tomorrow can be spent organising ourselves so we can be ready to set out first thing in the morning the day after.'

'Where's the list of supplies we need?'

'Here.' She rummaged through one of the piles and found the list. 'I've added a few more things I thought we might need, but it's all on there.'

'So, all we need to do now is work out how we're going to get to them without exhausting ourselves, because we need to be at full strength when we arrive. There's no point conducting a rescue mission when we're half asleep and exhausted.'

'Well, I think I've come up with a solution that I wanted to run by you.' Jem nodded for Lily to continue. She leaned over the map and pointed at a section of their route that ran through a patch of thick woodland, relatively close to where they hoped the Shadow Sect were hiding. 'I propose we make our way here before nightfall. According to this map, the area is large and wooded, which means it will be easy to hide in there. We can make a small camp, far enough away from the Sect that we won't accidentally draw their attention to us, and stay the night there. Then we get up at daybreak and make our way to their lair first thing in the morning. It also means that if ... *when* we escape with Alice and Grace, we still have half a day's worth of light to begin the journey homeward.'

'Have you ever even slept outside?' Jem stifled a smirk.

'Don't patronise me please, Jem. I slept many a night under the stars with Alice at her cabin, thank you very much.' They both smirked.

'A night in the forest it is then!' Jem agreed.

The two of them pulled up their chairs so they were sitting beside each other and started poring over their research materials. They circled vital pieces of information in pencil, flicked through the heavy books, and drew up several possible routes to their camp in the forest.

Occasionally, when Jem was fascinated by a book or was examining a map, she'd steal a glance at him. She wanted the image of him, relaxed and almost happy, with his hair in a careless bun, his furrowed brow almost invisible and his full lips pulled into a satisfied smile, to remain etched in her memory forever.

She had thought, when she had first met him, that hiding under his careless smiles, he was a thunderstorm, all power and rage and darkness. But Jem Rafferty was the calm stillness after the storm has passed. He was gentle and peaceful. He had that storm inside of him, yes, but he kept it contained. His sheer determination to be a solid unchanging force of good to support those who most relied on him morphed the stormy seas into a still, warm azure ocean. Lily realised she wasn't alone at all; she never had been. She hated that her journey was necessary at all, but she was inexplicably glad to have Jem by her side now.

They sat like that, talking occasionally but mostly in a comfortable silence, until the sun started to set. Lily looked out across the sea, admiring the rusty glow over the world. The ocean was white-tipped and angry; she had learned enough about the sea in her time at the lighthouse to know that it was going to be a fog-coated, stormy night.

Jem broke the silence with the scraping of his chair against the wooden floor. 'All right,' he said, standing up. 'Shall we go and see what everyone has managed to collect today then?' He offered her a hand, which she took, and helped her out of her chair. He held onto her hand a few seconds longer than necessary, just long enough to make Lily's heart do a little somersault in her chest, and then left the room. He glanced back to make sure she was following, and the two of them headed towards the main building.

Chapter Thirty-Two

Grace Rafferty was running. Running and running and running. But all she could hear in her mind were the echoes of Alice's screams from the hall below.

The training room that she favoured was in the very depths of the lair, but Merryck and Arasgain were already in there, pummelling each other in the name of combat training, and she didn't have the heart to stroll in and demand they leave. They had struggled to settle far more than Grace had, but they had finally seemed to relinquish their hopes of escape and had thrown themselves headlong into learning everything they could.

This had meant that, for Grace to be able to exercise away her feelings, she had to use the training room directly above the great hall. And that was why she was now sprinting from wall to wall, panting, desperately trying to drown out the sound of Alice's anguish.

Running wasn't working. She glanced around the room

until her gaze settled on the grain-filled dummies hanging from the ceiling. Perfect.

Wrapping off-cuts of material around her knuckles, she sauntered over to the figures and looked them up and down. In her mind, she placed Hecate's face over the head of the first one, and Blayne's over the second. All right, so maybe Blayne just did as she was told, but she had been the one to knock her unconscious as she tried to protect Alice. So she was as good a target as any.

Expelling one heavy breath, Grace danced on her tiptoes and, after she had psyched herself up, threw a punch square across the jaw of the inanimate dummy. It swung pathetically.

It was taunting her.

She let out a cry of frustration and battered the dummies, no longer caring for technique or practise. All she wanted was to hurt something, anything, like she wanted to hurt Hecate.

Shrieks echoed around the cavernous lair. Alice's shrieks.

Grace felt bile rise in her throat. Was this kind of visceral reaction to a witch's pain normal for a Protector? She had only heard of such a connection between witches and Protectors who were bonded ... but she couldn't ask the one remaining bonded pair; they kept themselves to themselves. And they were *terrifying*. Hecate herself was scared of those with bonds; she had already banished two sets of them in Grace's short time with the Sect. It wasn't safe.

But Alice had changed everything. *Everything*. What if she and Alice had...

Grace flinched. A searing pain spread over her hand, and the pale material around her knuckle was now saturated with red. Lost in her thoughts, she had pummelled the dummy until the skin on her hands could take no more. The figure hung limply from its neck, as lifeless as ever. The only proof that Grace had touched it at all was the flecks of blood splattered across its head and torso.

'Argh!' Grace yanked the dummy from its noose, its head dropping to the floor. She flung the body across the room where it sprawled, helpless and broken, on the floor. A final growl escaped her lips and confirmed to Grace that training was only exacerbating her agony.

She stormed out, letting the heavy wooden door slam behind her. She shouldered her way past anyone she encountered, ignoring the tuts and the threats, until she reached the door of her room.

The pain had ebbed away. She could no longer hear Alice's cries. She breathed a sigh of relief and pushed open the door into her safe space.

Only to find it had been infiltrated.

Grace swore.

Lying on her bed, feverish and asleep and glowing bright red, was Alice. Around her body there were singe marks on the bedclothes. Her brow was saturated with sweat and she was tossing and turning in her unconscious state. Grace had only witnessed one other witch fresh from her breaking, and that girl hadn't survived. But that girl hadn't had a Protector.

Her own selfish fears disappeared and were replaced

with strong resolve. If Alice was going to make it through this, she would need Grace to be unwavering in her care. There was no time for whimpering.

She dashed from her room to the nearest washroom, filled a large bowl with cool water and grabbed a cloth, before returning as fast as she could back to Alice without spilling a drop. She sat herself next to Alice on the bed, lifted her head so it rested on a soft pillow, and dabbed the cold water onto her forehead and temple.

Although Alice was asleep, Grace knew her magic would be strong; there was no harm in borrowing a little of her power to heal the wounds; if Alice had been conscious, she could have done it for herself. She placed a hand on Alice's arm and felt the magic channel through her own body, making her fingertips tingle with flames. She placed a careful finger on the gruesome gash on Alice's temple. The skin covered over the wound and the redness faded almost instantly.

Grace soaked the cloth once more in the cool water, ignoring the throbbing in her own knuckles. She stroked Alice's head with the damp material in an attempt to lower the girl's raging temperature. She knew she had to break the fever soon, and she wanted to make sure Alice felt comfortable and safe when she woke up.

Footsteps echoed outside her room, hurrying past in quick succession. There was whispering, too. Suspicious whispering. Grace climbed off the bed and locked the door. She didn't want any uninvited visitors watching as Alice regained consciousness. She would be uncontrollable, reckless even. Waking up and seeing someone threatening would surely release more of her untapped magic. Who knew what damage that could cause?

As she turned back to Alice, Grace heard her mumble. She was waking. The mumbling evolved to whimpering, and that evolved to screams. Grace rushed over to the bed and knelt over the writhing Alice, holding her head in her hands, gently but firmly.

'Alice. Alice!' She shook her, trying to bring her back to consciousness with as little pain and trauma as possible. Alice began to thrash around and fought against the strength of Grace's hold. Alice's eyes flashed open. They were watery, blood-shot, and the pupils were dilated. Combined with the growls that were rattling in her throat and her wild, black hair that was strewn around her pillow, Alice looked fearsome, terrifying, powerful.

Grace winced. Every fibre of her body wanted to run out of the room as fast as she could.

She wanted to be both far away from Alice and also never, ever apart.

Just as Grace was about to leap off the bed, Alice's fierce expression crumpled and she started to cry. What began as soft little sobs grew to a crescendo of full-volume weeping.

Grace pulled Alice to sit up and wrapped her arms around her, allowing her to cry into her shoulder. She rubbed her back, whispering to her that it was all going to be all right as she rocked the girl back and forth, lulling her into a quiet calm.

It broke Grace's heart to see Alice like this. To see her scared. To see her in agony.

It was in that moment that she swore to herself that she

would protect her for as long as they both lived. She would protect her from the Sect, she would protect her from herself, she would protect her from anyone on this earth that wanted to harm her.

If they wanted Alice Blackwell, they'd have to go through Grace Rafferty first.

Chapter Thirty-Three

As Lily and Jem approached the living room, they heard lots of excited chatter and laughter. Any awkwardness that had hung in the atmosphere from the events of the night before had disappeared. Lily and Jem entered the room to see all five of the children – even Glenn had dragged himself from his bed to join them – sitting in a crescent shape around the fire. Brenna looked up as they walked in and jumped up from her sitting position, running full pelt at Lily with a grin on her face.

'Lily! Lily!' she shouted, jumping up and down in front of her. 'We did it! We got *everything* you asked for!' Brenna lifted her chin proudly.

'Well,' Lily took her hand and led her back to the group, 'I am incredibly proud of you all, but I had no doubts that you'd manage absolutely fine without Jem and me to guide you, because you're all so sensible and responsible. Isn't that right, Jem?'

'Oh, oh yes!' He smiled at them all, subtle creases

forming around his eyes. 'I'm very proud.' He found himself a spot next to Morven and sat cross-legged.

'Have you got everything you foraged here with you now?' Lily asked the group, who all rushed to different parts of the room, bringing back baskets full of the things they'd collected. There were myriad plants, flowers, and rocks, several jam jars filled with paint and river water, sand and seaweed. Everything was laid out in the middle of the semi-circle, a cornucopia of ingredients and supplies. They really had managed to find everything she'd asked for. Lily was thrilled. 'Wonderful! Gather up your supplies and follow me to the kitchen…'

On the oak table that dominated the kitchen space, Lily placed three cast-iron pots. She collected her mass of thick curls on top of her head and stuck a pencil through the knot, just about holding it in place enough to keep it out of her eyes. She then rolled up her sleeves, cleared her throat and began: 'We are going to be making three very different potions this evening. First, we have a very simple healing ointment that will speed up the healing process of any type of wound. I brought lots of this with me, but unfortunately I had to use a little bit more than I'd anticipated in order to get our lovely Glenn back to feeling himself again.' The boy smiled, still shy and quiet. Lily gathered up several types of flowers and the seaweed, then drizzled the river water on top. She used a large wooden spoon to mix everything together and then carried the pot over to the ancient range oven. The fire was already lit inside, and so the pot began to heat immediately after Lily placed it on top of the stove.

'While that one is brewing, the next one we're going to

make is a potion that will be a huge advantage to us when Jem and I attempt to infiltrate the Shadow Sect's lair. We're going to play them at their own game. If they like shadows, shadows are what we will give them. This is the Draught of Darkness, and when brewed correctly, a simple sprinkle of this onto the rocks in the cave will create a shroud of darkness. To those who aren't expecting it, it will be disorientating and terrifying, but to Jem and to me, who will be in possession of this,' she pulled a tiny bottle out of her trouser pocket, 'we will be able to enter unseen, as this little potion that I brought with me from my uncle's apothecary will make us immune to the effects of the draught.'

Everyone in the room was staring at Lily with expressions ranging from intrigue and fascination to sheer delight. They were hanging on her every word. She scooped up an armful of seaweed, emptied the tin of black paint and the river water into the pot, and sprinkled in the sand. She lifted the pot onto the space on the stove and let it simmer next to the healing potion. She rooted around in her bag for a tiny bottle of unlabelled viscous liquid and poured the entire contents into the bubbling pot.

'Finally, we have a potion that we absolutely cannot heat. Please, if you remember nothing else I'm teaching you, remember not to heat this one. I'm about to show you how to make a potion that is violently explosive when it comes into contact with heat or open flame. This potion is only to be used in dire situations: if you are under attack, or if you need to destroy something quickly and efficiently … like the lair of an evil coven of witches.' She smirked at Jem, who was looking at her with a mixture of fear and adoration in his eyes.

Lily gathered the rest of the ingredients on the table and placed them all into the final cast-iron pot. She used a heavy marble rolling pin to crush all the flowers and plants into mulch, until she was left with an unrecognisable but seemingly innocent concoction of ingredients.

'Glenn, can you do me a favour and bring me some of those small glass bottles from the pantry? Brenna, Maeve, go with him and help please.' The three of them obediently got up and wandered off to the pantry. Lily thought she heard Glenn heave a sigh, but ignored it. She still hadn't figured out that boy.

They returned holding armfuls of brown and green bottles. Lily handed out half of the bottles to everyone crowded around the table and instructed them to fill the bottles with the mixture. When they were all full, they returned them to the pantry, and then proceeded to fill the rest of the bottles with the mixtures from the stove. By the end of the evening, the kitchen was filled with a group of very tired, very satisfied children who felt like they had learned a great deal from Lily's potions lesson.

Maeve and Brenna both fell asleep at the table almost as soon as the bottling process was finished. Jem asked Morven, Cass, and Glenn to clean up the kitchen whilst he helped Lily put the twins to bed. Lily scooped Maeve up into her arms and Jem lifted Brenna, and the two of them wandered down the quiet corridor, trying to walk as slowly and carefully as they could so as not to wake the girls. They reached the room Maeve and Brenna shared and placed them in their respective beds, tucking them up with blankets and pillows so they were warm and comfortable. Lily watched Jem as he kissed them both on their foreheads. It was a carefully constructed routine that Lily didn't want to disturb, and then they were tiptoeing past the girls' beds and closing the door behind them.

'They're lucky to have you,' Lily observed. It was a fact, not flattery. Jem smiled and then nudged her shoulder gently as they walked side by side.

'We're all lucky to have you, Lil. The way you captivated that room tonight ... I've never seen anything like it. None of us knew how much we needed you until you arrived. Especially me. I'd forgotten what it felt like to have someone around who understands, who can tell me when I'm being an idiot, someone to have a proper conversation with.'

He paused and stopped walking. They were alone in the corridor, standing just outside the living room. Jem reached out and took Lily's hand and held it tightly, as if he were scared that she might disappear.

'Thank you. There is no one I'd rather have with me, with us, whilst we go through all of this.' He stepped closer. Lily could feel the warmth of his breath gently on her face. 'And ... I hope that, maybe, once this is all over ... you'll consider coming back.' He pressed her hand to his heart and she felt that, like hers, it was beating like a fluttering hummingbird inside his chest. He leaned closer and—

'Jem! Jem, can you help me light this fire please! I think the wood is too damp,' Cass called from inside the living room and Jem took a step back, looked into Lily's eyes for a millisecond longer, and then charged in to help Cass.

Lily stood there in the empty corridor. She was all of a sudden lightheaded and her hands were shaking. *Did that just happen?* she thought. *Did Jem just ask me to ... stay?* She leaned against the cold stone wall, trying to catch her breath, a smile tugging at the edges of her lips, her heart aglow.

Chapter Thirty-Four

'G race...'

Alice started to re-emerge from the nightmare.

'I'm here, I'm here.' Grace continued to rock her gently, still holding Alice tightly against her chest.

'It was horrible,' Alice said between sobs. 'She said all these awful things about my mother and about me and ... I just lost it. I don't know what happened. Everything hurts; every inch of me is burning. And the noise! I can hear so much, I can hear mice in the walls, I can hear them talking outside, I can smell the kitchens from here. Everything is so loud and bright and strong. I can't ... I can't cope!'

'I know, I know. It will get easier, I promise. I'm here, all right, I'm here.'

Alice drew back from Grace's arms and gulped in air, trying to stop herself sobbing. Her throat was scratchy and her eyes were dry and sore. She still felt like she was burning from the inside out.

Grace reached out and held Alice's face in her hands, a

gesture that comforted Alice more than she could ever explain. They looked into each other's eyes, unblinking.

'I promise you, Alice Blackwell, that I won't ever leave you. They'll have to kill me first.'

A sob broke free from Alice's mouth. 'I can't stand it. It hurts…'

Grace shushed Alice, wiping her brow. 'I've got you… It's all right.' She pulled Alice back into a tight hug, rocking her gently from side to side. 'There is nothing on this earth that can make me leave you now.'

Alice felt her heart stop at those final words. It stopped for several beats, and then when it started up again, it was beating so fast, she felt like her chest couldn't contain it any longer. A tear ran down her flushed cheek, as the magic burned in her veins.

'Ali, I've realised something, while you were in the hall with Hecate…'

Alice sniffled and pulled out of Grace's arms to look her in the face. She couldn't read her companion's expression. 'What is it?' She wiped the tears from her cheek with the corner of Grace's soul cape that still sat crookedly around her shoulders.

'Have you heard the others talking about bonding?'

Alice shook her head, a single tear running down her face. The burning in her body was almost unbearable and it took all her strength to sit calmly when what she wanted to do was writhe and cry.

'It happens – not often, but sometimes – between a witch and a Protector. It starts when there is a match between the soul cape and the colour of the magic wielded by the witch. Yours was red, wasn't it?'

Alice frowned, sniffling. 'How do you know that?'

'It had to be, for my theory to work. Witches and Protectors with aligned sympathies towards a certain element can "bond". Your red magic, my cape, it means we align with the fire element. It also means we align with each other.

'In normal circumstances, I can protect any witch that needs it. However, I'm stronger when protecting a fire witch than I would be protecting an earth witch, for example. I can still protect her, but it's not as easy. However, when a witch and Protector are bonded, all of my energy as Protector flows towards you, the witch. I can still physically defend other witches, but I can't work anyone else's magic except yours.

'It sounds a bit rubbish, until you realise that when I *can* channel your magic, and when you and I are working alongside each other, we are both infinitely more powerful. Everything is heightened. Everything is strengthened. As a team, we are almost undefeatable.'

'And ... you think we've ... what was it? "Bonded"?' Alice didn't understand.

Grace nodded. 'Yes, I think we have. Today, when you were with Hecate ... I can't explain it, but it was *horrible*. I realised, then, that what we have isn't the norm. I don't know when it happened, but we need to keep this to ourselves. The strength gained from bonding terrifies some people – Hecate included. There's only one existing partnership still living here; the others were stripped of their powers and flung out into the night.'

'I wonder...' Realisation flowed through Alice, momentarily quietening the coursing pain.

'What?'

'I wonder if Hecate and my mother were bonded... That's why I'm here; that's why she wanted *me*.'

'But ... bonds between two witches are even rarer than with Protectors.' Grace was frowning.

'Rare doesn't mean impossible.'

'I guess...'

'What if she thinks she can recreate the bond she had with my mother? Imagine the power she thinks she can wield with me by her side. It makes perfect sense. That's why all of this has happened; that's why she's put all this effort into tracking me down.'

Grace was nodding now, a look somewhere between understanding and horror etched on her face. 'Alice, she can't find out. If she knew ... about us...' she reached out and took Alice's hand, as if looking for reassurance in her own feelings, 'I'd be a goner. She couldn't let me live.'

Alice dashed across the room without warning and vomited violently into Grace's chamber pot. She stood, tears coursing from her eyes for a few moments, before wiping her face and turning back to Grace. 'I won't let that happen,' she whimpered. 'I won't.'

Chapter Thirty-Five

'I don't understand why you won't let us come with you. You could use all the power you can get! We're strong, and we're only a few years younger. Please, Jem. *Please*.'

Jem had already explained, as had Lily, that it just wasn't possible, but Morven was obstinate. They had already told her that she and Cass needed to lie low, and that a young couple going about their business would look miles less suspicious than a group of children skulking around. She hadn't been convinced.

Morven had followed Lily from the kitchen, all the way across the courtyard, relentlessly begging her to change her mind.

'No, Morven,' Lily finally snapped. 'We've said no. Please respect that.'

She stomped off in frustration, muttering under her breath. Both Morven and Cass always liked to feel included, be part of the action, but this was far too dangerous and they were still both barely fifteen. No, Lily knew they were right to keep them here, especially because they needed them to look after Maeve, Brenna, and Glenn.

Lily entered Jem's study with her worn carpet bag slung over her shoulder. Between them they were going to share the research materials, maps, lists, as well as blankets and food and any other essential items that they would require on their journey. Jem had his leather bag already open on his desk by the window and was attempting to organise everything.

'Are you nervous?' Lily asked him, for her own stomach was churning with the fear of the unknown. They didn't know if they had tracked the location of the Sect correctly, or what they would be faced with when they arrived. Jem was always strong and unflappable, but in this instance, she needed reassurance that it wasn't foolish to be afraid.

'I'd be an ignorant fool if I weren't nervous, Lil. But we're prepared, aren't we?'

Lily nodded. 'Yes, of course. In fact, I'd even say we're probably overprepared. We have planned for every outcome.' Then, with a smirk, she added, 'What could possibly go wrong?'

Jem rolled his eyes at Lily as she dropped her bag down on the table. As the evening winds whipped the waves outside, they both worked by candlelight and the glow from the fire; their faces had a warm orange radiance that crowned them both in a blaze of firelight.

'Tell me about Alice. I feel like I've only really spoken about Grace, but it's both of them we're going to save. I'm sorry I haven't asked sooner.' His true purpose was distraction. They were both anxious.

Lily looked up, tears sparkling in her eyes. Every time she thought of Alice, an icy iron hand broke through her brittle ribcage and took hold of her warm beating heart, clenching it hard.

'She's...' Lily paused, trying to find a single word that defined her best friend, her Sister of Shadow. 'Rare. She's a rare gem, glittering amongst dull rocks and blunt metals. She shines: her heart glows like a cold star, the brightest in any constellation. She's a force of darkness itself; she is fierce and strong, but she is also really vulnerable. She has always been desperate to find her roots, to connect with her lost parents and the magic that she wanted so dearly.'

'Magic?'

'She was never able to connect to it, unleash it, I guess. If she even had it at all. I didn't believe in any of it before I set off on this journey. But she always did. She leant heavily on her tarot cards and tea leaves. I think she felt that if she could make herself useful in telling the future, in predicting events, then she could lead herself to her own destiny. Find it, in her way. I used to read stories to her when we were little.' She smiled, despite her heartache. 'She always hated the part when the princess was set off to meet her destiny by a person who told the princess what her destiny should be. She used to say "Why believe the ravings of superstition and fate when you could forge your own path and make your own destiny?" and I guess she had a point, but it's only recently that I've come to understand what she meant.

'I think, for a long time, I was expecting her to up and leave, in search of her family, of her roots, of her magic. But not like this, not stolen away in the night. That, surely, is the opposite of making your own destiny. It's trying to fit in with someone else's.

'My Uncle Alf used to say we were two sides of the same coin. She's dark, like a glimmering night sky, a foggy forest, a mist-shrouded mountain. I'm light, made from river water and sun-drenched fields. But without the darkness, I could never shine, and without my shine, Alice could never find her way.

'The village we lived in was full of the superstitious old grumps that Alice despised, and they despised her in return. They called her a witch and spread all sorts of rumours about her. Rumours that developed into tales, and tales that became a part of our folklore. Years from now, they'll still be whispering about the witch in the woods, blaming their misfortunes, their illnesses, their bad luck on her.

'She stopped coming down to see me in the village when we were still small, so we could only see each other when I wasn't working and could walk up to her cabin. Still, we saw each other three or four times a week. I couldn't imagine, I never could imagine, that I'd be able to survive any longer than that without her. Being apart from her now, not knowing if she is all right, if she is healthy, if she is even alive … it kills me. It has been killing me, slowly eating away at my heart.'

'You'd know.'

'What?' Lily had been speaking every word that entered her head and hadn't really been paying much attention to her own words.

'You'd know. If she were dead, I mean. Bonds as close as

yours, as close as mine and Grace's, we'd know. We'd sense it. We'd feel a part of our heart as it was ripped away. I promise you, she's alive.'

'You're right, I hope. It's just a strange thought that … two or three days from now, we will see them again. I'll get to meet Grace…' She couldn't decide if she was excited or terrified to meet the famous, incomparable Grace.

'I really hope they're spending time together, drawing strength from companionship, as we are.'

They both sealed their bags closed, every document, map, and book they could possibly need piled up inside, along with the bottles of potions that Lily had made the night before and other essentials.

They were ready. All that was left now was safeguarding the lighthouse and making sure the children knew exactly what was expected of them.

Tomorrow, their rescue mission would begin.

Chapter Thirty-Six

A lice Blackwell was growing stronger. Hours and hours of physical training followed relentless mental training and she had no choice but to keep up or suffer the consequences. She'd start the day with three solid hours of combat, which would roll into another brutal 'training' session with the other witches, a process that was closer to emotional torture than actual training.

Time crawled by. Hours felt like days, and days felt like weeks. Soon, Alice had no idea what day it was, nor could she guess what kind of moon shone outside in the night sky. How she missed the languorous days in her cabin; the predictable flow of each day, the fire in the grate, the books on the shelf, the birdcalls outside the window. She missed Lily, too. She missed how her friend couldn't visit without bringing a freshly picked posy of wildflowers. She missed running about with her through the forests until they were so warm they would dive into the cool brook that sidled by her home. She smiled as she recalled all the time they'd spent splashing around in the crystalline water. She missed planning to bake all sorts of wild fruit pies, and then eating all of the wild fruit between them before the pie crust was even made.

Imagining the things she loved helped ease the pain from the unyielding training. Alice had taken to lying on her bed with Grace, the two of them dreaming aloud about the rusty orange beauty of autumn, or the crisp crunch of winter. It wasn't the training that was helping Alice grow stronger. It was Grace.

The priestess had noticed that Alice and Grace had developed a connection, though the girls suspected she wasn't aware quite how deeply that connection ran, and so they were allocated as each other's training partners. From dawn until dusk, the two of them trained ceaselessly, and after a few days of this new routine, they knew each other's strengths and weaknesses intimately.

One morning, they were both roused by a summons. Alice and Grace met in one of the serpentine corridors that snaked through the coven's lair and their hands came together, as if magnetised. They marched with their chins raised and shoulders back, an air of confidence and power ebbing from them like sparking electricity. They moved as one entity and had learned to interpret each other's movements, expressions, thoughts, and feelings simply by glancing.

The other witches in the Shadow Sect whispered about them, for even amongst the magical community, their connection was rare and unnerving. They were isolated from everyone else, and whispering and gossip followed them everywhere. They both made a concerted effort to downplay their relationship so that people wouldn't guess they were bonded, but their energy was impossible to hide.

Alice pushed open the huge door into the great hall and she and Grace walked without hesitation towards the priestess who sat casually on the altar table, just as she had when Alice had first arrived.

'Ah, my precious girls. Welcome, welcome. How are you both this morning?'

This politeness was strange and Alice and Grace glanced at one another, a barely visible but identical frown appearing on their foreheads. They smiled and nodded, waiting with bated breath for the priestess to reveal the real reason she had summoned them.

'Now, I do believe that the two of you have a *bond* quite unlike anything I've witnessed in all my years leading this coven. You are both fierce and powerful. We know, from experience, that Alice's magic is strongest when she is under some form of'—she paused, licking her lips—'stress. Today, I'm going to test just how much power we can extract from you. Which is where you'—she pointed at Grace with a carved fingernail—'become useful. Guards!' She gestured to the hooded women who lined the walls in a defensive stance. 'Put Rafferty in chains.'

'WHAT?' Grace yelled, hands clasped into fists, ready to fight.

'NO!'

Alice rushed towards Grace in a futile attempt to protect her.

The guards were too great in number for either girl to

have a chance. Grace put up an admirable fight, but was very quickly overpowered. The guards surrounded her and battled her to the floor, where she was pinned until she stopped squirming. When the guards retreated, Alice knew that Grace was already suffering, but the pain was so subtle, almost invisible, that to the priestess she just looked defiant, fierce, ready to breathe fire. She was slumped onto her knees, hands weighed down by cast-iron manacles attached to chains that ran along the stone floor which were in turn attached to the walls on either side of the great hall. She didn't beg or plead; she didn't cry or whimper. She refused to show any sign of weakness.

'Now, shall we play a little game? I have just perfected a spell that will make your strong, fearless *friend* scream like a baby. And I've perfected another spell with very different but just as destructive consequences. Which would you like to see first?' The High Priestess was enjoying herself. She appeared to be getting some form of sick thrill from torturing them.

'Neither, you beast,' Alice spat.

'Now, now, watch your language, Blackwell, or I'll have you in chains too. Actually, that's not a bad idea.' She called the guards over again and Alice found herself face to face with Grace, both on their knees, hands manacled to chains that spread their arms like human sacrifices.

'I won't let you do this,' growled Alice, trying to crane her neck to look the priestess straight in the eye.

'I'm afraid, my dear girl, that you don't have much choice. I want to see your power. I want to know how far I can push you, how powerful you really are. Grace here is …

useful, but she won't be a leader; she won't amount to much. I expect you'll grow bored of her someday soon; you'll want a companion who's a little more ... experienced.'

A guttural growl was vibrating at the back of Alice's throat as her anger began to grow. She risked a glance into Grace's eyes and saw pain etched there, as clearly as if Alice herself had carved it into her face.

'Grace,' Alice whispered, her throat constricted with emotion. 'Grace, don't listen to her. It's not the truth. Don't listen to her.' Grace could only nod.

'It appears,' the priestess announced, trying to regain the girls' attention, 'that I may have to take a more forceful approach to encourage your magic to really break free of the constraints you have placed upon it.' She came to stand on Alice's left, staring at them both with fierce intensity. She lifted her hands in front of her, her fingers flexing and shaking with the effort of the spell she was in the process of conjuring.

For a few short seconds, nothing happened. Grace and Alice locked eyes, confusion clear in their faces.

Then thick black smoke started swirling around Grace's legs. As soon as it made contact with her, she shrieked and began to writhe in pain. The smoke continued to climb up her body, clinging to her limbs, sticking to her bare wrists and throat. Alice could only fight against her chains with helpless abandon as she watched Grace suffer.

Grace's skin was just about visible through the swirling burning haze and it had turned red raw and bloody. The smoke was ripping into her, peeling the skin from her bones, flaying her alive. Grace screamed and screamed and screamed...

Until the fog made its way into her eyes, through her nostrils, and down her open throat. Grace's eyes rolled into the back of her head and her entire body started to shake and jolt. Grace had lost all autonomy, she had lost consciousness, and she had lost the ability to cry for help. No, she had not *lost* it. The High Priestess had taken it from her.

As Grace flopped backwards, her chains barely keeping her upright, Alice finally lost control. Like the last few times when the priestess had pushed her to the limit, her arms were involuntarily flung outwards and an ear-splitting cry tore itself out of her throat. But this time, the flames that coursed through her body made her feel powerful, unstoppable, strong. She no longer felt the agonising burning or the fear. She was the mistress of her own magic. Something dark had snapped inside her soul.

The feeling of the magic pulsating through her was euphoric. She smiled, sinister and fearless, and yanked her arms inwards, snapping the reinforced iron chains from the walls. She did not know any spells, any words or phrases she should utter to create magic. All she knew was vengeance. All she could do was channel this beautiful rage towards the one soul who had tortured Grace.

Alice leapt to her feet, chains still dangling from her bleeding wrists. She ran, full-force, at the priestess who had backed against the wall. The priestess had her arms out in front of her, her hands stretched wide, and she was furiously muttering something inaudible. When Alice was just a metre or so away from the priestess, she bounced backwards off a solid, invisible wall. The priestess had managed to construct a shield of magic to prevent even Alice's sheer unbound strength from penetrating it. Alice screamed in frustration, punching and kicking the invisible boundary that was preventing her from avenging Grace.

The priestess watched, a satisfied, if slightly anxious, smile spreading over her face.

'Nicely done.'

She turned away from Alice and went back over to the altar, where she sat herself in a cross-legged position.

Alice dropped to her knees, exhausted and unable to move. The shield spell that the priestess had constructed was not just a wall in front of her, but a transparent cage that prevented Alice from moving even a step or two away from the spot on which she stood. As the magic ebbed away, she turned to see Grace's unconscious form.

The smoke had faded and Grace's wounds were invisible. Had they even been there at all? Alice looked on helplessly, unable to move, as the hooded guards surrounded Grace's lifeless form, lifted her, and carried her out of the room.

'Where are you taking her?' Alice shouted. She couldn't bear the thought of Grace waking up alone and in pain, without Alice there to comfort her. Tears she couldn't control streamed from Alice's burning eyes.

'Nowhere that you need concern yourself about. She knew the dangers of becoming a companion of yours; she knew the risks. Let's see if she can cope with the repercussions.'

'W-what do you mean, *she knew the risks?*' Alice blubbered.

'Well, when you arrived, I saw how protective she was of you, so I instructed her to gain your trust, to win you over, to get close to you. All this time she's been reporting back to me everything you have done together. *Everything.*'

Alice felt nauseous. Had any moment she'd spent with Grace been real? Or had they all been a part of the priestess' plan to infiltrate her defences and manipulate her into releasing her dormant magic?

Images of the time she and Grace had spent together flashed before her eyes. Moments of laughter midway through intense training sessions, falling asleep together after difficult days, midnight feasts, laughing so hard they could barely breathe... And then there were those moments she couldn't bear to think about, the moments when she felt sure that Grace had wanted something more, the moments that kept her awake at night: when their hands brushed all too often, when Grace spent a little too long gazing at Alice's lips. All of those times she had woken up drenched in sweat after dreaming about Grace doing things to her she wasn't even sure were possible...

Were they bonded at all? Was every moment, every gaze, every almost-kiss founded on misinformation and betrayal? Had everything been a lie?

Alice fought back tears. *This is what comes of being vulnerable,* she thought: *pain and betrayal.*

'Guards, you know what to do.' The priestess waved a nonchalant hand and disappeared out through a hidden doorway behind the altar. Alice was manhandled and dragged kicking and screaming from the room, terrified about them taking her back to the dungeons.

Instead, the guards deposited her at her bedroom door, dropping her on the cold stone floor and disappearing into the shadows. Her muscles felt like they were bleeding, but she managed to pick herself up and, sobbing, drag herself into her safe haven.

As she crossed over the threshold, a blurry figure rushed towards her, sobbing uncontrollably. It was Grace.

'Alice, what did they do to you? What did she say? Are you all right?' Grace bombarded her with question after question. All Alice could do was stand there, arms firmly stuck to her sides, until Grace unfurled herself and limped backwards, staring at Alice in confusion.

Her left eye was overcome by a blackened bruise that was shimmering on her dull, usually glowing, skin. There was still a crust of dried blood around her nostrils and on her top lip. Her thick russet hair was unkempt and wild. Instead of her usual loose shirt and trousers, she was dressed in just a white floor-length nightgown. There were charred marks on her collarbones, her throat, her wrists. She looked like a ghost, intent on haunting.

'Is it true that the High Priestess told you to get close to me? To gain my trust?' Alice's voice was shaky, but strong. She would not be lied to.

'No, Alice, no. Don't believe her. She was trying to trigger a reaction and she saw that I was the way to make you break. In the beginning, I was assigned to be your guardian, yes, but that was because I begged, on my hands and knees, when we returned from the journey to collect you. I went in there and I threw myself at her feet and I begged to be appointed as your Protector. I couldn't stand the thought of you suffering alone. I couldn't leave you to deal with this on your own, Alice.'

She reached out to take Alice's hand but Alice flinched back.

'Alice…' she pleaded. 'Please, believe me. In that room, she was manipulating you, manipulating *us*. What she said about you looking for someone more experienced, someone better than me, that was her way of trying to creep into my mind and release my demons. She wanted you to see my suffering. My fears are built upon how much I couldn't stand losing you. This,' she gestured to the two of them, 'what we've built, what we have, it's real.'

She stepped closer, but Alice couldn't shake the unease that had settled in the pit of her stomach. She needed time. Swallowing the lump in her throat, Alice dragged open her bedroom door and gestured to Grace to leave.

'No, no, Ali, please don't do this.' Grace was red-faced, her eyes filled with tears that she refused to let fall.

A tear rolled down Alice's cheek. 'I'm sorry, I just … I need to be alone for a while. I've got a lot to think about.' She held her head high but she couldn't look at Grace for fear that she would see how broken she felt inside.

Grace didn't plead again. She nodded once, wiped a tear on her sleeve and marched from the room without a backward glance.

As soon as the door clicked closed behind her, Alice crumpled to her knees. Sobs wracked her body and she couldn't breathe from the pain of the spasms.

She dragged herself onto her bed and yanked the covers over her. She didn't bother undressing – what did it matter now anyway? She grabbed a pillow and clawed it to her chest, hoping it would fill the void that had opened up in place of her heart.

Her hand brushed something that felt odd beneath the pillow. Trying to regulate her breathing, she sat up and felt around until her fingers closed around a torn-off piece of paper.

Alice frowned, sniffling as she unfolded the parchment. She recognised the handwriting immediately as Grace's, and felt her world collapse in on her.

You're the strongest, most courageous person I know.
When you're by my side, I'm home.

Sweet dreams,
Your Grace x

She dropped the note, her hands shaking. How could she have ever doubted the sincerity of Grace's affections? How could she have turned her out, when all she had ever shown Alice was kindness, patience and ... love.

Alice screamed into her pillow, tears flooding down her cheeks.

She had ruined everything.

Chapter Thirty-Seven

'Morven, you're in charge of keeping the lamp lit. Maeve, Brenna, I need you to make sure everything stays clean and tidy. Glenn, I'm trusting you to make sure everyone has three square meals a day, and Cass, I need you to be my second in command. Your job is to keep everyone safe until we return. Does everyone understand?' Jem was regimental, marching up and down the room, allocating duties, pacing, wringing his hands.

Everyone was sitting around the fire, as they always were, but they were facing outwards towards Jem, with the fire warming their backs. Jem and Lily should have left an hour before, when the sun was still yawning. Now it was creeping up over the ocean and Lily was growing increasingly nervous – and from his twitchy behaviour, she could tell that Jem was too.

Cass and Morven were sensible, but the others were so young to be left alone for any amount of time, and with the tension that had built and culminated in Glenn and Cass's fight only a few days ago, they were both dubious about leaving them unsupervised. Ever-responsible Morven would ensure Maeve and Brenna were kept away from anything dramatic, but when the boys were violent, she wouldn't be able to restrain them both. She was strong but she was only one person.

Something else was niggling at her mind though, and Lily hadn't felt brave enough to mention it to Jem. What if, for whatever reason, they couldn't come back? What if they were kidnapped as Alice had been, or worse, killed in the attempt to break out Alice and Grace? It was a horrible thing to consider but a necessary consideration, nonetheless. They were walking directly into enemy territory – an enemy more prepared and more powerful than the two of them. But she hadn't come all this way to back out now; Alice needed her, and Lily was thankful that she had Jem by her side. Yet she hadn't really considered the actual process of a rescue mission until very recently and suddenly it seemed impulsive and foolish, especially since there was a lighthouse filled with children who relied on their safe return. Not to mention the innumerable children still to be saved and cared for.

Jem glanced at her as he paced the room and her worries were mirrored in his furrowed brow. He, too, knew how dangerous this journey was going to be. Lily was brought back to the present as she felt a warm, tacky liquid flow from her hand. She looked down and saw the mess she had made by absentmindedly picking at the torn skin and hangnails on her fingers.

She excused herself from the room and went to the

kitchen to wash her scarlet hands in the copper sink. Her fingers were throbbing with a constant, dull ache. There was a roll of gauze next to the sink which she tried, unsuccessfully, to wrap around her hands but the flow of blood was still too heavy. She looked up as Jem appeared in the doorway. He looked as worried as she felt.

'What have you done?'

'My fingers. I picked them to shreds. I do it when I'm—'

'Anxious. I know. I've noticed.' He looked sympathetic and then noticed the gauze that was half-heartedly wrapped around her left hand. 'Do you need a hand?' he asked, and then laughed in spite of himself.

Lily laughed too. 'I need two – ideally two working ones – that aren't bleeding. But, failing that, I'd like some help wrapping them. Thanks.' She kept hold of the gauze and Jem went to grab a damp cloth, poured some of the warm water from the kettle over it, and then dabbed at her fingers. After a few minutes of this, the bleeding became less profuse. Jem then tightly wrapped her hands in the gauze. The bandages still looked a little red from the blood, but at least it had been suppressed.

'How are you feeling?'

'Aside from nauseous, anxious, terrified, stressed, upset to be leaving the kids, and worried about what state we're going to find Alice and Grace in? I'm feeling great, thanks.' She didn't know where the acid in her voice had come from. It was as if all the emotions she had been attempting to keep bottled up were spilling over into a venomous outpouring of fear.

Jem didn't flinch or take offence at her tone. Instead he

just nodded, placed a friendly hand on her shoulder, and said, 'Yeah, me too.'

They couldn't avoid it any longer. They had miles to walk and they needed to make camp way before nightfall. In late autumn, they didn't have as much time or light as they needed, so they had to swallow their fears and set out on their journey.

Everyone gathered outside on the shale beach that Jem had dragged the unconscious Lily onto by the light of the full moon. How different the world felt now. She had experienced friendship and companionship from every single person that stood on this beach and, in a strange way, she felt almost thankful that events had led her to this stormy lighthouse.

Almost.

Lily was wrapped in her own heavy emerald cloak, and underneath that was a thinner, lighter, more insulating cape of Grace's. She wore high-waisted, fitted trousers the colour of burnt umber, tucked into thick socks and her trusty worn leather boots. A thick taupe fisherman's jumper was pulled down over her torso and climbed up to roll around her neck. She felt warm and comfortable and much more ready for a fight than if she'd have been in one of her heavy plaid dresses. She pulled the hood of the cloak up over her strawberry-blonde tresses, which she had left loose; she hadn't been in the mood to try and tackle the bird's nest today. She felt like Mother Earth herself, wild and turbulent, ready to face whatever it was that stood between her and Alice. But inside, she felt like a little girl in a world that was far too big and scary for her to cope with. She hoped it didn't show on her face.

Jem was dressed similarly, in warm black woollen trousers and dark leather boots. A grey shirt poked out of the neck of his thick black jumper and his cloak was floor-length, like a black cloud following him as he walked. His hood was also pulled up over his russet hair, the usual unkempt strands falling over his face. He looked firm and unflappable. When Lily looked at Jem, she knew that his strength was a rock for her to lean on, but she had to remind herself that he, too, needed a rock, and she would try to be that for him. She had to. Maeve tugged gently on Lily's cloak hem, and Lily kneeled down so she was face to face with the little girl.

'Are you going to bring back Aunty Grace?' Maeve asked, tears welling in her eyes.

'Yes, my love,' Lily said in a voice that she hoped was comforting. She could not reveal her fear, especially not to Maeve. She knew that Maeve and Brenna would worry each other to death if they could, and she refused to give them anything more to worry about. 'Yes, in a couple of days' time, me and Jem, and Aunty Grace, and my lovely friend Alice, we'll all be back here and we'll cook a big family meal and everything will be happy and normal again. How does that sound?'

Maeve just nodded. Lily stood and turned to Jem. 'Right, we need to be on our way, I'm afraid.' She turned back to the children. 'We've got a long day of travelling today and a big day tomorrow, so cross all your fingers for it to be an easy rescue.'

Each of the children took turns to say good luck, and they all came and hugged them both. Even Glenn, who was still quiet and brooding most of the time, was smiling. He hugged Lily and whispered, 'I'm sorry.'

Lily frowned, but Glenn stepped back and wouldn't meet her eye. They all walked down to the rowboat and Lily and Jem climbed in, taking an oar each.

'See you all for dinner in a few days! Be safe, make sure you behave, all right?' Together, Glenn and Cass pushed the boat off the shingled shore and a gentle wave caught the craft, carrying them out onto the sea. The children all stood in a line on the shore, waving, trying their best not to look forlorn.

'Did Glenn say anything to you when he hugged you?' Lily asked Jem as the children faded from view.

'No, why?'

'Ah, no reason.' For some reason, Lily found herself hiding Glenn's apology from Jem. She decided she'd ask him about it when they returned, but for now, she pushed it from her mind. They had more important things to worry about. Like raiding the lair of the most notorious murderous coven this land had ever seen.

After half an hour of relentless rowing, they heard the tell-tale crumble of the bottom of the boat hitting land. Jem leaped out of the back of the boat and dragged it up onto shore. It was still early and the town hadn't yet woken. The sky was alight with fuchsia pink and violet streaks as the sunrise twirled across the horizon. They secured the boat to a post that was driven deep into the sand and then walked into the centre of the village. Instead of following the path back up the cliff, the path Lily had nearly fallen down the week before, they went west, following the path through Kelseth and up a much less steep path that led to a different part of the moors.

For late autumn, the temperature was eerily cold and their heavy breathing from the walking created dancing patterns of mist in the air. Lily's hands became red and sore with the chill, and she took to walking with them cupped over her mouth to collect the warm breath, instead of letting them slowly freeze by her sides. The smoking tendrils that escaped her mouth and nose made her feel a little like a fire-breathing dragon. Lily tried to embody that thought and take on the strength of a dragon, too.

She tried not to think about the fact that they wouldn't have a roof over their heads tonight.

Once they had summitted the hill, they both turned slightly to look back down over the bay, their beloved lighthouse glinting in the early morning light. The beacon at the top of the striped tower called out to them. Lily could almost hear its strained voice crying out over the bay, through the light layer of sea fog, across the crumbling rooftops.

'Don't leave me here alone,' it cried. 'Come back to me, come back to me.'

It was a wrench to turn away from their sanctuary, not knowing whether or not they would actually return to see its welcoming glow once more. The children had disappeared back inside now, and with a heavy heart, she imagined them trying their best to do the chores and keep themselves busy. She knew the absence of Jem would be especially hard for them. Without Jem or Grace, that lighthouse surely lacked the soul that made it 'home'.

'Do you think you'll ever leave here? When we come back, that is. With Grace and Alice.' They had turned back towards the little, narrow track over the moors and were walking side by side, which meant that every time one of them took a step with their outward leg, it was lost in the heather branches.

'I don't think so. It's been my one solid sanctuary since I was ten years old. Everything in there, everything we've built, it has memories, significance. Plus, I always want to be there if any of the children who were with us a few years back decide they need to return for one reason or another. Or if anyone new arrives in Kelseth in need of help or guidance. I want to be there for the lost children always, whenever they need us.'

Lily nodded in understanding. 'You never told me what you and Grace were doing before you washed up here. Where are you from?'

Jem, rather than being taken aback by her question, just lowered his chin and nodded, smiling slightly. 'I was wondering when you'd ask. I'm surprised it's taken you so long; you're such an inquisitive person.'

'I didn't want to pry, but now it's just you and me and an open road with a destination I'd rather not think about. I'd appreciate the distraction of a good story.'

Jem cleared his throat dramatically, earning him a gentle shove in the shoulder from Lily.

'Well, the truth is, I honestly remember very little. Grace is worse because when we washed up on the shore, she had a really dreadful head injury. She still has a gruesome scar across her face; a reminder of how long we've been here, and what it took to get us to safety.

'Thankfully, there were some ancient and dusty medical textbooks in the lighthouse which I consulted whilst I cared for her, but she had ... still has, pretty serious problems with her memory. She recalls nothing from our past. Her memory begins from that day we washed up on the beach.'

'Have you tried to remind her?'

'I've tried everything, but I also remember very little. In the end we both just accepted that her memory was lost forever and our new life started there. It was easy to pretend that she and I had been born, fully grown, there on that beach. But that's not quite true. I also hit my head pretty hard and ingested a sickening amount of sea water, so my memory comes back to me in snippets, flashbacks, stolen moments. I remember red dust everywhere. On my skin, under my feet, covering my clothes, swept up in the gusty, warm winds. It wasn't in the Shadow Lands, that's for sure.

'It was a temperate place, but I remember the sea breeze, which I think is why the lighthouse immediately struck me as home. The smell of the sea grounded me.

'I have snippets of memories, but nothing solid. I remember evenings crowded round a huge campfire with terrifying flames that made everyone's faces glitter and glow in the lowlight. We all shared similar features: a strong nose, russet hair, and furrowed brows. I think that was the family we left behind. You'll know Grace as soon as you see her because we're both so similar. Except I think she's a lot more patient than I am.' Jem paused.

'We'll get her back, Jem.'

He nodded, his eyes swimming with the tears of lost memories. 'You're right. All this walking, all the heartache of leaving behind the children. It's for her. For them both.'

Lily reached out and placed a comforting hand on his back, and then pressed him further. She was eager to think about anything other than her aching feet and tired eyes. They still had so much further to walk. 'Do you remember anything else?'

'I remember the day we left – or at least most of it. Grace and I were dragged from our beds in the dead of night. We were tied up and blindfolded, and the next thing I remember, we woke, still tied up but able to see. We were moving up and down in a kind of motion I'd never experienced. We were on a boat, you see, in the middle of the ocean, with no land in sight. It was terrifying. There were so many of us there, all young and wide-eyed and too terrified to ask what was going on or where we were. We were crammed in, body upon body, manacles scraping the walls and each other's cold, bare arms. We were surrounded by hulking men and we were only allowed out of the hold in the ship once a day to stretch our legs. Other than that, we were kept tied up below deck. I can still remember the stench of seaweed and human waste. It was so strong that our eyes were constantly watering and we never really had an appetite.

'I don't remember how long we were aboard that ship. Every day was monotonous, never-ending. All I cared about was Grace's safety and making sure we got enough food and water.

'I remember the night it sank though. How could I forget it?

'There were flashes in the sky that screeched above our heads. The roaring of warring giants in the clouds. I've never felt such conflicting emotions. I was terrified. The ship was flying around as if the ocean couldn't hold it down any longer. It wanted to be free, and so free it became. It came to a deafening halt as it smashed itself into a rock, and the water flooded our hold faster than you could ever imagine. The force of the jolt snapped the manacle loops off the walls and allowed us at least to move about through the rapidly rising water, wrists still chained together. I dragged Grace up the wooden steps and shouted to everyone else to follow, but so many of those captured alongside us had already gone far, far away to their new lives at the bottom of the ocean.

'The manacles had always been on the big side, designed for larger prisoners, fully grown men, and the water made our skin slippery. Once out onto the mangled disappearing deck, I managed to yank the manacles from Grace's wrists, and she did the same to mine. The saltwater stung and gnashed at the blisters the shackles had given us, but we were free. Holding on with all my might to Grace's strong hands, we leaped from the wreckage into the inky water. In the distance, we could see a lighthouse in the gloom and I tried my hardest to point to it, so Grace could swim alongside me. But I must have been hit by some more falling flotsam, or simply have swallowed too much water, because the next thing I know, I'm choking up blood and salt on a rocky beach beneath the very lighthouse we'd been aiming for. Grace was next to me, inanimate and bleeding profusely from her temple. There was a thin layer of foam at her lips and her chest lacked the rise and fall of her breath. I thought she'd left me, too.

'I remember tearing up my shirt to wrap the wound on her head and doing everything I possibly could to wake her up and make her breathe again, to make her return to me where I could keep her safe from harm.

'Impossibly, and to my great relief, she retched and vomited, saltwater streaming from her nose and mouth. She took a deep but raspy gasp of air and opened her eyes. She must have seen me kneeling above her because her wide eyes closed again and she surrendered to sleep, safe in the knowledge that I was there.

'You know the rest of the story. I haven't ever really said any of that out loud before.'

He looked at the ground, kicking stones as they walked and avoiding eye contact. Lily could tell he'd let his mouth get the better of his brain, and he was suddenly worried he'd been too open.

She took his hand in hers and entwined their fingers. 'You've been through far too much for someone so young. When we get Grace home, let's work on sharing some of that load you have sitting so heavily on your shoulders.'

Their eyes met and he half smiled, exhaling his relief.

Chapter Thirty-Eight

A lice paced back and forth, rehearsing aloud how she planned to apologise to Grace. It was the middle of the night, but she dared not sleep for fear that she'd forget everything and have to remember it all over again in the morning. She couldn't bear the thought of those few sleepy seconds of blissful ignorance before her world caved in once more.

She couldn't take it anymore. She pulled a heavy black velvet overcoat on over her nightgown but left her feet bare; she didn't want to risk the heavy thud of her boots betraying her. Grabbing the bronze candlestick, which had a candle in it that still burned brightly, she fled her room and tiptoed down the corridor. If she could get past the rooms in this part of the lair, she'd be away from the sleeping quarters and, thus, away from any prying eyes.

The smell of bubbling porridge and rich chocolate filled the air, and Alice knew she was approaching the kitchens. She pressed herself tightly against the wall and peered round the corner, checking for any other midnight wanderers, but she was entirely alone.

A few more tiptoed steps and she pushed open the door to the kitchens as gently as she could. As she suspected, the porridge was bubbling unattended on the stove, with a vat of warm chocolate drink by its side.

Rolling thunder sent dust dancing down from the stone ceiling. She hated storms. Alice paused, shivering, listening out for any signs that she'd been followed. She allowed herself a few deep, calming breaths and her heart slowed its ceaseless hammering. That was when she heard the trickle of rain. Drip. Drip. Drip.

She hadn't heard rain, or any weather, since arriving at the lair. The stone was thick and all-encompassing; they lived in their own isolated kingdom without any hint of the existence of the outside world. So why could she suddenly hear the storm?

Placing the candlestick down on the worktop, Alice followed the sound of the rain. And then she saw it. There was a round vent close to the ceiling, hidden from view by the shelves upon shelves of kitchen ingredients. And it was swinging open on its hinges.

Before her courage could desert her, Alice hitched up her nightgown and began the precarious climb onto the worktop and then up the sturdy shelves towards the vent. The smell of the falling rain and the fresh, fresh air gave her the strength to ignore how high up she was; she was glad that all those years spent climbing trees hadn't gone to waste.

Just as she thought her muscles might give up on her,

she heaved herself up and out through the vent, stumbling onto the saturated, mossy ground. She lay there on the damp floor for a few moments, enjoying the feel of the cool water hitting her face. She closed her eyes and could almost imagine she was back at the cabin by the brook, when it was warm enough to swim even in a rainstorm.

'Alice?'

A voice broke her reverie and shook her awake. She scrambled to her feet, her heart racing. Her overcoat and nightgown were soaked through and she suddenly realised how cold her bare feet were, exposed as they were to the rain.

Out of the darkness, a figure appeared – hair soaked through, wrapped up against the elements, scar glinting in the broken moonlight. Grace.

'Alice?' She spoke again, firmer this time. 'Alice, what are you doing out here? Where are your shoes?' Grace stomped over to her and grabbed her by the shoulders, shaking her. 'Are you mad? You'll catch your death!' She had to shout over the deafening thunder.

Alice could only gaze into Grace's wide, terrified eyes. *She still cares.*

'Alice, for goodness' sake! What's wrong with you?'

There was something bursting within Alice. It had roused her from her pacing; it had sent her out of her bedroom in the middle of the night. It had convinced her to climb up and out through a vent in her nightgown to stand in the pouring rain. And it had led her here, to Grace.

Grace let go of Alice and stepped back, running a

nervous hand through her soaked hair. She could sense it too, Alice knew she could.

Before she could lose the courage that had been building and building within her, she finally did what she had been waiting for Grace to do ever since they met.

She covered the distance between them in two strides and their lips touched for the first time. The kiss was gentle, tentative. Alice pulled back to check that Grace was all right and found her glowing. They pressed their foreheads together, hands intertwined. Alice could no longer feel the pouring rain falling upon them. All she could feel was Grace.

'I've been waiting for you to do that for a while...' Grace smirked, pulling Alice into a tight embrace.

Alice laughed. 'And I've been waiting for you!'

Grace shook her head and chuckled.

Alice began to cry softly, not from sadness, but from an overwhelming, all-encompassing swell of emotion. She felt warmth flow through her bones and around her veins, the warmth of magic, the flow of power, and Grace leapt back, her eyes round, inquisitive. Alice was quite literally glowing. A warm scarlet light was radiating from every inch of her skin. It wasn't hatred, anger, pain, or stress that really allowed her to tap into her magical roots.

It was love.

Grace stepped forward and embraced Alice once more. The two girls were alight: a fiery beacon, a lighthouse lamp glowing bright as an exploding star, despite the storm raging around them.

'Shall we go inside before we freeze to death?' Grace

asked, and Alice could only nod, still flying high up in the rainclouds.

They managed to sneak back along the silent corridors until they were safe inside Alice's room. The fire was still lit in the grate and its warmth was blissful after so long shivering in the rain. They spent every evening together, so why did Alice suddenly feel so awkward? Nothing had changed and yet ... *everything* had changed.

Grace kicked off her boots and wrung out her hair. Alice was in awe that such a woman could exist, let alone feel any kind of affection for her. Grace's billowing white shirt had come untucked as she'd thrown off her soaking overcoat, and her rolled up sleeves revealed strong, muscular arms. Alice had spent her life in high-necked, long-sleeved dresses, and she'd forgotten just how beautiful skin could be. The firelight made Grace radiant.

How could she want a scrawny, pale girl like Alice?

She looked up into Grace's eyes and saw a hunger she'd never seen before. It scared her and exhilarated her. She decided then and there that she wouldn't question Grace's feelings ever again. Alice exhaled deeply; her heart was hammering in her chest. She didn't know what to do next.

Almost as if Grace sensed her unease, she stepped across the room and took Alice into her arms. With a smile, Alice leaned into her once more, kissing her again, neither worried now about rejection or humiliation. Grace overpowered Alice's lead and pushed her backwards onto the bed, climbing on top of her, running her hands through her ebony hair. They were intertwined, moving and breathing and loving as one entity. Everything made sense now.

Alice had never been kissed, had never wanted to be kissed. Not unless it was with someone who made her feel safe, who made her heart sing, who felt like home.

Grace Rafferty felt like home.

Chapter Thirty-Nine

L ily and Jem walked with a fierce sense of purpose for the rest of the day, as the landscape changed around them. They left behind the salt-soaked coastline, moved through moors carpeted in a dingy brown long-dead heather and found themselves deep in a forest that stretched out endlessly on all sides. Lily at once felt at home and stopped to untie her boots. Jem watched her with a confused expression as she stepped with her bare feet onto the forest floor. Lily took the laces and tied them together around her waist so that she didn't have to carry her boots in her hand.

'Aren't you worried you'll cut yourself?' Jem asked as they started walking again. The light was fading and the forest was filled with the burning glow of the sunset.

'I trust the forest. I've wandered through ones like this my whole life. For years, the forest and our little village were all I knew. My world didn't stretch much further. I learned how to adapt to my environment, as you adapted to yours. I'm made to exist amongst the trees. They have been my companions for as long as I can remember. They'd never hurt me.'

'You speak as if they're sentient, as if they could choose not to harm you,' Jem said, smiling not unkindly.

'Well, they are. I've always felt like they speak to each other, and to us, if you listen. Respect nature and it will respect you.'

Jem shook his head slightly as they continued, but Lily could spy the smirk tugging at the edge of his lips. The long day of walking was showing in his face; his cheeks were flushed and his brow glistened. He had long since removed the hood from his cloak, but in doing so, his hair had been pulled slightly out of the leather tie he used to keep it all off his face. Strands like raven feathers fell across his face and he absentmindedly ran his hands through his hair every now and again, which only pulled more hair out of the tie. He glanced up and caught her eye and Lily looked away, her stomach clenching and colour rising to her cheeks.

She was suddenly gripped by panic that they were going to have to make camp soon and sleep alongside each other. The thought did not help the clenching feeling in her stomach. She swallowed and felt her heart rate quicken. She had never been one for the strangled conventions of society, such as chaperones keeping men and women at arm's length from each other at all times. That was one advantage, she'd heard, of life beyond the Shadow Lands; they'd moved on, progressed, laughed at the principles to which those living in the Shadow Lands remained chained. Yet, there in the gloaming, she couldn't help but feel it would be much easier if they weren't alone.

The sun had almost completely disappeared and both Lily and Jem were waning beneath the dazzling, rising moon. Their pace had slowed and Lily's back ached with a dull constancy. She stopped and leaned against a tree, rolling her shoulders and her neck to loosen them. Jem pulled a dog-eared map out of his pack and consulted it, his brow creased with concentration.

'Where are we?' Lily asked. Jem sighed and turned the map upside down, clearly reluctant to admit his confusion.

After a few more moments, he looked up and shrugged.

'Honestly? I haven't a bloody clue.'

He started laughing and the laughter spread through him; he threw his head back, his guffaws echoing through the trees. Lily joined in; his amusement was contagious and the anxiety and tension that had built over the course of their journey, the responsibility of finding Alice and Grace, it had all become so heavy. The laughs came freely, a tonic to the stress of the situation in which they had unwittingly found themselves. They crumpled to their knees, eyes watering, stomachs aching from laughter.

They finally got a grip on themselves and their laughter died down. A barn owl flew overhead, a sentinel of the oncoming night, and the urgency of their situation returned once more. Lily moved to take the map from Jem's hands.

'Here,' she said, a soft caution in her voice, 'let me have a look.' He surrendered the parchment and watched her as she studied it. She gazed up to the canopy and found a streak of silvery moonlight shimmering through the leaves and, walking to it, she knelt down in the underbrush and placed the map under the pillar of incandescent light to study it further.

Jem followed, patiently waiting for her analysis. She pointed to a deep green section of the map, to the north-west of the coastline they had left behind. The patch of green was slender but long and stretching further northward. 'I think we're somewhere here. If you follow our path'—she pointed to where they had marked the lighthouse and moved her finger across the moorland and into the forest that she believed they were in—'then we only have this distance'—she gestured to a point on the map that was an inch or two away from their current location—'left to walk. Here'—she tapped on a grey area that they had marked with red ink in their preparations—'is where we're headed, right? That must be less than half a day from here. I think we should set up camp where we are now, or at least somewhere near here, and then make the final journey at first light. Agreed?'

Jem nodded with fervour. 'We need to find somewhere more sheltered than this though. If a weather front closes in, or if anyone is patrolling these woods, which they very well could be, then we need to be somewhere a little less open. Did we mark anything on the map?'

Lily shook her head and then stood, rolling the map and handing it back to Jem. 'I think we're going to have to figure the rest of this out on our own. The map isn't detailed enough for that kind of information, and we'll already be playing a guessing game in the morning to find their lair. We know the general location, but it isn't going to be signposted, is it? We'll just have to trust our instincts.'

'I think we head towards where the forest slopes upwards. If nothing else, at least being high up will give us a better vantage point to keep watch tonight.' Jem shouldered his pack and set off walking, glancing behind to check that Lily was following.

They scrambled up the slope and were greeted with a hulking grey ledge of slate that curved over their heads, creating a shallow cave. It wasn't much, but it was exactly what they needed. It provided shelter from the elements, a place to hide and it was angled in such a way that it was easy to see down into the forest valley, while keeping the two of them hidden. Lily and Jem glanced at each other and grinned, a wordless acceptance passing between them. In unison, they dropped their packs on the floor.

The light had completely faded and they were relying on flecks of moonlight to see in the darkness. Jem wandered off with a small axe, muttering that they needed to get the fire lit as soon as possible. Lily suspected that he, too, was concerned about the gathering night and the thought of being alone, in the dark, together.

Kneeling on the grubby cave floor, Lily opened her pack and began to lay out some of the essentials they would need to get through the night: blankets, their water canteens, slices of tough seeded bread which was buttered and wrapped in paper, their notes and map, a small lantern. She left everything else in the bag and placed it at the far end of the cave, intending on using it as a pillow later.

Clambering to her feet, she unrolled a couple of the

blankets on the cave floor, covering and softening the hard dirt. It was going to be a long night. She sat back down and wrapped herself in one of the remaining blankets, before throwing her hair into a careless knot on the top of her head and bending over her notes, inspecting them for the millionth time, hoping that this time she'd notice a new clue or shred of information that would prepare them for the mysteries of the following day. Flicking through the notes, she reached for her water canteen before taking a long swig. When the liquid touched her mouth, she gagged and spat it out, her lips and throat burning. It obviously wasn't her canteen, and it appeared that Jem had not filled his with water.

True to his swashbuckling, murderous Lightkeeper reputation, Jem's canteen was full to the brim with something much stronger than water: rum. She choked and gasped, the burning liquid lighting a fire all the way down her throat and landing, still flaming, in her belly. Spluttering, she placed the canteen down and took a deep breath, throwing several muttered swearwords about Jem to the wind.

After the initial shock subsided, Lily could feel the warmth that had creeped through her insides thanks to the dark, thick liquid in the canteen. Guilt tugged in a quiet but unmistakable way at her heart as she lifted Jem's canteen back up to her lips, deliberately this time. Rather than the violent burning she had expected, the rum was gentle and deliciously warming. After one more quick, guilty swig, she screwed the canteen lid back on and hid the bottle back in Jem's pack, hoping that he wouldn't notice.

Her heart fluttered and her head swam with the alcohol; a shiver tickled her spine and the muscles in her neck rippled – a strange but not unpleasant side-effect. As much as she wished it would, the rum didn't settle the sense of unease that had sunk deep in her heart, not just for the approaching night but for tomorrow as well.

Tomorrow, if all went to plan, she'd see Alice again. Jem would find Grace. Soon, the four of them would be walking, or running, from whatever it was that had stolen Alice and Grace away. She hoped.

The temperature was dropping rapidly now, as the autumn air swirled around her, nipping at any uncovered skin. Lily's hands were stiff with cold and her muscles were groaning from the day's endless walking. A raven flapped its wings somewhere far up above, screeching and cawing into the dusk, breaking the otherwise deafening silence of the autumn evening. Time passed with painful slowness, but just as Lily was beginning to grow unsettled and concerned for Jem, he reappeared. Or at least, his legs did. His body from the waist up was obscured by the mountain of logs he carried.

'Are there any trees left?' Lily asked with a playful glint in her eye. Jem snorted but resisted biting back at her and instead dropped the pile of logs at her feet.

'When you don't freeze to death tonight, you'll have me to thank! Help me light it?' Jem asked.

Between them, they constructed a simple fire structure, with kindling surrounded by dry logs. After a few attempts with Lily's flint and steel, the fire caught and a warm glow filled the cave. The light of the disappearing day had long since vanished, and the warmth and light from the fire were a welcome atmospheric change. They huddled together, a blanket thrown around both of their shoulders, soaking in the heat from the burning logs. Lily stretched out her hands, rubbing them together. They were still stiff but the tingling at the end of her fingers was starting to fade.

Jem leaned over Lily to grab his bag and liberated his canteen. He sat up and unscrewed the top before taking a long, deep swig.

'Fire not providing enough heat?' Lily asked, wondering whether he'd pick up on her tone.

Jem wiped his mouth with the back of his hand, frowning. 'What do you mean?'

'Rum. That canteen is filled with rum, instead of water.'

'Ah … yeah.' He placed it to the side and looked down at his empty hands. 'I just thought … I don't know. If it gets any colder, or if we're nervous tomorrow, it just felt like a good idea, I guess.'

Lily smiled. 'I'm not mad! I'm just curious why you didn't tell me back at the lighthouse. I'd have told you that it's a bloody brilliant idea and that we should've both brought water *and* rum. Anyway, I'm hardly in any position to judge you since I already – accidentally, I might add – had a pretty huge mouthful of the stuff.'

'I'd have done anything to see your face if you were expecting water!' Jem chuckled.

'Honestly? I nearly *died*.' Lily dramatically opened her eyes wide, and then broke into a sarcastic grin. They laughed together, thankful for a break in the tension. As it grew later, they became more and more aware of the mountain they had to climb in the morning.

Lily and Jem muddled together a quick dinner of buttered bread and tea made with boiled water and pine needles before settling down on the makeshift bed of blankets. They'd both rolled up their rucksacks, which transformed them into makeshift pillows on which to rest their heads. To begin with, there was a gulf between them, an abyss. Neither one wanted to breach the gap, both wanting to avoid any awkwardness. The longer Lily lay there though, the colder she became, until her whole body was wracked with uncontrollable shivers.

Whether he sensed her discomfort or simply heard her teeth chattering with violent vigour, Jem edged closer and stretched his arm out, encouraging Lily to draw herself close so they could share their warmth under the same blanket. She didn't need asking twice. Lily was tentative but deliberate with her movements as she closed the gap between them and pressed against the warmth of Jem's torso. His core heat hadn't been affected at all by the plunging temperatures: he was still burning hot. Lily felt relief flood through her as she closed her eyes, finally warm, and drifted into a welcome sleep as Jem wrapped a comforting arm around her back, pulling her closer.

Chapter Forty

R ain tore itself from the heavy grey clouds with terrifying force. The cave provided adequate but not perfect shelter and Lily was awakened by rogue icy droplets dampening her exposed skin. She scrunched her face against the cold and shifted her weight, only to find that she was still trapped inside the cocoon of Jem's arms. He was fast asleep. He looked like a different person to the one she knew. His furrowed brow and stern demeanour had disappeared. Sleep was his only refuge. Lily hoped that, after today, this peacefulness would spread over his whole being and he might finally be able to relax and enjoy being a young man, without the pain and the responsibility that he had borne so bravely, alone, for so long.

Today was their chance…

Lily rolled herself out from under Jem's arm and wrapped another blanket around her shoulders, before standing up and stretching her aching limbs. They'd left the fire burning through the night and a tin of water had been gently warming, so she poured the water into a spare metal mug with some more pine needles and juniper berries and wandered towards the mouth of the cave. On her way, she grabbed a hunk of bread from her pack and stood leaning against the cave wall, gazing out at the treetops, shrouded in fog and thick clouds. It had been a while since she had been able to just be still, quiet, thoughtful. She often spent her mornings back home under her tree, lost in her imagination. She valued those quiet moments more now than she ever had before.

As Lily stood there, she watched a peregrine falcon soaring and swooping through the low clouds. It danced on the wind, fierce, elegant, slight but powerful. It was a creature whose energy she knew she had to channel if she was going to survive the day.

Survive.

She had never thought about this as a matter of life and death; she had never allowed herself to think about any other outcome than them breezing in, taking Alice and Grace by the hands and swanning back out. But Alice and Grace had been kidnapped by ruthless, dangerous killers. Killers who, without a doubt, would slay her and Jem without a second thought. She could die before she made it out. Or worse, Jem could die. Alice and Grace could already be dead. She might never see Uncle Alf ever again.

Her heart quickened in her chest and her throat constricted.

Lily closed her eyes and tried to float away with the falcons. She imagined flying far above the treetops, gazing down at the raging rivers cutting their paths through the forests. She sat a while on a cloud to rest. But no matter how far she flew or how high a cloud she chose, she could not escape the storm on the horizon.

Even at this distance she could feel its fury, rushing headlong towards her. Just before it engulfed her, she felt a pain in her hands which ripped her from the intensity of her daydreams.

Shaking her head, she looked down at the source of the pain.

Her hands were covered in blood again, scarlet and shimmering, a stark contrast to the grey glow of dawn. She held them out of the cave and let the rain wash away as much of the blood as possible, gritting her teeth. Once her hands were rinsed in the rainwater, she tore off a strip of her petticoat and used it to wrap around her hands to dry them and stem the bleeding. She wiped her rain-drenched face on her sleeve and tucked tendrils of her damp hair behind her ears. The day was starting to break and she could deny the morning no longer. She and Jem would have to set out sooner rather than later if they wanted any chance of getting in and out alive in a single day.

Turning away from the mouth of the cave, she poured another mug of steaming pine and juniper tea for Jem and grabbed him some bread. She knelt by his side and, pushing a strand of hair from his face, gently roused him.

'Good morning.' She handed him the tea and bread as he sat up, still hazy-eyed with sleep. 'It's time.'

Jem smiled, wordless but grateful. He sat and ate, drinking his tea in intervals. Lily went to stand but he stuffed the remaining crust of bread into his mouth to free his hand and grabbed hers. 'Wh-dd-y-do?' he spluttered; mouth still full.

'I think you might have to repeat that one.'

He finished chewing, his eyes glittering in the early morning light. 'I said, what did you do?' He was still holding one of her hands, the throbbing persistent through the makeshift bandages.

'Ah, the usual.'

'Again?' he asked.

'I don't know what you mean.'

'When you arrived, when you were still unconscious, after we'd made sure there was going to be no lasting damage to you from the water in your lungs, the next thing we noticed was your hands. They were in pieces then too, and they weren't injuries you'd sustained from the boat.'

Lily was touched that he'd noticed such an insignificant detail, and also furious because there was pity in his eyes. She shrugged.

'So ... you're not worried then?'

They locked eyes. Their expressions were mirrored on each other's faces. 'Of course I'm worried. I'm worse than worried. If I think about it too much I might actually throw that bread straight back up.' Lily shrugged. 'But we haven't come this far to give up now. We can't. We have two people who rely on us, and a whole bunch of people back home at the lighthouse who need us to come back in one piece. Jem'—she leant forward and took his hands in hers—'it's normal to be worried. But you're strong. So strong that sometimes it completely floors me. You have more courage and goodness in a single strand of that stupid, beautiful hair than most people have in their entire bodies—'

'You think my hair is beautiful?' Jem interrupted, teasing.

'That,' Lily smirked, 'is entirely beside the point. Anyway, I was being supportive. Would you mind not distracting me?'

Jem saluted and winked at her.

'Grace needs you. But so does everyone back at the lighthouse.'

Frowning, Jem opened his mouth to say something, but closed it again when he saw the flash in her eyes.

'What I mean to say is this: be strong, be courageous, be good, but do not, under any circumstances, risk the air in your lungs today. You. Cannot. Die. And I don't say that lightly. You mean too much to all of them, to me, to leave us behind. No chivalrous sacrifices, all right? Promise me.'

'I promise. I promise I won't ever leave without your express permission.'

She rolled her eyes and nodded. 'Quite right. Now, let's be off, yes?' Lily stood, still clutching Jem's hands, and then pulled him to his feet. He squeezed her hands affectionately and then dropped them, gathering up their belongings.

It wasn't a long way to the Shadow Sect's lair, but in that moment Lily wished it was still days of travel away. All of a sudden, she felt unprepared, like a scared little girl with a big impossible plan. They had spent all that time scouring their maps in Jem's study. Late nights, early mornings, headaches from the intense concentration, sore eyes, aching hearts, they'd battled it all. They'd done all of that for this day, for this moment. Doubt was a luxury they could not afford. *No*, she thought, *I specialise in impossible plans. If anyone can do this, we can. Because we must.*

Lily had memorised the final part of the journey, so the two of them set out with their packs on their backs, feeling barely ready for the day ahead. The chatter between them had vanished and a nervous buzz surrounded them, like a whole hive of honeybees stalking their every movement. This wasn't a time for small talk, for laughter or jokes. They had to focus. They couldn't lose their nerve.

After what felt like a hundred thousand strides, they spotted what they had been looking for: a vast but unremarkable edge of stone jutting from the hillside. Nothing about it suggested that it housed the most dangerous group of people known in this land. In normal circumstances, Lily would have loved nothing more than to clamber onto the top of the ledge and gaze out at the landscape, relishing the wind in her hair and the fresh air in her lungs. But these were not normal circumstances, so she quashed that yearning and turned to Jem.

'I think we should leave our packs hidden here amongst the underbrush. We don't want to be carrying bags that jangle with our belongings every time we take a step. Plus, it'll be easier to move and sneak around if we aren't weighed down.' She was already swinging her bag to the ground. Jem just nodded and followed suit. They found a patch of bracken and ferns that acted as an adequate shelter for their packs and, making sure they were completely out of sight, they left the bags behind.

They climbed and clambered for what felt like an age, but finally reached the bottom of the sheer stone cliff. They followed their meticulously researched route and headed to the right of the cliff, edged around its furthest side and, to their immense relief, they spotted the slim cave entrance that marked the beginning of their rescue venture. Just before they were about to march inside, they heard scuffling, voices, footsteps. Lily turned to Jem. His face had drained of colour and his eyes were wide; he looked like a cornered animal.

'Hide!' Lily whispered with desperation, and pushed Jem back around the corner of rock in the direction they had just come.

He disappeared, and Lily was left alone.

Chapter Forty-One

L ily dropped to her knees and rubbed some of the mud from the ground onto her face and hair, hoping to make herself look vulnerable. She racked her brains to think of a convincing cover story and hoped against hope that Jem had managed to hide.

An idea shot into her mind. If there was one thing Lily Knight was good at, it was being underestimated, and that was what she would rely on. She dug her nails into her palms, the pain making her eyes water, and then rubbed her bloody hand across her cheek. She was still on her knees when two women appeared at the mouth of the hidden cave entrance.

'What the—?'

The first woman walked headlong into Lily's crouched form and tripped, tumbling to the ground with an almost amusing lack of grace. She quickly regained her feet and brushed herself off, her face glowing like it had been branded with the humiliation she felt.

'Who are you? Why are you here?' the woman asked. She sounded firm – confused but not unkind. When Lily looked up with her bloody, tear-stained face, the woman stepped back, shocked. 'Do you need help?'

Lily stuttered. She surprised herself at how choked up she sounded. 'I was sent a letter,' she sniffed. 'It told me to come here. That I had powers... I've been travelling for five days. I had a terrible fall two days ago and I wanted to arrive here looking presentable but, well, I am as you see me.' Lily looked down, inwardly praying to the universe that they'd believe her.

The two young women exchanged concerned glances. The one closest to her had a kind face, with large dark-green eyes. She reached down to help Lily regain her feet, much to the clear chagrin of her companion who rolled her eyes.

'You really ought to stop taking in lost causes.'

'The last one hasn't worked out so badly though, has it?' The woman fired back, smirking at her companion. She then turned her attention back to Lily, who was brushing herself off, trying desperately to keep up the appearance of a lost injured girl in need of assistance. The more vulnerable she looked, the easier it would be to hoodwink whoever she was about to face. If they all thought her harmless, that could only be a good thing. She wondered what Jem would do though, and hoped he wouldn't decide to charge in after her.

The nicer of the two guards took her arm and led her into the cave. Inside, it opened into a long corridor, but it wasn't dingy or damp like the interior of the cave in which she and Jem had spent the night. Instead, it was well-lit with flaming lanterns attached to the wall with iron, and underfoot, the floor was paved with flat, highly polished stone. The general impression was one of quiet, understated opulence. The corridor snaked through the rock, until Lily felt sure they were in the middle of the mountain, miles from any escape route except the winding one down which she was currently walking, the one taking her further and further away from Jem and any hope of liberation.

The woman guiding Lily must have sensed her lost sense of direction, because she dropped her arm, safe in the knowledge that she wouldn't be able to leave even if she wanted to. *They don't fully trust me*, Lily thought. *But they don't have to; they just have to get me to Alice and the rest will come later.*

The other woman, the less kind one, turned unexpectedly and disappeared down a separate narrow corridor to the left. Now they were alone, Lily was able to get a better look at her guide. She was dressed unlike any woman she had ever seen. She wore clothes similar to the strange garments Lily had found herself wearing at the lighthouse. Instead of heavy skirts obscuring her legs, this young woman wore black trousers which were fastened with a thick leather belt around her waist. A flowing white shirt was tucked into her waistband and an oversized woollen overcoat was slung lazily around her shoulders. At her waist sat a holster, from which hung a variety of weapons Lily couldn't begin to name.

'Do you always dress like you're about to go and murder someone?' Lily asked.

The woman shrugged. 'Most days. I'm what they call a

Protector. I'm assigned to a witch and it's my responsibility to make sure she's safe. If what you say about yourself is true, this will all make sense soon. If you're lying, you won't be alive long enough for me to worry about what you know.'

'Why aren't you with her now? Your … witch.'

'She sleeps in. She doesn't usually surface for an hour or two yet, so I was going for some fresh air when I bumped into your sorry-looking self. I hope you've got a better story prepared though because I'm definitely not buying the one you gave us.'

Lily's heart sank. She tried to calm herself. 'What do you mean? I told you the truth.'

She rolled her eyes. 'What's your name, anyway?'

Lily paused. It might be dangerous to reveal her real name, but there was a chance this girl knew Alice, and maybe she could help.

'I'm Lily.'

The woman stopped in her tracks. Then, in one swift movement, she had Lily pinned against the hard stone wall, a knife at her throat. 'For the love of the earth, please tell me you are not Lily Knight.'

Lily looked her dead in the eye, but said nothing.

'Why are you here?' the woman spat, her teeth clenched. Her entire face had turned a deep shade of mauve and her hand was shaking with fury.

'I'm here for Alice. And I'm here for my friend's sister. I've come a really bloody long way and I'm not being frightened away now, so,' she warned, revealing her own hidden weapon and pressing it into the young woman's side, 'drop the knife before I make you.'

The other woman stepped back, raising her hands in a faux-apologetic stance. 'Where's your friend?'

Lily rolled her shoulders and rubbed the graze on her neck where the knife had nicked her. 'What? You tell me. I literally just got here.'

'Not Alice, you half-wit. You're here to save your friend's sister too, so where's your friend? Why are you here alone?'

'He's finding another way in.' Lily put away her knife and inspected the woman's face properly, for the first time since she'd arrived. Her hair was shoulder-length, dark as molasses, and just as thick. It was heavily parted to one side, obscuring her left eye. As if aware of Lily's invasive gaze, she ran a hand through her hair, pushing it back out of her face. A thin scar snaked from her eyebrow down to her cheekbone. It looked like it was from an old wound; it was silvery and pearlescent, barely visible.

Lily's stomach clenched with recognition. The sea-glass eyes, the dark, thick hair, the scar that was evidently the result of a head injury sustained years ago. This girl wasn't just some random passer-by. She was *Grace*. Just a much less patient version than the one Jem had described. 'You're Grace Rafferty, aren't you?'

'How do you know that name?' she snapped, fear flashing in her eyes.

'You're famous, where I've come from.'

Grace frowned and narrowed her eyes, Lily's answer

obviously not satisfying her. 'Who are you?' she pressed. 'Where do you come from? How do you know me?'

'My name is Lily Knight, and you are going to help me rescue Alice Blackwell.' Lily puffed up her chest and shook her wild hair behind her shoulders, proud and fierce. Two words she never would have associated with herself a few days ago. Whether she wanted to admit it or not, she had changed.

'And why would I do that? Alice and I are happy here … happy enough anyway, for me to want to keep it that way.' Her cheeks had reddened slightly, either through anger or something else Lily couldn't recognise.

'Because my friend who's here with me, his name is Jem Rafferty, and I have a sneaking suspicion that even if you won't help me, you're going to want to help him.'

Grace's shock gripped her, and she opened her mouth to retort, but her voice caught in her throat. Before Grace could regain her composure, a figure appeared at the end of the stone hallway in which they had stopped. Lily's statement had caught her off-guard, and now the two of them had to convince this newcomer of Lily's story, otherwise they'd be in trouble before they'd even begun.

'Grace, what are you doing? Who is this?'

'This is Lilian Day. She was summoned. I'm just taking her to freshen up before presenting her to the High Priestess. Is that all right with you, Blayne? Or would you like me to sign a warrant?' she spat. Grace clearly didn't have much patience for Blayne, or anyone else as far as Lily could tell. Lily was highly impressed by Grace's ability to create aliases and made a mental note to thank her later, if they pulled this off.

'Well she's ready now, so take her in, we don't have time for you to dawdle and enlist her as your next victim ... I mean ... *friend*, right?' Blayne growled back, a cruel smirk tugging at her lips. The way she said 'friend' made Lily wonder what kind of friends Grace had a habit of making.

Lily glanced at Grace. She noticed a thin line of perspiration had appeared on her forehead and upper lip. She was stressed. Nervous. Maybe even scared? Lily gulped. In the few minutes since she'd known Grace, and from the days she'd spent hearing about her courage from Morven and Cass, she thought Grace wasn't the kind of person who'd be easily frightened. Yet, here she was. Scared. Scared for Lily, not just for herself. Grace caught her eye, nodded slightly, and gestured for her to follow Blayne. Grace fell into step by her side. Her entire demeanour had shifted from defensive to protective. Grace walked barely an inch from Lily's side and stood tall, her broad shoulders several inches above Lily's own.

As they walked through the snaking corridors, the ceiling seemed to creep down to meet them. It was dark and oppressive, as if the tunnels were trying to squeeze out every ounce of defiance Lily possessed before she even reached her destination. With each step, her brain grew increasingly foggy and her energy seemed to drain out of her, dissipating into the damp and shimmering dark-orange walls. By the time the small party reached an aged wooden door at the end of the corridor, Lily was slumped onto

Grace, whose arm was wrapped around her waist, keeping her just about upright.

Lily didn't even have the energy to wonder about why she was feeling so weak; all she could focus on was staying conscious, even though every fibre of her was desperate to fade away, to succumb to the force that drained her.

'Stay with us,' Lily heard Grace whisper into her ear. 'Keep Alice as your focus and you'll survive this. Lose your purpose and you'll lose yourself. *Remember Alice.*'

Lily nodded, her eyes fluttering. the guard lifted a heavy metal bar that kept the wooden door sealed and pushed it open, gesturing for Lily and Grace to enter.

Remember Alice.

Remember Alice.

Remember.

Remember ... what?

She blacked out.

Chapter Forty-Two

Rolling over, Alice reached out to find Grace's hand in the mountain of blankets that covered the bed. The pressure of Grace's hand in hers helped her to ground herself, to remember who she was, what she was, and why she was there. It helped her to push away the nightmares that plagued her head and the dreams that rose from the guilt that sat deep in the chambers of her heart.

Alice's hand fell on emptiness. Jolting awake, she scrambled around in the dark room, searching for the familiar pressure of Grace's weight by her side, but she was alone.

After their night together, Grace had left early.

Alice stretched and lit the candle by her head, before clambering out of bed to throw a black silk dressing gown around her shoulders. She shook her head to rid the tiredness from her eyes and lit the lamps around the room, bathing the space in a rusty glow. Now she was fully awake, she was aware of the chattering and whispering from outside her door. There were several people walking up and down the corridor outside and Alice focused hard to listen in and discover the source of the commotion.

'—New arrival apparently. No idea where she's come from of course.'

'Well, she must have some idea?'

'No, none at all, if I heard right. Sounds like someone on the inside has tipped off an outsider about our position and what we do here.'

'Who would do that though?'

'The new girl, I reckon. Never trusted her.'

Alice's heart sank. She hadn't contacted anyone outside the Sect, and she had no idea who it was they were talking about. She needed to get up and ready fast. She needed to find Grace so they could work out what the hell was going on.

She pulled her black velvet dress down over her shoulders and struggled to tie the fastenings around the back. Where was Grace when she needed her? Underneath her dress, she tied the laces of her boots. They were made from soft and supple leather, well-worn, perfect for running, and comfortably hugged her calves, ending at her bony knees. She didn't know why she thought of running in that moment, but something made her feel like she might need to do that today. The only problem was that she didn't know if she was going to be running towards something, or running away. The unease of that thought made her stop to fasten a knife to her thigh, hidden by the folds of her dress.

Just in case.

She smoothed her dress down in the mirror and brushed

her hair, before pinning half of it up into a braid that crowned her head. The rest of her hair fell in a shimmering waterfall to her waist. Alice couldn't help but notice the changes she'd experienced, for they showed themselves on her face. The girl in the mirror was an entirely different person to the girl that had been stolen away on a rainy night all those weeks ago. It was true, the blue-black bruise that circled her right eye eliminated any chance of Alice looking completely restored, but she certainly had gained a lustre that had previously been absent.

Turning away from the mirror, Alice jumped as her door was flung open, the lock that secured it now hanging loose, obsolete. Two of the priestess' guards stood silhouetted in the doorway, wearing her symbol around their necks. She recognised one of the women as the toad-faced Blayne, whom she'd met on her first day. Their eyes were lined with thick black kohl and on their faces they wore twin expressions of hatred and disgust. Alice searched their eyes for mercy, but found nothing. Together, the two women strode forward and grabbed an arm each, fastening Alice's wrists together with heavy rope. They didn't speak, they didn't offer an explanation or even question her, they just dragged her out of her room and into the darkened corridor.

'Where are you taking me? What's going on?' Alice demanded, no longer shy or reserved, as she had been on her arrival. The women escorting her stayed silent. The one on her left, the taller of the two, simply looked Alice dead in the eye and snarled. They were taking her to see Hecate Winter, the High Priestess, that much was sure. Grace had told her that occasionally they'd hear of a girl who'd digressed from her training or who had displayed transgressive behaviour being escorted, like Alice was now, to the great hall. The girl, more often than not, was never seen again.

But Alice hadn't done anything wrong. Had she?

She barely had time to wrack her brains over what she could have done. She was dragged through the hallways and corridors and then through the open doors into the great hall. They flung her onto her hands and knees, ignoring her cries and her struggles. Her dress was covered in dust and grime from being dragged relentlessly and her once-neat hair had fallen from its pins. Everything ached.

'A-Alice?' she heard a weak voice stutter. It came from the darkened corner at the back of the room.

Locked in chains, slumped backwards against the wall with her arms outstretched awkwardly and her legs crumpled beneath her was Lily. Her Lily. The Lily she had left heartbroken but healthy, the Lily she thought would be fine without her. How could she possibly be here?

Panicked thoughts rushed through her brain faster than she could process them as she fought to get to her feet and run towards her friend. She barely covered three feet of ground before she felt herself dragged backwards by an invisible force. She landed on her back, the air forced out of her lungs with the violence of her fall. She lay there desperately trying to catch her breath when a shadow obscured her vision.

Not a shadow.

Hecate.

She stood above Alice, scowling. 'The longer it takes for you to give me answers, the more pain your friend will have to endure. Do you understand?' She didn't wait for Alice to reply. She simply raised a hand and focused it on Alice's chest, dragging her upwards with her magic until they were face to face, Alice's feet barely scraping the floor. 'How did you tell her where we were?'

'I didn't ... I didn't know she'd come here.'

'Liar.' Hecate nodded her head at one of the women who had brought Alice from her room. She stalked over to Lily and struck her across the face, but Lily bit her lip and didn't cry out, even though her nose was bleeding profusely.

'Leave her out of this, please.' Alice struggled as an invisible python wrapped itself around her slender neck, constricting her throat and making it almost impossible to breathe. 'Punish me, leave her.'

'Oh, I will punish you, don't worry, child. But first, I need the truth. The longer you waste my time, the more pain you inflict on your friend.'

The woman who had hit Lily was still beating her mercilessly, but she still wouldn't cry out. Instead, she was attempting to splutter something through her blood-filled mouth. Hecate held up a hand and the woman stopped, allowing Lily to speak.

'She didn't send for me. You think I'd come all the way out here for her? She abandoned me.' Lily sniffled. 'I'm here because I want to be one of you. I want to learn magic. All of this, everything I've done to get here, has been a lie. I'm here because I want to stay.'

Hecate paused, intrigued. 'How did you know we were here?'

'I followed … I don't know, a feeling? A sense? Like there was a string of lightning pulling me towards you. I've felt it for years but as soon as Alice disappeared I knew where she'd be so I followed the pull I'd been ignoring my whole life.'

'You weren't helped?'

'No.'

'Well, there's one way to find out…'

Chapter Forty-Three

T *hwack.*

Blood ran in streams from Lily's nose as her assailant once again struck her across the face. The pain and the rubbing chains on her wrists were making it increasingly difficult to think of new convincing lies. She didn't even know if this woman believed her. All she cared about was clearing Alice of blame; she didn't want her to have to suffer for Lily's mistake.

With the promise that Hecate would find out the truth of Lily's claims, she was released from the wall-chains, only to be cuffed again and dragged to the middle of the hall. The walls were made of ancient stone, damp and streaked with copper ore that reflected and refracted the torchlight. The entire room looked to have been carved directly from the rock, and the furnishings, if they could even be called that, seemed to have been dumped there in an attempt at creating a more grandiose atmosphere. There was a huge, rusty chandelier hanging from the arched ceiling, an altar at the back of the room covered in a variety of weaponry and bottles filled with all manner of strangely coloured, swirling liquids. The theme of battle continued throughout the room: attached to the walls were swords, staffs, bows, and quivers filled with arrows. The door she'd come through, which she now faced, was reinforced with a huge contraption made of steel bars, ropes, and pulleys. This was no hideout.

It was a fortress.

'Look at me, child.' Hecate's rich, slimy voice forced Lily back into the moment. She was pushed to her knees by invisible hands and refused to make eye contact, instead choosing to stare intently at the witch's leather boots. 'I said,' Hecate growled, 'look at me. Did the Brotherhood send you?'

Lily slowly raised her head and met Hecate's eyes. She could hear Alice's struggles in the background, but the woman obscured her view. With a flick of the wrist, Lily's hands were thrown outward and fastened to wooden posts that hadn't been there seconds previously. On her knees with her arms outstretched, she was helpless. *Where is Jem?* she thought. If there was anyone who could give her the last ounce of strength she needed to survive this, it was him. She closed her eyes and pictured him standing by Alice, the two of them smiling at her with kind tenderness in their eyes.

All of a sudden, Lily felt warmth on her face that didn't come from the joy of her wishful thinking. Opening her eyes, she found herself face to face with a roaring fire that was burning without fuel, right in front of her. Through the flames, Hecate leaned towards her. 'Talk, or this fire gets hotter and it gets closer. The longer it takes you to tell us what you know, the longer you'll be trussed up, slowly burning on a pyre of your own making.'

'I don't know anything,' Lily pleaded. 'Please, I don't know anything. I came alone. I followed my heart. Please...' Smoke clutched at her throat, choking her. The more she coughed, the more smoke she inhaled. Suffocation would kill her faster than the flames if she continued to hyperventilate, but she couldn't catch her breath to try and calm herself. Panic filled her, threatening to force her into unconsciousness.

'If you don't know anything, girl, then why do you look exactly like Alfryd Knight? He sent you, didn't he?'

'No ... no.' As Lily drifted, barely conscious, Uncle Alf's name echoed around her mind. What did Alf have to do with any of this? Just as she felt herself being drawn irretrievably into a hole of darkness, she was jolted by the sound of those huge doors being thrown open. The room was filled with shouts, threats, and growls. Chaos broke loose, but Lily couldn't see the source of the commotion through her barely-open eyes.

The pain from the flames was excruciating. It felt like they were slowly melting the skin from her bones and the more smoke she inhaled, the less she could fight it. The pressure in her body was building. It felt like something was desperately trying to claw its way out of her, like it had always been there, looking for a way out.

Lily felt her consciousness slip away, and as it did so, the overwhelming urge to surrender came over her. She fell forwards, into the flames, ready to be engulfed. But she felt nothing. As she hit the ground, the room exploded around her. Power flowed from every inch of her, enveloping the room.

Everything was silent. Her chains disappeared in the blast and the whole room turned to stare at her. She felt like she was a lightning bolt. She didn't know what had happened, but she knew that it had come from her and she didn't know how to stop it happening again. She felt powerful for the first time in her life, as she looked around the room and saw fear and confusion painted on every single face.

Before she had time to think what to do next, Hecate ran at her, screaming. Lily stretched out to defend herself and experienced the rush of power again. It felt like warm glistening honey running through her veins and out of her fingers. The golden light ploughed towards the woman, but just before it hit, Hecate spun on her heels, making strange shapes with her hands.

And then she vanished.

The beam of golden light hit the wall at the back of the cavernous room and shattered it. There were a few short seconds of terrifying silence before the roof started to grumble and dust fell ominously from the ceiling. The room was going to collapse in on all of them.

The fighting stumbled to a stop when Hecate vanished; the other women were cast adrift without their leader. Witches and Protectors alike scattered, and a panicked mass of bodies exited the great hall, leaving only the weak and suffering behind.

As she looked around her, Lily realised Alice was

manacled to the wall, barely conscious. Beneath her tragic frame was Grace, crumpled at her feet, sobbing. *No*, she thought, *no, she can't be*. She tried to move towards Alice, but her legs gave way beneath her and she crashed to the floor, her energy levels dangerously low. She felt a strong arm wrap around her waist and lift her to her feet. She leaned against the solid unwavering form that kept her upright and helped her to stumble across to Alice. Her vision was blurred and patchy, but she recognised the faint smell of seawater, pine, and oil. Jem was here. Jem was holding her up and helping her save Alice, like he'd promised.

The three of them gathered around Alice. Jem's presence filled Lily with hope as if he, simply by being there, had given her the strength to carry on. Grace tried to pull at the manacles, but they wouldn't give. She pulled and she pulled, but they remained enclosed around Alice's wrists.

'I can't free her. I can't … I don't…' Tears streaked her face. She was helpless. Lily's heart sank. Too much pain and anguish had already fallen upon them today. She couldn't lose the one person she'd come all this way to rescue. She felt the air buzz with electricity and the golden light filled her veins once more.

'Move,' she choked out. The heartbroken girl looked over her shoulder at Lily in confusion. 'Move!' Lily cried, and Jem threw himself forwards and knocked his sister to the ground, shielding her. The light burst from Lily's hand once more, but instead of shattering the wall, the shackles, and Alice's arms with it, the glow danced around her unconscious friend, shimmering and swirling around her bloody wrists. Her face was illuminated by the warm light and the chains melted away. Alice dropped from the wall and fell into Lily's arms. Her eyes flickered and she looked up into the face of her best friend.

'Lily?'

'It's me. I'm here. I came for you.' She held Alice to her chest and sobbed into her raven hair.

Their embrace was interrupted by another deep rumble, and a piece of rock fell from the ceiling and shattered right by Jem's foot.

'Everyone,' he said tentatively, 'Lil, Grace, we need to leave now. Get Alice. NOW!' he shouted and dragged Lily to her feet. Grace lifted Alice from the floor and carried her, one arm underneath her shoulders and the other supporting her legs. Alice's arms wrapped around Grace's neck, and they followed Jem and Lily as they sprinted from the dark room as the roof began to disintegrate.

They ran through the rabbit warren of corridors. Lily felt weak and paused to lean against the damp wall, struggling to catch her breath. Jem whirled round in a panic when she stopped.

'Lil, you need to keep moving. Please, come on, you can do this.' He stepped towards her and held his hand out. She took it and wrapped it around her shoulder, leaning into him. With his arm around her and him supporting her weight, they stumbled through the final few snaking tunnels and pushed themselves out into the open air, Grace and Alice following close behind.

A deafening rumble filled the air and rocked the very earth beneath their feet.

The lair was no more.

Hecate had vanished and her followers had bolted.

The foursome had survived, by the very skin of their teeth. Once they were clear of the entrance, protected by a gathering of trees, Lily stumbled to the ground. It was only just nightfall, but her eyes felt like they were filled with sand and she couldn't move another step. Grace placed Alice down by Lily's side, both of them resting their backs against a rounded rock that kept them upright. Alice rested her head on Lily's shoulder and closed her eyes. They were holding hands, afraid that if either one let go, they'd lose each other again.

Neither girl could cope with that.

Chapter Forty-Four

The warmth of sunlight woke Lily from a deep, dreamless sleep. For a little while, she kept her eyes closed, watching the shadows behind her eyelids dance in the early morning light. As she broke free from her slumber, she smelled burning. Panicked, she snapped open her eyes, ready to fight whoever was threatening her friends, her newfound power flickering at her fingertips. She jumped to her feet and looked around with wildness in her eyes and heard a low chuckle. The final glimmerings of sleep fell away as she remembered they'd escaped.

They were safe.

Jem was kneeling in front of a fire, stoking it with deliberate care. Their bags were at his feet; he'd obviously taken the time that morning to liberate the packs from their hiding place.

Lily looked around at her sleeping place and stared, wide-eyed. The patch of grass on which she had slept was singed and black, as though someone had set fire to it. She looked down at her hands, and noticed her fingers, too, were covered in painless burns. She hadn't just had a feverish sleep; this must be the *magic*.

Magic. That word still felt weird. Her own magic. Not Alice's imaginary, yearned-for magic that didn't actually exist in any world, let alone the Shadow Lands. Her very own. That was going to take some getting used to, but at least, she hoped, Alice could help.

Jem whistled quietly to catch Lily's attention. He'd rolled the sleeves of his grubby white shirt up to his elbows and tied his hair back carelessly, the usual strands falling in his face. She stepped over Alice, who was sleeping soundly, and Grace, who was curled up close to her. The two girls were almost nose to nose, with their hands clasped together at their chests in between them. Grace's other hand was resting gently on Alice's cheek, as if she'd fallen asleep stroking her face. Lily felt a strange tug of understanding in her heart when she saw them together.

She finally understood.

Lily tore her eyes from the sleeping lovers and tiptoed across to Jem, a smile tugging at her lips. Jem glanced past Lily at Grace and Alice, his face mirroring hers.

Lily's entire body still ached with sheer exhaustion from the battering she'd faced in the Shadow Sect's lair. She could still feel the crusty dried blood on her face and neck. Jem noticed that she was struggling and reached out a helping hand to guide her to the ground next to him. He held it a fraction of a second longer than necessary and they locked eyes. He swallowed and went back to tending the fire absentmindedly.

'I never thanked you, yesterday. For saving us all,' Lily whispered, keeping her voice down so as not to wake the others. 'But you took your time!'

'Sorry, I got waylaid. But we did it. *You* did it. You did all the hard work.'

Lily snorted. 'Hardly. I don't know what I did. I certainly had no control over it. I'm sure I'd have collapsed to the floor and died amongst the falling rubble had you not carried me out.'

'You saved yourself, Lily Knight. The power flowing from you as I carried you out of there kept me upright. It was almost as if your energy was flowing through me, giving me the strength to move forwards. Without you, I'd have died on the floor by your side.'

'You came here for Grace though. You could've taken her and run. You saved what you came to save, so why waste your time?'

'I stopped doing this just for Grace a long time ago, Lil. There was never going to be a scenario where I came out without you. If you'd died in there...' He took her hand again, gently tucking a strand of hair behind her ear. Lily's heart hammered against her ribcage, desperately trying to free itself from her chest and find a new home, huddled right next to Jem's. 'Lily—'

Grace yawned loudly and sat up, peering across the flames to Lily and Jem. Jem dropped her hand and stood, instinctively moving towards his sister. Quelling her disappointment, Lily watched as Jem went to sit by Grace and was struck by how similar they were, and yet how different. They looked like twins – they had the same large, dark eyes that sat beneath a strong brow, framed by sharp cheekbones. Their hair was the same shade of deep brown that glistened bronze in the light of the sunrise, but Grace's was shorter than Jem's, and less wild and unkempt. He let it down from his hair tie and the waves fell to his shoulders. Lily liked it best like that.

They were deep in a mysterious conversation. Lily noticed that where Jem had a softness to his demeanour, Grace looked fierce and solid. She couldn't help but feel slightly terrified of her. After all, they hadn't met in ideal circumstances, and she was Jem's sister. If Grace didn't like her, so much would change.

Conscious that she was staring, Lily was about to look away when Jem caught her eye and smiled, gesturing for her to join them. She limped over tentatively, and Jem helped her to the floor again. She crossed her legs as she sat next to him.

'I feel like we might've got off on the wrong foot...' Grace began. Lily was surprised to see that she looked nervous.

'Circumstantial. You were doing your job. I'm glad we can start again.' Lily held her hand out in a gesture of friendship. 'I'm Lily, it's a pleasure to make your acquaintance.'

Grace grinned, her smile lighting up her face. 'Grace. The pleasure is mine.'

At that moment, Alice stirred and groaned. Grace immediately shot to her side, as if a string in her ribcage was tied to Alice and compelled her to be by her side at all times. She knelt by Alice's shoulder and gently ran a thumb over her cheekbone, brushing Alice's hair from her face. That small gesture proved to Lily that she didn't have to look out for Alice in the same way anymore. It felt strange ... almost sad. The bittersweet acknowledgement that her best friend didn't need her so much anymore. She had someone else to love her now.

After a few minutes of conversation with Grace, it was clear that Alice was going to make a full and quick recovery. Jem warmed some pine tea over the fire and poured it into the metal cans they'd brought with them from the lighthouse. Grace gazed at the cans with a nostalgic glint in her eyes. 'I can't believe we're going back. I honestly never thought I'd see it, or you, ever again. And I certainly didn't think that if I did make it back, we'd be dragging along a pair of freeloaders with us for the ride...' She smirked.

Jem grinned at Grace's quip as he reached into his pack. He pulled out several packages that looked like they had been haphazardly wrapped in brown paper and string, for they were crumpled and squashed. 'If anything can get us all up and moving, it's these. Why did you think it took me so long to come to the rescue?'

'Ha! Rescue? Lily had it in hand, didn't you?' Grace smiled.

'Of course, if I hadn't been tied up and set on fire, I'd have broken us out of there in a matter of minutes...'

'Anyway, before you steal any more of my glory, take a look at these.'

Jem unwrapped the packages to a cacophony of joyful shrieks. Inside each parcel was a different baked treat. The first he opened was a huge, gooey bun that smelled of warm spices and sugar. The next was a beautiful, round loaf of bread, made with light, pale flour rather than the tough, hard rye. In the others was a variety of cakes and loaves of different sizes, colours, and flavours. He then pulled out armfuls of apples, a hunk of cheese and some other fruit that Lily didn't recognise. It was a feast the likes of which none of them had seen before nor were likely to see again. Their empty bellies growled at the sight.

Grace helped Alice to sit upright, and she and Lily each took one of Alice's arms in their own so she was supported. The sweet smell of the spiced, gooey rolls seemed to have properly awakened her, and her eyes lit up at the banquet.

'Where did you get these?' Alice asked. Grace leaned forward and tore off a piece of the pale bread, throwing on a piece of cheese before stuffing the whole thing into her mouth.

'The kitchens. I had to find another entrance instead of the one Lily managed to go into, so I figured I'd look for a vent: all kitchens need one, especially if it's underground, otherwise they'd all cook themselves, rather than just the bread. So, I found the kitchen vent; it was open anyway.'

Grace and Alice exchanged a knowing look, and Lily could have sworn she saw Alice blush.

'I found the entire place empty; presumably they'd all gone to watch the commotion unfold. I thought if we were going to make it out alive, we'd need sustenance. Lily and I finished the last of our food on the walk yesterday morning so I grabbed whatever I could, and wrapped it all up so my bag didn't get sticky—'

'Hang on,' Lily interrupted. 'You knew something was

going on with us, something potentially awful, and you still made time to *wrap* the food?'

'You should know by now never to get between my brother and his stomach,' Grace replied, glancing between Lily and Jem, clearly attempting to figure out their dynamic.

They all laughed amongst themselves. It felt like years but also just a matter of days since they last saw each other. So much had happened, so much had changed.

Once they'd all eaten their fill, there was still enough to take home to the lighthouse and share with the children. The sun was just creeping over the treeline and they knew they had to start moving if they were going to make it back before nightfall, and they were all keen to return to the coast – Jem and Grace especially. They had saltwater in their veins. Too long away from it was never healthy.

The food had brought about in Alice an almost miraculous recovery. She was able to stand and walk unaided, although Grace made it clear that if she struggled, she could lean on her shoulder. Lily wondered whether they ought to have a spell or something to make her feel stronger but didn't dare ask; she didn't know what they had been through at the hands of Hecate Winter and she didn't want to pry while the wounds were still fresh. There was plenty of time to hear their story when they were ready to tell it.

They all helped pack up the bags and started walking, buoyed by comforting thoughts of warm beds, an open fire in the grate, the companionship of their left-behind friends, and the sound of crashing waves around them.

Chapter Forty-Five

The world shone a brilliant orange, and Lily felt like they'd been walking for days. The sun was setting, slowly disappearing over the unseen horizon and it was hard to believe that it was only yesterday that they had been suffering at the hands of Hecate Winter.

Thoughts of Hecate's disappearance kept rearing their ugly heads whenever Lily allowed herself to feel joy or relief at having Alice back. Everything felt like it should be perfect but something niggling at the edge of her consciousness told her that this wasn't the end. She had unlocked a power inside her that she didn't know existed until yesterday and she was going to have to learn to control it. A band of dangerous and even potentially murderous witches was still stalking the land and it was only a matter of time before they had to face them again.

She would have to adjust to a new life, figure out where she wanted to be and who she wanted to be with. After all this, could she really go back to making up potions in her uncle's apothecary? Could she disappear into a life of obscurity, of normalcy, now she knew what else was out there?

Lily looked around at the faces of her companions. She was terrified, confused, and conflicted but she had never felt safer than she did now, amongst this tiny band of misfits. Ahead, Alice lightly brushed Grace's arm and whispered something softly into her ear. She then hung back and let Grace wander ahead, Alice herself falling in step with Lily. Instinctively, the two girls joined hands, as they had done so many times over the years of their friendship.

'Why did you do it?' Alice asked.

'What?'

'Drop everything to come and find me. I was about to leave of my own volition; you didn't know I'd been taken, or where I'd be, or who I'd be with. It was a suicide mission.'

'You're my best friend. My Shadow Sister. I wasn't going to stop looking for you. I was never going to give up on you. You were in trouble and that's all there was to it.' Lily squeezed Alice's hand affectionately. 'Enough about that. It's over now; we're together again, and for good this time. We have more important things to discuss.'

Alice frowned. 'More important than the life-or-death situation we found ourselves in these last few weeks? More important than the fact that you dropped everything and travelled halfway across the Shadow Lands on your own to find me?'

'Yes. Far more important.' Lily turned to her and

grinned, 'I want to know everything about you and Grace. Every detail. How did it happen? Who kissed wh—'

'Lily!' Alice exclaimed, her face reddening.

'What? This is the most exciting thing that's happened to you in years – minus the whole abduction thing. I want to know everything!'

'Ugh,' Alice rolled her eyes, 'you are incorrigible. I'll tell you everything once I've had a long soak in the bath and an even longer sleep, I promise. As long as you promise to tell me everything about … y'know…' She flicked her eyes towards Jem and raised her eyebrows.

Lily was suddenly wracked by a very loud coughing fit. 'I have no idea what you mean,' she said, avoiding Alice's knowing look. 'Nothing to tell, nothing at all.'

At that moment, Jem caught up with them, flanking Lily's other side. 'Everything all right?'

'Yeah, everything's fine.' Lily accentuated the final word so strongly that it became immediately evident to Jem that he'd interrupted something.

Lily, eager to change the subject, linked one arm through Jem's and the other through Alice's. 'I've just realised that you guys haven't been formally introduced. Jem, this is Alice, who is, as you know, the reason I ended up at the lighthouse in the first place. Ali, this is Jem, without whom I'd probably have died about three times by now.' They reached across Lily and shook hands, sharing a knowing glance between them.

'Only three times?' Jem smirked. 'I expect I'll be seeing a lot more of you around, Alice, what with Lily staying with us and Grace living there too.'

'Lily is staying with you?'

'Well,' Lily panicked, 'it was something that was mentioned in passing... Um...'

'And you guys would be okay with me being there? Is there enough room?'

'There's always room for friends. Grace and I would be lucky to have both of you around. Mainly because trying to clean a bloody big lighthouse with the kids running riot is a nightmare: two extra pairs of hands would definitely be a blessing,' he teased and Lily lightly nudged his shoulder. She felt like she'd known Jem at least as long as she'd known Alice. He was a true kindred spirit, but there was something else there. Something that made her veins flow with golden honey when they met each other's eyes.

They were so nearly home. Over the final couple of miles, they were all lost in thoughts of home comforts and a long undisturbed sleep. The hillside that led them down to Kelseth was just up ahead and the blazing sunset had now faded to a bright orange glow in the distance.

Lily smelled burning for the second time that day. Jem tipped his head back. He'd clearly caught the scent as well. It didn't smell like a log fire. It smelled heavy, consuming. Jem dropped Lily's arm and ran ahead, disappearing over the crest of the hill.

Moments later, a pained cry shattered the silence.

It was Jem.

Lily sprinted forward, followed closely by Grace and Alice. The three of them crested the hill and saw Jem on his knees, sobbing at the horizon. He was illuminated by a rusty glow, but it wasn't the sunset. The lighthouse – their home, their sanctuary – was a burning beacon off the shore.

The entire tower was engulfed in flames.

Their presence seemed to break Jem from his shocked state. He regained his feet and set off, hurtling himself down the rocky, treacherous path to Kelseth, heading straight for the beach. Before Lily could even stop to check that the others were following, before any of them could process what was happening, they all set off after him.

They ran as if chased by rabid wolves, their emotions overridden by concern for Jem, for the children, and for their home.

Lily dashed down the precarious cliff path, rocks and scree falling off the edge and crashing to the ground far below. Her pack was impossibly heavy on her back and her muscles, still sore from Hecate's torture, screamed as she moved. A glance behind saw Alice and Grace close by, but Alice was limping and wincing with pain and Grace was torn between following her brother and helping Alice.

When they finally reached Kelseth, Lily had to force her way through the throngs of people on the crooked street. They were all staring as the lighthouse burned; some of them were even cheering.

Of course, Lily thought, as she elbowed her way through the unrelenting crowd, *they think the end of the lighthouse will bring an end to their curse.*

They reached the shoreline as Jem dived into a rowboat. He had obviously been slowed down enough by the mob to allow the rest of them to catch up. They barely had time to climb into it before he was ploughing mercilessly through the water towards the flaming lighthouse.

As they sat staring, with nothing to distract them from the horror of the moment, Lily prayed to whoever was listening that the children were safely out. She strained her eyes, the smoke affecting her vision, but couldn't see anyone on the pebble beach. Please, she thought, please let them be okay. She couldn't bring herself to think about what this would do to Jem. If any of the children were hurt, or worse … it would destroy him.

The boat barely scuffed the pebble beach before Jem was out. He ran directly towards the flames. In a matter of moments, a coughing and spluttering Morven appeared, clutching the hands of Maeve and Brenna, from the spot into which Jem had plunged. Grace ran to them, sobbing through smoke-stained eyes. Alice and Lily stood back, clutching each other.

The tower was completely overwhelmed by fire and smoke. The thick black stripes that Jem had painstakingly painted were now completely invisible; the contrasting white bands were entirely caked in ash and soot.

As they gazed upwards in horror, the precious, beautiful glass of the lantern room shattered. Lily loved that room, that view. She loved the calmness of a quiet sea reflecting in the sunlight, casting patterns on the white painted floorboards. Now the room that had been such a comfort to her rained down upon them in brutal, jagged shards.

'Take cover!' Lily cried, and saw Grace throw herself over the twins to protect them from the falling debris.

A few more minutes passed and Lily couldn't take it anymore.

She squeezed Alice's hand, let go of it, and ran.

She ran as fast as her legs would carry her, through the door that Jem used.

'Jem!' she cried, choking as the smoke clawed at her throat. A beam from the ceiling, eaten by the flames, fell inches from her head, blowing dust and ash into her face. The air was so thick, she felt her head spin with the lack of air to breathe. She shielded her eyes and pushed forwards. Someone was running towards her. As the figure grew closer, she saw the cropped hair and height of Cass. He ran at her and shook her.

'WHAT ARE YOU DOING HERE?' he shouted over the noise of the flickering flames. 'YOU NEED TO GET OUT IMMEDIATELY.'

'But, Jem!' she cried, trying to push past him. She couldn't stop coughing from the smoke inhalation.

'HE WILL BE FINE. WE NEED TO LEAVE.' Before she could protest, Cass had scooped her up and carried her back in the direction she'd come. When they got outside, Alice ran to her and helped her to her feet. Cass still clung to her side, the two of them holding each other up.

'What happened here, Cass?' Lily managed to choke out.

'I can't ... I...' He was lost for words. The shock crashed over him in a wave as they watched the building begin to crumble. 'It was Glenn... I didn't think he would actually do it but...' He burst into tears and fell to his knees.

Agonising minutes passed. Lily's mind was reeling.

Glenn? Was that why he apologised to me before we left? she wondered. *Had he planned this?*

All of them were on the floor now, gazing blindly into the fiery beacon that was once their home. Grace stood ashen-faced, a single tear rolling down her cheek. Maeve and Brenna clung to her, quietly crying.

Then, impossibly, a figure appeared out of the black smoke. Actually, one figure carrying another.

Jem.

Covered in ash, burns, and grazes, he stumbled forward and Lily rushed to help him.

When they were free of the flames, they all moved to the very edge of the beach, the waves lapping at their ankles. Jem laid the figure down on the pebbles. He was almost unrecognisable, covered in soot, blood seeping from a multitude of wounds: Glenn.

He was perfectly still, peaceful, calm. Lily looked for the rise and fall of his chest but saw only stillness.

He was dead.

Nausea washed over her at the sight of his lifeless body. Her fingertips flickered with the potential of her new powers, but she had nowhere to channel it. What could she do to make any of this better? She could never ask him why he had done this. She couldn't fathom why she was more upset about that than the fact that he was dead. All she could see in his body was unanswered questions. And that made her angry, so deeply angry. Red hot tears rolled down her cheeks.

What would this do to Jem?

What would this do to all of them? Their home gone.

Their lives ruined. And Hecate was still out there, waiting to make her next move. Now they were vulnerable, broken.

Cast adrift.

Jem clutched the limp form of his most difficult ward, the boy he'd felt sure he could have reformed, and sobbed with abandon. Lily reached out to touch his shoulder but he flinched and moved away, his arms locked around Glenn.

The waves continued to creep up the shore as the final light of day faded. With a deafening rumble, the lighthouse collapsed and fell inward, covering the courtyard in its blackened bricks.

Everything was destroyed.

The home they had spent years building, the lives Jem and Grace had salvaged at first for themselves, and then for the children who needed their shelter the most, it was all a disintegrated ruin on an abandoned island.

Alice found her way to Lily's side, as Grace attempted to pry Jem away from Glenn. Lily's face was sparkling with tears in the low light and Alice held her to her chest, where the tears flowed freely. They held on to each other for dear life.

They had nothing now but their love for each other, and their shared grief.

Jem finally looked up from Glenn's body into the faces of Lily, Grace, Alice, Maeve, Brenna, Morven, and Cass. His family.

'I'm going to find out who did this. I'm going to find out, and I'm going to kill them.'

'You'll be looking until I let you find me, Rafferty,' a voice said, cutting through the darkness.

They whirled around to see the shimmering figure of Hecate Winter hovering above the black sea.

'Glenn was far too easy to manipulate. Oh, poor little Glenn with his tragic backstory. Glenn, who never felt truly loved, who always had to fight with the others for attention. He was all too happy to know he was wanted, to know he could be useful to someone, somewhere. It was just a matter of time and manipulation.'

'No…' Grace spat.

'Oh yes, and don't think you two have got away with it either. I know of your bond, and I know exactly how to break it. You're all just sitting ducks now, with no home to call your own.' Hecate started laughing maniacally. 'Oh, this is all going to be far too easy…'

Jem got to his feet and ran towards her, into the foamy waves, but as he clawed at her, the apparition disappeared. He whirled around, looking this way and that, but she was gone.

Lily gazed up at the burning wreck, cinders whirling to the ground like ash keys from a tree. They had lost everything.

But at least they had each other.

She looked around at her friends scattered across the beach. Morven and Cass were holding hands, staring lifelessly out to sea. Brenna and Maeve clutched at Grace like lost lambs reunited with their mother. They looked afraid that if they let go, she would disappear again, like Hecate had. Alice stood nearby, looking at Grace with fierce admiration in her face.

Jem trudged back to dry land and collapsed, letting the

waves lap over his legs. He stared at the sky, unblinking. Lily dragged herself over to him and lay by his side. She took his hand and this time he didn't flinch. He clung to it, intertwining their fingers, and held it to his chest.

From there on the beach, looking up to the night sky, the dancing ash was almost pretty. A thousand tiny ballerinas twirling around the stars.

Lily exhaled deeply. Their home was destroyed. Their plans were in tatters.

But for now, Hecate was gone.

They were alone in the silence once more.

Author's Note

Hello, dear readers and friends!

Firstly, thank you ever so much for picking up this book, for reading it. *Sisters of Shadow* has lived in my mind for more years than I care for admit. For a long time, I wondered whether it would ever find itself into the hands of readers, or whether it would continue to be my own little secret world, hidden away forever.

The idea for this book (and its sequels!) came to me painfully slowly; it was always bubbling away in the back of my mind, like a forgotten cauldron. Occasionally it would boil over, and I'd have a flash of inspiration, and then it would go back to quietly simmering for another few weeks. I had flickers of ideas: the lighthouse, a shadow of Lily, crashing waves, lightkeepers blackening their light.

The only thing I was ever set on was that I wanted the story to follow queer female characters. Growing up I couldn't see myself in any of the books I was reading, which meant it took me longer than most to realise, understand and accept myself as bisexual. I wanted to read about girls falling in love with girls, but I also didn't want those books to revolve around the "coming out" romance, I wanted it to be treated as any other romance is treated within a book: a part of the plot, not its defining feature. I wanted to read books that normalised queerness, so I decided to write them. First and foremost, *Sisters of Shadow* was written for twelve-year-old Katy who was beyond frazzled from trying to work out her feelings. I hope she'd be proud of who she grew up to be.

So, those ideas stayed just as ideas for a couple of years. Then, one sunny afternoon overlooking Bassenthwaite Lake with my mum, in a 19th century hotel I'd got a last-minute deal on, the ideas began to grow. The hotel had a window seat, and anyone who knows me will know I am a total sucker for a window seat. I sat myself in that window, warmed by the late afternoon sun, and jotted down what is now the first few lines of Lily's opening chapter in *Sisters of Shadow*. I've just scrolled back through my Instagram and found the exact date of that inspiration breakthrough: 6th of July 2015. Almost 6 years ago to the day, at the time of writing this note to you, dear reader.

So, I began to write. Around university commitments, through my master's degree, in the back of the campervan I bought with my partner, in a tiny cabin without any electricity in northern Norway, to now, around my (very understanding) full-time job, in the garden of my own little miracle house in the countryside. The one constant has been this story, these characters.

You may recognise some of the landscape inspirations in the book. The lighthouse on the windswept island came to me because I've always been obsessed with the idea of living in a lightkeeper's cottage. That idea developed into something that vaguely resembles the stunning, completely mystical Godrevy Lighthouse in Cornwall, that I stumbled across while holidaying there. I couldn't believe my eyes when I saw it in the distance; there it was, Kelseth Lighthouse, in real life!

The village of Barley I mention a few times is a real-life village in my home county of Lancashire, and sits very close to Pendle Hill, famous for its witches. The heather-strewn moors and forests are taken straight from the countryside I grew up running wild across, but are also inspired by the bleak Yorkshire landscape made famous by the Brontës. I won't mention just how many "inspiration trips" I took to Haworth, just to wander the cobbled streets or twirl in a pretty dress out on the moors.

So, that's the story of this story. But the tale doesn't end here. I can't wait to show you where my beloved characters go next. There are new landscapes, new characters and there's plenty of trouble on the horizon. I hope you'll join me there!

Until then,

With love, light and a bunch of fresh wildflowers,

Katy

Sisters of Shadow: The Playlist

- *The Mystic's Dream* by Loreena McKennitt
- *Granuaile's Dance* by Celtic Woman
- *Morrígan* by Adrian von Ziegler
- *Annabelle Lee* by Sarah Jarosz
- *Jenny of Oldstones* by Florence + The Machine
- *Smoke & Mirrors* by Agnes Obel
- *Moving* by Rolf Løvland, Secret Garden
- *An Historic Love* by Trevor Morris
- *Birdsong* by Emma Langford
- *Hard Road* by Johnny Flynn
- *Tha Mo Ghaol Air Àird a' Chuain* by Julie Fowlis

Acknowledgments

First, I'd like to thank the amazing team at One More Chapter, who have made all of this magic happen. You made realising my dream the most enjoyable experience and it's a genuine joy to be a part of the OMC family.

On that note, I'd like to thank my inimitable editor, Bethan Morgan. For believing in me, and this story, for understanding all of my niche *Anne of Green Gables* references, and for always being up for a natter about *Hamilton*. Bethan, your confidence in me has helped me grow in so many ways and I genuinely don't think I'll ever be able to thank you enough for everything you have done.

I'm also sending a huge heap of thanks to Bethany Davidson, Jen Rossall, Anthony Barrett, Ingrid Melle Åkernes, Leanne Downs and Lydia Crook and for letting me send you the first three chapters of this book way back in 2019, and for all of your brilliant, helpful feedback (and support, love and friendship ever since). I count my lucky stars every day to have such a lovely bunch of people in my life.

To the rest of my dearest friends who have plied me with coffee and cake and words of support and encouragement over the years, and who still miraculously want to hang out even after I disappear into a writing hole for months on end: Chelsea Coyne, Jessica Blake, Rosie Cunniffe, Beth Cocking and the entire Cooper family (aka my 2nd family). You guys are the greatest.

Thank you to Adam Joice for being quite possibly the best boss the world has ever known. Your support at work, and your understanding during the stressful book weeks, has been invaluable. Also, sorry to Caroline Joice for how much this mention is going to inflate Adam's ego... Will you ever forgive me?

To my incredible, long-suffering parents, thank you for everything and more. Mum, you read this book when it was in its most skeletal form and still believed in me and the story I wanted to write. Thanks for all the trips to National Trust properties and for all the time we've spent lost in period dramas. You have kept me sane and I couldn't have done any of this without you. Dad, this will be your first time reading this book as you've been "saving it"! I hope it was worth the wait. Thank you for the fabulous midnight pub debates, for introducing me to the fantasy genre, and for being my biggest cheerleader. I promise I'll read *Magician* soon. Honest.

Finally, to my better half, to the person who has motivated me, cheered me on every step of the way, the person who encouraged me to send this book out to publishers in the first place, the person who believes in me more than I ever could. Arron, you are my hero. You make me strive to be a better person every single day. Thanks for all the freshly baked loaves of bread and cups of coffee, for the words of encouragement and unfailing belief, and for dragging me outside for a bike ride or a dog walk, even when I insisted I didn't need it. I always do, and you always know.

ONE MORE CHAPTER

YOUR NUMBER ONE STOP

FOR PAGETURNING BOOKS

One More Chapter is an
award-winning global
division of HarperCollins.

Sign up to our newsletter to get our
latest eBook deals and stay up to date
with our weekly Book Club!
<u>Subscribe here.</u>

Meet the team at
<u>www.onemorechapter.com</u>

Follow us!

 <u>@OneMoreChapter_</u>

 <u>@OneMoreChapter</u>

 <u>@onemorechapterhc</u>

Do you write unputdownable fiction?
We love to hear from new voices.
Find out how to submit your novel at
<u>www.onemorechapter.com/submissions</u>